LUISA DOMIC AND SHAWNO

BOOKS BY GEORGE DENNISON

Luisa Domic and Shawno
Temple
A Tale of Pierrot and Other Stories
Oilers and Sweepers and Other Stories
The Lives of Children
And Then a Harvest Feast

LUISA DOMIC

AND

SHAWNO

GEORGE DENNISON

INTRODUCTION BY HAYDEN CARRUTH

STEERFORTH PRESS

SOUTH ROYALTON, VERMONT

For information about permission to reproduce selections
from this book, write to: Steerforth Press L.C., P.O. Box 70,
South Royalton, Vermont 05068.

Library of Congress Cataloging-in-Publication Data
Dennison, George 1925–1987
Luisa Domic ; and, Shawno / George Dennison ; introd. by Hayden Carruth.
p.   cm.
ISBN 1–883642–49–3
I. Dennison, George, 1925–   Luisa Domic.   1994
II. Dennison, George, 1925–   Shawno.   1994
III. Title: Luisa Domic. IV. Title: Shawno.
PS3554.E55L6   1994
813'.54—dc20   94–6469

Manufactured in the United States of America

First Edition

TO MY FAMILY

$\begin{bmatrix} \text{C O N T E N T S} \end{bmatrix}$

George, with tears streaming from his eyes, told me once of a time when he had visited a Russian Orthodox church in London during the midnight Easter service, possibly with his friend Ivan Tolstoy. As George was standing at the back of the church a roughly dressed man, a Russian working-class émigré, had come hurrying in and had immediately thrown himself on his knees and flung out his arms toward the candlelit altar, the cross, the figure of Jesus, smiling radiantly, his whole posture expressing utter confidence and happiness. "I've never seen such a strong image of the joyful human spirit in any painting," George said to me that day.

This was when he was dying. Again and again during those final days his mind went back to similar fleeting memories of gladness and goodness from his past.

A few years earlier in one of his letters to me he had written about his experience in rereading Melville's short stories. He was particularly impressed by the story called "Cock-A-Doodle-Doo," which is not a story at all but a rhapsodic account of an Oriental rooster whose song at morning resounded over the neighborhood where Melville lived. George called it "glorious" and went on to demonstrate his idea of *glory,* how it is related to *splendor* and *light,* to the Divine manifestation in human awareness, to the Hebrew concept of the *Shekinah.* He regretted that the critics in their earnestness had spent so much effort on "Bartleby the Scrivener" and "Benito Cereno," as fine as these stories are, and had said scarcely a word about "Cock-A-Doodle-Doo."

Melville was one of the most important writers in George's pantheon, along with Hawthorne, Kafka, Tolstoy (a distant relative of his friend Ivan), Proust, and a few others. He would have said that although the keenest images of the human spirit are given to us in the behavior of living people, such as one's children and neighbors or complete strangers, like the man who burst into the Russian church when George was there, these are also the rarest and most evanescent, so that the job of the artist is to come as close as possible to capturing them in a more durable order. In this George was unlike most writers who tend, at least in practice, to exalt literature above life.

Don't get me wrong, George was not a believer, certainly not in the conventional way. He was a complicated, sometimes violent, person who could and did provoke many people, including his friends. He could be withering in his attacks on those who he thought, sometimes unjustly, were shallow thinkers or hypocritical exponents. In his relationships with women he was sometimes abusive and often unreliable. In spite of his brilliance and his obviously acute talent for language—and he was a good painter too—he was unsure of himself, always self-reproachful, often filled with remorse, which nevertheless did not prevent him from punching someone in the snoot when he felt like it. His life as a young man in the city was a succession of failed love affairs, including two marriages; his friendships there were often close but often edgy or troubled as well. He wrote continually during those years, yet saved little of what he produced.

When George moved to the backcountry of Maine, however, he found in at least some of his new friends and neighbors qualities he had always esteemed but seldom encountered, qualities of loyalty, tenderness, imaginative resourcefulness, humor, hardihood, and forbearance. And he found also, I think unexpectedly, a connection to the natural world that touched him deeply, the alternating violence and loveliness of the seasons in northern New England, the woods and fields and ponds, the hills and valleys. He became a gardener. He kept dogs and horses and other animals. He spent long periods of solitude in the outdoors, skiing and snowshoeing, hiking, fishing, and canoeing, cutting, splitting, and stacking firewood. He learned his region well, the village of Temple and its surroundings. It was still, when he arrived there, a rough and in some ways primitive area of poor farms, many of them abandoned, of forests slashed and tangled, of old fields eroded to gravel and grown up in hardhack, chokecherry, and alder. Yet parts were uncommonly attractive too, a stand of magnificent uncut beech here or a long emerald slope of timothy there. Through it all ran Temple Stream, clear water flowing over the granite, raging and flooding in spring freshet or murmuring in the summer doldrums. George took to it all and found it, pristine or ravaged, equally moving, equally beautiful and pathetic.

This was the key—beauty and pathos combined, the yin and yang. It was the key to his mind, the key, he thought, to reality and art. Beauty could not appear to those unaware of its indwelling sorrow. The pathos of change was always the underlayer of his vision. A resplendent field of dandelions in the spring, a forest blazing with color in the fall—these magnificences were for George imbued with evanescence, yet no less magnificent for that. It was not loss that bothered George as much as unattainability, the projective loss. In art—and when he set up his slide projector he could be a marvelous informal critic of painting, just as in his letters he was an astute, ingenious critic of literature—human aspiration always falls short. We never make it. In all endeavor and in nature itself inadequacy is the flaw. Reality for George Dennison was failure—not immediate failure, not complete, not unmitigated, but necessary, and of course at last catastrophic.

Beauty is joy and gladness: it comes from them and reverts to them. Hence, since beauty contains pathos, joy and gladness are conveyors of pathos. George had a great capacity for pleasure, a great talent for comedy, and he smiled more than he frowned, though he was a famous frowner. For him joy almost escaped the bounds of pathos; it was always straining at the limits. His problem, like Tolstoy's and Proust's, was to separate the poignant from the sentimental, and to keep them separated, which in the nature of things is a failing endeavor too.

This is what some critics of George's novel, *Luisa Domic,* pointed out. They said the setting of the story in a New England Indian Summer is idealized, and the life of the family in the book, before the brutal intrusion of international politics, is too happy. But anyone who has lived in northern New England knows that for a few days nearly every autumn it simply *is* the most beautiful place on earth, hands down. And, at such a time, is it impossible that a family should experience tranquillity, that a house should be filled with affection, that the tragedies of the past should be put aside, the oppositions of the present overridden, the uncertainties of the future forgotten? It happens. As for the politics, *Luisa Domic* is the best North American memorialization of the overthrow of President Allende in Chile that we possess.

Quite coincidentally, I was visiting other friends in Temple the morning when the *New York Times* brought us news of that event in triple six-column headlines, like the outbreak of war. It was a somber and dreadful morning. I think everyone in the village felt it, even those normally unaffected by remote disasters. During succeeding days and years, as further news emerged of the savagery of the junta and the collapse of political sanity, along with more and more evidence of the covert, utterly illegal involvement of our own maniacal government—waves of despair, fury, and enervating alarm passing over us—the intellectual and artistic community, and indeed many other elements of the general population, came to see that the destruction of the elected government in Chile in 1973, with all its consequences, was both the archetypal and most appalling political event of our time. Not improbably, my best friend today in upstate New York, where I live, happens to be, like Luisa Domic, a Chilean refugee.

George Dennison was a handsome man with strong features, black hair, dark eyes, a powerful body, of average height. He played football enthusiastically in his youth. His movements were rapid, his tastes impulsive. In conversation he went after ideas with the kind of quick persistence that is both passionate and pragmatic at the same time. He was fierce and competitive, yet moody too—he could fall into reverie in the midst of an argument. He came from western Pennsylvania, meaning Pittsburgh primarily, along with such other tough and witty artists as the poets Jack Gilbert and Gerald Stern, the painter Bill Baziotes, the musicians Ray Brown and John Heard. In other words he knew working-class America in one of its oldest and most ago-nized strongholds—if that's the right word—and some of his most moving stories and plays came from that knowledge. His mind and temperament took to radical thought as a matter of course. But I don't mean conventional radical politics; George never belonged to any party or committed himself to any program. I mean radical thought in all its possible applications, thought searching for betterment through change. When he went to New York in the late 1940s he became associated with Paul Goodman and his circle, with Julian Beck and Judith Malina and their Living Theater, with such painters as De Kooning and Jack Tworkov; he became interested in gestalt therapy and the ideas of Wilhelm Reich, in alternative education, in civil rights, and communitarian politics. In short he belonged among the left-leaning but non-Marxist and multi-lateral intellectuals of the time who were redefining American radicalism, breaking down the European-oriented politics of the 1920s and 1930s, paving the way toward the more broadly native and problem-specific rebelliousness of the 1960s, in which most of them were participants and leaders. George's first book, *The Lives of Children,* was an account of an alter-native school founded in the 1960s on the lower eastside in Manhattan by Mabel Chrystie. It became a popular book, a primer for the free-school movement. For a while George was in demand as a speaker at educational conferences and a writer for educational journals, until he came to see that his work in education was sidetracking his main business in life. He was a writer. Owing to lack of funds Mabel's school failed, but by that time she and George were married and had had their first child. Then they decided to move to Maine.

They were not pioneers. Moving to Maine had become, metaphorically, the whole project, ideological and practical, of the counterculture. George's friends Peter and Elka Schumann were in the process of moving their street theater, the Bread and Puppet Theater, from Manhattan to northern Vermont. Paul Goodman had spent his summers for some years in New Hampshire in a rural environment that became increasingly important to him in his later writing. Jules and Helen Rabin, radical friends of George, were establishing themselves in Plainfield, Vermont. Many others were moving as well. By 1970 scores of communes and hundreds of artists and intellectuals had moved into the previously remote and "backward" region from Lake Champlain on the west to the coast of Maine on the east. George and Mabel chose Temple, Maine, a very small town in the center of the state. The poet Theodore Enslin was already there. Other writers— Denise Levertov, Mitchell Goodman, Henry Braun, Michael Rothschild, John Irving—were either in the area or soon would be, along with many painters and musicians. The tide of earlier years, when poets like E. A. Robinson and Louise Bogan had fled their origins in the poverty of rustic Maine, had been reversed. Rusticity had become fashionable.

George and Mabel bought a farm on a hill four or five miles from the center of the village and characteristically added a huge wing to the farmhouse, containing a single barnlike room with an immense fireplace at one end, a well-equipped kitchen at the other, and dining tables, work tables, game tables, sofas and chairs, carpets and beanchairs, spread out in between. As I knew it this room was always filled with children, townspeople, visitors—an immense, untidy, very comfortable space, the scene of many parties, readings, theatrical performances. It even contained a ping-pong table and a machine for serving and returning shots. Gathering the hundreds of balls from all over the room and returning them to the machine became a continual chore. In his later years George practiced table tennis ardently; he became good enough to play against a number of regional champions, mostly Chinese or Korean immigrants. "Wretched Orientals," he would say. "They have all the advantages"—George being too stocky to match their litheness.

George lived a good life in Maine until cancer destroyed him when he was still relatively young. He was planning a big comic novel, epical, about the conjunction of traditional culture and the counter-culture in Maine, about the historical, philosophical, and political importances. It would have been an extraordinary book, very likely a masterpiece—hilarious, trenchant, passionate, touched with pathos. But George was too slow, the cancer caught up with him.

Meanwhile we have two other masterpieces. *Luisa Domic* is the political novel par excellence of our time, meaning the novel of our real lives in this world—not as flashy or violent as many of the other fictions that have compelled our attention in the past twenty years, but of far more enduring value. *Shawno* is the best work of its kind I know, and I'm not forgetting Thomas Mann's charming *A Man and His Dog (Herr und Hund)* of 1918. Both *Luisa Domic* and *Shawno* are fictions, they bring together experiences which were not together in actuality, but they are closely, very closely, attached to George Dennison's actual existence, inner and outer. They are works of a supremely moral sensibility, impelled by the energies of great talent and profound feeling. They are what we truly need.

—HAYDEN CARRUTH

LUISA DOMIC

$$\begin{bmatrix} \text{P A R T} \quad \text{O N E} \end{bmatrix}$$

A month after the military coup in Chile we received a phone
call from our friend Marshall Berringer, who for the third
time in ten days was escorting a Chilean refugee from New
York to Canada. His previous trips had been to Montreal. This time
he was going to Quebec City, and since we lived in central Maine,
three hours from the border, he asked if he could stay with us on the
way. The following morning Patricia and I ate an early breakfast and
she drove off to her antinuclear conference in Augusta, an hour to the
south. She expected to be back in the evening, perhaps in time to
welcome Marshall.

It was early in October, a Saturday. The days had been sunny and
clear, and the hillsides facing our own across the valley had reached
their peak of color and were blazing with reds and yellows. This day,
too, promised to be warm, but since the children would be in the
house alone, I built a fire of slow-burning yellow birch in the cast-iron
stove before going to my cabin studio half a mile uphill through the
woods.

The town road ended in our dooryard, and was maintained all year,
though ours was the only house it served. The woods road, however,
hadn't been used since the time of wagons, and had become almost a
tunnel, the trees beside it were so numerous and tall. Crisp leaves rat-
tled at my feet and it wasn't until I turned into the grassy little field
before my cabin that my footsteps were silent again.

Several times during the day I heard the dogs barking and heard cars and trucks arriving at the house. I had been writing of rural occupations, the old life that had vanished into the economic networks of the cities. My papers had grown numerous and needed to be organized, yet each time I heard the dogs, I went out of the cabin and walked up and down in the sunny little field . . . and each time, feeling the freshness and warmth of the air, I stretched out lazily on the grass. There had been a freeze the week before that had blackened leaves in the garden and had covered the puddles by the barn with delicate sheets of ice, which the children had lifted carefully and had held before their faces, peering at one another as through panes of glass, but now the sun was warm, and the sky was a lucid blue. The insects of summer were gone. Most of the birds were gone. I could hear the voices of adults in the stillness, and—more clearly—the ringing voices of children, among them my own. We would be pressing cider in a week, and our friends, acquaintances, and neighbors had begun bringing apples. There was scarcely any breeze, yet once while I lay there the gleaming long filament of a migrating spider drifted by me just a few feet from the ground, bellying deeply and changing shape continually. The spider clung to the end of it. We had seen several of these shining strands drifting over the nearby pond just the day before, when I had taken the children for one last ride in the canoe and we had glided over water so quiet and so crowded with images of hills and clouds that we seemed to be floating on air, and the usually boisterous children had knelt before me silently on the floor of the little boat.

I went back to the house late in the afternoon, stopping first at the barn to see what had happened. The fragrance of apples was strong. Blades of sunlight gleamed in the cracks between the boards, and the whole of the dusky, lofty space was striped with molten lines, vertical in the sides and horizontal in the gables. A week from today perhaps twenty people, adults and children, would be working and chattering here, some feeding apples to the motor-driven grinder in the loft, others pushing the pulp down a wooden chute, still others levelling it in layers on the platform of the huge old press. The fragrant, many-colored apples, in the meantime, were waiting in boxes and feedbags by the grinder, and I went up to inspect them. I remembered the elderly neighbor, dead now, who ten years ago, at our first pressing, had turned the apples in their boxes with the rubber-tipped point of his cane, identifying each orchard (most of them abandoned) by its fruit.

"I see you been up Soames place," he said.

"What?"

"Them Black Oxfords and Twenty-Ouncers is from the Soames place, ain't they? And that lot there is from Carpenter's. Them trees won't last much longer. It's good you're gitten 'em. Ayeh . . . you've got Baldwins and Spies all together in these boxes. Them are drops, ain't they? That's how I know." (He had begun to smile at my amazement.) "I grafted them trees. Them are the six trees by the house . . . pie trees. Well . . . you'll git good cidah. Bettah cidah than with all one kind. . . ."

The floor had been swept. The big press of stout maple timbers had been scrubbed and covered with sheets of plastic. Later in the week parts of it would be waxed.

The unhurried, firm blows of the ponies' hooves sounded on the plank floor below me, and at the same moment the piano struck up in the big room in the house, just forty steps away. It wasn't music, quite, but a whimsical, droll jangling, in which, nevertheless, I could hear phrases from *Peter and the Wolf*, which Liza had been practicing for several weeks.

I took some apples from one of the bags, and tossed them to the ponies, having chased them ahead of me into the sunlight. They had been eating enormously for two months, first husks and tidbits of sweet corn, that had ripened progressively, and that I had always shucked kneeling on the grass by the garden, the ponies waiting restlessly beside me; then they had eaten "drops" from our own small orchard; and once had enjoyed a feast of slightly rotten pears. They seemed to have doubled in size, yet they were handsomer and more vigorous than ever. Soon their winter coats would be complete: richly colored, deep-piled hair that was almost fur, a mixture of soft and coarse that would bring them through our many nights of twenty below zero, and our few of forty.

The velvety black little mare, swinging her head and peering from one eye, pursued the apple I tossed to her. She ate it from the grass. Her full-grown foal, however, the handsome chestnut gelding, ate from my hand. He threw his head against me playfully, and rested its full weight in my hand while I scratched the grinding huge muscle at the base of his jaw. The warm, clean, pungent odors of his breath and barrelled sides were oddly heartening.

As abruptly as it had started up, the piano fell silent.

I whistled as I neared the house, and our powerful, black-and-white Bernese mountain dog, who slept outside all winter long, leaped up and whirled, as if hit with a stone. He had been sleeping in the sun. He braced his legs and barked at me and then, rocking enthusiastically fore and aft, bounded toward me. Immediately, from within the house, there came the muffled barking of the golden retriever, and the throttled howling of the malamute, and there appeared at the window and vanished from it, like the flashing of a light, Jacob's eager six-year-old face.

Three cardboard boxes, each big enough to hold all three children, lay in the center of the large room, not far from the piano. Sticks and bits of rope were nailed to two of the boxes, and one was draped with an old sheet. Two bright yellow raincoats lay nearby. Toys and dolls, two bongo drums, a broken guitar, crayons, paper, coloring books, clothing, and more, much more, lay scattered about the room. Handles of knives projected from jars of honey, peanut butter, mayonnaise, and jelly. Nothing had been put away. Butter and milk, bread and eggs, cheese, lettuce, laundry. . . .

Three guiltless, elated voices called, "Hi, Dad!"—or rather, the girls called; Jacob only glanced at me and bent again over the long table, copying something. "Wait! Wait!" he shouted. "Let me, Ida!"

The aging retriever, in the meantime, wagging his tail and whimpering loudly, brought me a stick, a rotten tree limb he had dragged in from outdoors, and while he pressed against my legs, moaning for attention, the young deep-furred malamute reared up and placed her paws daintily on my chest. A fire smoldered in the fireplace, and I could tell from the mess down there, and from the odors, that the children had toasted marshmallows and made popcorn. All three faces were glowing, were bright-eyed and calm, and were lightly touched by perspiration.

Ida, who was twelve, was laughing at something. She was leaning back against the sink. She caught my eye with her glance that characteristically combined elation and tenderness. "We had another fight, Daddy," she said. "He pulled my hair again. . . ."

"That means you started it," I said, knowing that Jacob, rowdy as he was, had never started a fight by pulling Ida's hair. Jacob shouted across to me, *"Yesss!"*

"No!" said Ida. "Daddy! Listen, Daddy. . . . He pulled me all the way from right about *there* to right about *here* . . . *by the hair!"*—but she said it rather admiringly.

Liza, who was propped up by pillows on the sofa at the far end of the room, near the fireplace, and who was nine years old, said calmly and definitively, "You started it, Ida."

"No I didn't, Liza."

Liza's posture and manner were regal, and she was entirely unaware of it.

"You did," she said calmly. "You gave him a wedgie."

"Yeah!" shouted Jacob. "She gave me a wedgie!"

"Well you gave me one too, didn't you?" said Ida.

"No, I didn't!"

"You tried to and then you got mad because you couldn't."

5

I asked them what a wedgie was, and all three laughed.

Liza said (she still lay in her regal pose), "It's when you reach inside somebody's pants and grab their underwear and pull it up so it gets wedged in their ass."

Again they laughed. Ida covered her mouth. She was blushing.

"Well he pulled my hair," she said.

"Ida!" said Liza. "You know damn well he pulled your hair because you gave him a wedgie."

"No siree, Liza. He pulled my hair because he got mad because he *couldn't* give me a wedgie."

Jacob had been listening to his sisters. He turned his radiant face to me and said, "You can't do a wedgie with girls' underwear."

"And you also punched him, Ida," said Liza.

"Well he punched me first because he couldn't give me a wedgie! Daddy, he's dangerous. He hit me with the broom."

At this Jacob's face clouded and his lower lip trembled. "I didn't *mean* to!" he cried. He adored Ida.

"Well you swung it all your might," she said.

"No I didn't, Ida!"

"And he hit me right here with the hard part. Look."

Her upper lip was red and slightly swollen.

There were tears in Jacob's eyes. "Well Ida," he shouted, "I didn't mean to!"

She bent her head toward him and said gently, "I know you didn't, Jacob. But you shouldn't swing something like that at anybody."

Still speaking in those soft tones, she said to me, "Jacob pulled his own hair after he hit me. He pulled a *hunk* of hair right out, Dad!"

Jacob was grinning again. He ran to me and hugged me. As far as I could see, he still had plenty of hair.

Liza called across to me, "And then he put the handcuffs on his ankle and wrist . . ." She meant his toy handcuffs, that actually worked.

"And you know what, Daddy?" said Ida. "Just then the phone rang and we all tried to get it. . . ."

6

Here again all three looked at one another and laughed.

"It was for me," said Jacob. "It was Mommy. And I couldn't get it."

"Jacob couldn't get the handcuffs off," said Liza, "and neither could I."

"You tried to help him?"

"No! I had some on me, too—"

At which very moment the telephone rang. Liza sprang up, and all three children, laughing and shouting, raced for the phone. Ida got there first, but Jacob clamored, "Let *me*, Ida! Let *me!*" and she stood aside and grinned as he leaped onto a chair.

It was this call—that I thought would be Marshall's, but was not; the caller was Harold Ashby, whose voice I heard with great pleasure, and whom I had known even longer than I had known Marshall—it was this call that set in motion the events of that weekend.

Jacob stood on the chair holding the phone with one hand and with the other balancing against the wall. "Hi!" he said. "Jacob. . . . Oh, yeah. Hi. Do you want to talk to my daddy? . . . Yes, he's here now. Do you want me to get him?" He called to me, and into the receiver said, "Here he comes," and, "You're welcome." (I was amazed to hear these civilities. We had not instructed him.)

I recognized Harold's voice at once, and said hopefully, "Where are you calling from?" He had stayed with us the previous Christmas, but we hadn't seen him since then.

"It's called the Blue Mountain Shopping Mall," he said. "I left a message with Ida. Make use of me now. What do you need?"

"Nothing. Nothing at all. Come ahead!"

I could see Ida in the other room whispering to Jacob, who seized the piece of paper he had been working on and came running. *Marshall will be late,* it said, in Jacob's own many-sized and wobbly letters. *Harold is coming.*

Harold had been driving since leaving his message.

I said to the children, "We have half an hour to clean up this mess!"

Liza and Jacob looked around them vaguely. The concept *mess* didn't quite exist in their minds. Everything their eyes fell upon seemed interesting and usable. Ida, however, took one look and laughed, and I could hear the throaty, ironic tones of her mother.

It was dark by the time I went into the garden to pick the vegetables for supper. Almost everything had been killed by the frosts that had preceded these beautiful, resurgent summer days, but the kale and brussels sprouts were thriving, the collards were still good, and some glossy little leaves had emerged in the clumps of wilted chard. I went without a flashlight, as I had learned to do, after the example of my country neighbors, just as I had learned to ignore all but the heaviest rains. I filled the shallow basket with greens. The congenial bulk of the house loomed beside me, and I could see Harold and the children through the yellow rectangles of the windows, all seated at the long table. The children faced him. They were leaning toward him and were smiling. He too was smiling and was leaning forward.

I was elated to see him. He was the only friend left to me from the time of my early manhood, but he was more than that; I thought of him, really, as an elder brother, a member of the family of the spirit certain friends become.

There was a photograph in the attic, a clipping twenty years old from the New York *Herald Tribune* in which Harold in evening clothes and I in a dark suit looked straight out at the reader. The occasion was the premiere of two new works of his, one of which—a choral piece—was a setting of a sequence of poems from my first book. It was not evident in the photograph that my suit belonged to somebody else, or that I had spent the day of the concert staggering up basement corridors with a hamper of rubble on my back. I was living from hand to mouth, as I had been doing for years, working slowly and with many misgivings toward my doctorate in psychology, writing poetry, and struggling unsuccessfully with fiction. I had been so hurried after work that I hadn't eaten, and then had rushed off on the subway in a lightheaded, euphoric state, filled with the optimism that had become chronic with me, and that both dulled and prolonged the terrible loneliness of my life.

Not a scrap of what I had hoped for came to pass. The woman of my longings was nowhere to be seen, nor were the new friends. I met a glossy, monied crowd, and at the party after the concert found myself repelled by their behavior. But it was on this night that I encountered Harold and his music.

Perhaps all art of consequence has the power of becoming self, or soul. But when the world of our own time is deepened or made brighter by art, we are not merely gladdened but are actually strengthened, as by a spiritual discovery, and there is an intimacy in this that can't be matched by the art of the past. Harold's music at first seemed light, as if it intended charm and not much more. It had the quickness and modesty of inspired conversation and, like inspired conversation, was filled with mind. Then feelings, of a sudden, seemed to be flourishing everywhere. One caught one's breath. It was thrilling. The feelings became emotions, and the emotions passions, the process all the while remaining spacious and lucid. I sat listening with a joyous shock of discovery. And when I recognized, in the first of the two pieces, words I myself had written not so long before, sitting at a white porcelain kitchen table, in the light of a student's gooseneck lamp, and with many tears . . . when I heard those words I felt a giddiness that almost made me laugh aloud. Far more than had the printing of the book, this public, social, sweet explosion of song took the poems away from me, freeing me utterly, and this was the last thing I could have guessed I wanted. Whatever those heartfelt things had meant to me, whatever I had suffered and perhaps had never understood, yet to some extent had requited, was carried away in the air, and momentarily I was unencumbered and as light as a bird.

At the party afterwards I had my first chance to look closely at the composer of this music.

Harold at that time was already famous. His fame was to grow, though his life, later, took two unexpected turns. I watched him that night with fascination. And I became aware that many others at the party were watching him too. One's eyes simply went back to him. There was a radiance about him, not only of intelligence, and gathered energies, but a simple brightness of eye and smile, and this was striking, because it was not the brightness of good health. On the contrary, there was something taut, thin-skinned, and overcharged about him. One guessed that had he been less strong some serious instability might have been evident.

He was tall, erect, and somewhat frail. His movements were both graceful and brittle, and this too, this minor drama of movement, was fascinating to watch. His hair was a sandy brown, and he wore it closely cropped in a military style. His skull was large and oddly shaped. The bony ridge above his eyes protruded, and his forehead slanted sharply. His nose was large, highly arched, and thin. His teeth were prominent and large, and gave a shy and boyish quality to his smile. The most striking feature, however, were his eyes. They were extraordinarily *noticing* eyes, gray, large, and round. One felt that nothing remained obscure to them, or hidden, yet his gaze was not probing, but encompassing and understanding. It was a maternal gaze, a "melting" gaze, and it freed his detachment of any hint of disdain. When I came to know him better I learned that this engaged detachment was even more defensive than I had guessed. Extreme emotions rose up within him continually, and he managed to live among people at all by what amounted to techniques of disengagement. But these were good defenses. The practice of his art was a powerful defense, and so were the simplicity and regularity of his life. I came to see that his modesty was the modesty of conscious abundance, and that the pride one sensed in him was made up of things powerful in themselves: admiration and outright love of the masters of his art, accountability to his own genius, and such ordinary virtues as patience and courtesy. One could not help but be aware of these many strengths. One felt that he would be true to himself under any pressure and to the very point of death. And yet one could not avoid the thought that, were certain fortuities to occur, he could quite rationally and perhaps without despair decide to cease to live.

All evening long a smile of happiness came to his lips. He was openly pleased by the praises of his friends. He was pleased by the musicians, the singers, and the conductor, and I overheard him several times express his gratitude to them. He came to me once, and in a friendly way said how well my lines held up under the pressure of singing. I thanked him, and remarked that Flaubert had tested his lines by shouting them, and his face brightened with interest.

Yet the pleasure one saw on his face never brought him closer to other people. He was pleased as from a distance, was pleased almost contemplatively. Among those who watched him was a handsome young man, who, so it seemed, watched him continually. I learned that the youth lived with him and was himself a composer. At times his lips were parted and his face pale with adoration. At other times a flush of anger darkened his face, anger infused with jealousy, and with envy as well, an envy so very hot as to look like hatred.

For a few years after that evening I saw Harold either by chance or at his initiative. Pairs of tickets came frequently. He disliked conducting, but on several occasions conducted things of his own in New York, and again I attended parties and receptions crowded with people whom otherwise I would never have encountered. He was prolific. One read of new work and of performances in Europe and England. Our song cycle was popular. A press pass arrived once for the festival at Spoleto, and I longed to go, but my life was in turmoil and I couldn't. Occasionally I met Harold by chance at the downtown, off-off-Broadway lofts and churches and made-over garages in which new theater, dance, and music were emerging, and to see him dressed informally was like encountering a high-ranking officer out of uniform; it always took me by surprise. But in fact we had acquaintances in common; and on one occasion he wrote some music for a modern dance company that I knew well indeed, since it was a member of this company whom I had come to love, and soon afterwards married. So great a happiness came into my life that I ventured to take seriously my innermost feelings about work, however impractical they might be. I dropped academic psychology once and for all and, with a hopefulness I hadn't known since youth, concentrated entirely on writing. Within eight months my marriage was ended and I was sick with loss and disappointment. The publication of my second book of poems, to which I had looked forward happily, was like the birth of a stillborn child. The prose fiction I had begun seemed unfinishable, and in my depression seemed not worth finishing anyway. I cured myself of at least the worst of my depression by plunging into a work that did use my powers, and that in itself—that is, without regard to the future—meant a great deal to me. This was psychotherapy with severely disturbed children. I could not have guessed, at the time, that this work that drew so much on specialized training would initiate a real friendship with Harold. I couldn't imagine that he would be interested.

It dawned on me only gradually that I had lost touch with him. I wrote to him, and telephoned, but the letter came back, and the telephone number was no longer active. And then I heard that he was living away from the country. And then I heard that he no longer wrote music.

My own life began to change, and soon it changed enormously. I took part in a two-year experiment with severely disturbed children, in which the therapeutic hope was placed in the specializations of a curative environment and in relations among the children themselves rather than in sessions with experts. The project was well-endowed, our staff was superb, and our results were stunning. I published several essays on this work, and was commissioned to write a book. To the extent that I was able to, I wrote from the point of view of the children themselves, and evidently some small part of the great poignancy of lives that made this work so moving did come through in my book, and this gave it a breadth of appeal I had not imagined it might have. By the time the book came out the project had ended, and I had cut my ties—it proved to be final—with psychotherapy. I was writing fiction, which I had come to love. I had married Patricia. Ida was two years old. In a matter of weeks the book became well-known . . . and one day there came a note from Harold Ashby praising it and asking me to call him. He was living in New York. I telephoned that night at suppertime and we made a date to meet, and then a mere three hours later encountered one another by chance at a party attended exclusively (except for us) by psychologists, not one of whom seemed to be aware of Harold's earlier fame.

His short-cut hair had turned gray, and there was a pallor, or rather a gray cast to his skin. But the same noticing, luminous eyes hovered as it were above his body, and the same interested, quick, forgiving, large-toothed smile came often to his lips.

I had both heard and read that he had stopped composing, yet it was oddly shocking to hear him say that it was true. I didn't question him, but he saw the questions forming in my mind, and smiled and nodded. A tremor agitated his eyes, a small tic or spasm in which the eye-balls seemed about to turn upward into his head. I couldn't tell whether he was aware of it or not. He had heard that my marriage had ended and that I had married again, but he was surprised to hear that I had given up psychotherapy, and he seemed to be disappointed. We stood in a corner of the noisy room talking loudly with complete privacy, as were the many others standing near us, all of whom seemed to be shouting, leaning toward each other, sipping from drinks.

He had been living in Majorca. He had never said much to me about his life and didn't now, only that the single event that had mattered to him in years was meeting his present lover, a psychologist and an accomplished amateur pianist, named Richard Rasmussen. They had met in Majorca, and Harold had left with him on a tour of British centers for retarded children. The tour had been financed by a grant. Harold was working now with Ricky, and had found a way of using music therapeutically.

Again he saw things forming in my mind, this time suppositions about the music, and pity for the (supposed) terrible descent to nursery-school piano-thumping.

He smiled at me, waiting for this mental process to reach its end.

"I'd like for you to see what we're doing," he said. "I'd love to talk with you about it"—and a few days later, in the basement rooms of a church off lower Fifth Avenue, I witnessed something so moving, and actually so beautiful that in telling of it later to Patricia I omitted to say that in a technical sense—that is, as therapy—it had seemed to me to be brilliant.

I sat in a chair, out of the way, in one of the two cheerful, simple rooms in the basement of the church. Harold sat at the piano looking back over his shoulder toward the open door, through which could be heard a strange wailing, louder and more desperate than the wailing of early infancy but with the same dense, impacted timbre. I could hear, too, a low voice speaking encouragingly. Ricky Rasmussen came into the room bending over and bringing along gently and yet by force a boy of nine, who struggled and braced his feet, tried to hide his face, and wailed that dense, thick sound that—I well knew—constituted his entire human speech. Finding himself brought implacably into the center of the room, he gave up struggling and wailed louder and unremittingly, drowning out the quiet voice of Rasmussen, who knelt beside him holding him by one arm.

There now occurred something that told me much about my own existence, and that moved me to tears and brought a gasp to my throat.

A flowing, beautiful music came from the piano at which Harold sat, looking back at the child as he played. The music imitated the crying of the child, resembled it uncannily in tone and pitch, rhythm, loudness, accent—except that all these things were woven into a simple and lovely song. And there was something miraculous in this transformation of lonely crying into a responding social voice of structured music. It was as if some evolutionary process had been laid bare and one were witnessing a primordial achievement of community, or the emergence upward from the inchoate into mind. The boy continued to cry, and he did not alter his position, but his voice registered his attraction and puzzlement. The song impinged upon him, one could well believe, with the minimal otherness of a warm small rain. To anyone familiar with autistic children, whose faces are placid as those of china dolls, and whose eyes seem never to perform the action of focusing, and who never by the slightest muscular twitch give evidence of human interest, this reflex of awareness was startling.

The crying continued, and the music accompanied it. But the boy's awareness of the music had altered his crying, and this small change entered immediately into the music. Again the boy noticed; the noticing was audible . . . and the music took up this new element and displayed it in the musical structure, which itself had no parallel in the boy's voice but was the otherness, or world, into which he was being lured. In later sessions that I witnessed, months afterwards, Harold added words to the music, and Ricky small actions, and to see the boy accept these things, however guardedly and on however small a scale, was like witnessing the dawning of human consciousness. One could not observe this and be unaware of the pain, vulnerability, and grave animal dignity of individuation. To the extent that Harold's music momentarily became environment, the boy found himself in a situation he had not experienced since infancy, when mere crying had had the status of action and had brought about change. And I could not help but believe that the beauty of the music was essential to the therapeutic task. All of it, conception and execution both, seemed to me to be a work of genius. And as was true of all such works, once stated, once displayed, it seemed inevitable, as if it had enjoyed some prior existence.

All during that first session, which was brief, a mere seven or eight minutes, Richard Rasmussen knelt beside the boy with an arm around his waist. At one point the boy was so intrigued by the responsiveness of the music that he really seemed to be testing it, using his crying in an exploratory way. Harold responded with a two-note phrase of his own, but the boy rejected it and began to cry again in earnest. Several musical instruments lay nearby on the floor, among them an expensive gong. Rasmussen drew it close, set it upright in its stand, and holding the boy's tiny hand in his own very large one, struck the gong with a mallet. The piano shifted into a rhythmic, playful invitation but the boy's thin, tense shoulders grew more rigid and he wailed loudly. I remembered the crying I had heard in the delivery room at Ida's birth, the small voice making such a familiarly human sound yet seeming so far away and scarcely human. Harold responded to the boy immediately, and for a short while played to this new crying, and then unhurriedly and with striking artistic fidelity came to a formal ending, and Rasmussen led the boy gently from the room.

Harold glanced at me. I indicated how moved I was, and he smiled.

In the fraction of a minute before Rasmussen came back, a memory that had been stirring beneath my consciousness broke through in full detail. I remembered a Sunday morning during the years of my early manhood when I lived alone and was estranged from my family, or at least from my father. It was a time of loneliness and yearning and painful confusion. I was listening that Sunday to a gospel service on the radio, broadcast from a black church ("Negro," as was said then), and I was washing the accumulated dirty pots and pans. The sermon gave way frequently to spirituals sung by a choir of women, who led the congregation. It was a music of fervor and power. One could imagine the many anguishes of the week that sought release in this music, the singing of which—so it seemed to me—was the very heart of the service, was prayer, community, was actually the church itself. I yearned for such a church as this. The congregation began to sing again, and as the singing heated an extraordinary thing occurred, though it must have been common in that church. A woman's screams broke out within the singing. They flared like a fire in the night—wide-open, bloodcurdling screams, a too-muchness of grief or terror tearing itself loose from a body and soul that simply couldn't bear it any longer. I went into the other room and knelt by the radio, listening.

To my astonishment, the singing went on. But those many voices shifted their pitch and rhythm so as to include the screaming voice. It seemed to me that the congregation had turned to face the sufferer.

She screamed again and again, and the congregation, led by the choir of women, pressed close to her with their voices, producing enormous chords that resembled her screams and yet were variations on a familiar hymn. The fervent *hallelujahs* went on, the many-throated compassionating voice holding, nursing, and restoring the suffering woman until her screaming subsided . . . and the uplifted voices went back by swift stages, and all were shouting powerfully again the same sweet song they had begun together.

I heard quiet voices in the hall. Ricky Rasmussen came back, pushing a wheelchair in which sat a dark-haired twelve-year-old girl whose face was radiant with expectation, and who—I could see at once—was blind. She held her head backward at a strange angle, and cocked it slightly. She was spastic. I learned that she was an orphan and had been diagnosed as autistic, though in fact she was not, but had been suffering a depression so severe as to have been fatal. Her soft full lips were lengthened joyously. Her pale cheeks seemed sensitive and— if this can be said of cheeks—alert. Her ears were almost translucent. They were her organs of awareness, and the set of her head gave them prominence.

The piano greeted her as she entered, and Harold turned to her and sang with the music. His words were as ordinary as might be, were nothing but the standard formula of nursery schools, but in fact he had composed a lovely and appealing little aria, and his playing of it and singing of it reached out to her across the room.

He sang, "Good morning, little Nora. We're glad to see you."

And she replied to him, singing heart and soul in a voice distorted by spastic convulsions, "Good morning to *you!* Good morning to *you!*"

He kept playing to her and speaking to her by means of song, and I saw that he was leading her this way and that through efforts of neural and muscular coordination she would not otherwise have attempted and in fact could not quite manage but attempted joyously in her great delight.

He questioned her, singing, "Where are *you?* Where are *you?*" and she replied ecstatically, "I in school! I in school!"

He sang to her again, repeating the refrain in different registers, and the music coaxed her to follow it, which she did, first in ascending notes, and she kept attempting them even after her voice had cracked and become the mere shrill squeaking of a mouse, and then back through the middle registers and down into the bass, which again she couldn't manage but eagerly attempted.

Ricky knelt beside her all this while. She touched his face from time to time excitedly. He spoke to her gently, and moved her wheel-chair closer to the piano. As he did this, Harold modulated to a more rhythmic song, which Nora recognized and seemed to have antici-pated. She shouted joyfully, "Hit the gong! Hit the gong!" Ricky placed a mallet in her hand and guided her first few strokes, but she jerked away in a spasm of excitement and struck the gong as fast as she could, very awkwardly, and with too much force, shrieking continu-ously, "Hit the gong! Hit the gong!"

Harold looked back at her, and improvised a music that echoed her excitement, and in fact was rather grand. He and Ricky exchanged a glance, and Ricky caught her hand and slowed the crashing of the mallet. The music slowed, too, and reverted gradually to the little duet that had provoked that outburst. Nora sang, "Here I am!" and struck the gong; and again, "Here I am!"—and Harold modulated toward quietness, singing to her more and more softly, "Here I am . . . here I am . . ." until, with great difficulty, and assisted by Ricky, she had achieved rudimentary coordinations of movement and hearing that I knew were the first and crucial stages in a regimen that, though it might take years, would alter her life. Ricky pressed his hand rhyth-mically against her diaphragm. Her breathing came more and more under control and she achieved a gradual subsidence in her squeaking, quavering voice.

A round-faced woman wearing thick glasses came to the doorway, and was joined by a tall young man. They watched attentively for several minutes, and then went back to whatever they were doing with the children in the other room.

When the session was over, Nora shouted piercingly, "I see Harold! I see Harold!" She kept her head tilted back, but moved it continually in tiny spasmodic adjustments, angling her cheeks and ears minutely, as an insect might its antennae. Her sunken, discolored eyelids alone seemed insensitive. "Nora see Harold!" she shrieked again, her lips drawn back in a smile of rapture.

Ricky wheeled her closer to the piano, and Harold got off the rotating stool and knelt beside her, saying, "I'm here, Nora." She reached with both hands, striking his face several times with the uncoordinated fingers of her left. She pried open his lips, felt his nose and eyes, the sides of his head, his chin, his close-cropped hair. Harold was smiling. He glanced at me happily and winked. Ricky, too, was smiling, but his face became grave; and when Harold turned to him a somber glow suffused his cheeks and he looked at Harold with deep, deep love.

After two more sessions Harold and Ricky went into the adjacent room, where they conferred at some length with the assistants I had seen in the doorway. The young woman, I learned later, was the granddaughter of an analyst who had been a member of Freud's Vienna circle. Even a generation ago her engagement in the present work would have amounted to apostasy, but now her father himself, who was a colleague of Rasmussen's, and had been his mentor, was encouraging her.

Rasmussen came to the door and asked me to join them, which I did. But my thoughts, during that conference, kept flying back to the time when I too had worked with disturbed children. I remembered how desperately unhappy I had been when I had taken up that work, and how it had been the children themselves who had cured me. I remembered the extraordinary dreams that had come to me toward the end of my first year with them, five or six in a row, night after night, and then they had ceased. In these dreams the children appeared to me as if they had been "cured" and were normal (no such thing was possible). Their postures, facial expressions, and gestures, but above all their voices, were of a kind they did not possess and could not achieve, and yet were distinctively and characteristically their own. An autistic boy explained to me confidingly in a sweet outgoing voice why he never talked to anyone, why he isolated himself from the other children, why he laid his head continually to one side and draped one arm over it, so that his hand dangled by his ear. He was twelve years old. His syntax, in the dream, was proper to his age, but the unreflecting, trusting sweetness of his voice was what one might hear in a child of four. Another boy, who was impaired neurally, and was so assaulted by spasms of excitation that he was continually gasping for breath and could scarcely speak, explained to me the patterns of the nerves in his arms. They were marked on the skin in branching lines of yellow, blue, and red. Nothing of his explanation survived my awakening—but the astonishing voice in which he had spoken stayed with me. He was standing in an unaccustomed posture, was holding his breath in a peculiar way, measuring it, tensing and relaxing the muscles of his torso. Certain things in these dreams led to therapeutic strategies. But more than that, they touched a deep chord inside me of peace and confirmation. Most important of all, they showed me that whatever my feelings had been, and whatever they were now, I existed in the world for others, and they for me, in ways that had nothing to do with the vicissitudes of self.

These were the things I thought of as I sat listening to Harold and Ricky talk with their two young assistants. But I had still another marvel to encounter on that day.

Spread before me on the table as I write are a dozen small pages torn from a notebook. On one, surrounded by stars like marquee lights, are the words *The Court of Hamzad and the Enchanted Forest.* The performers of this play, who arrived just as we finished our sandwich lunch, were retarded boys of thirteen, fourteen, and fifteen, so-called mongoloids, who for several months had been coming down to the church twice a week from a facility outside the city. There were twelve boys. They dressed rapidly, pulling on hooded robes over their blue jeans and sweat shirts, and this moment, for me, was the first of many surprises. The costumes were beautiful. They were artfully designed and expertly made of expensive fabrics. An incandescent zigzag of lightning divided the black velvet robes of one performer, dark as the night sky. The same sky, but with stars and a crescent moon, abutted the blue sky and round yellow sun of day on the robes of another. On still another were fish and water plants; on another, birds in flight; on another, walking bears; on another, against a white ground, six hands of peace and blessing, upraised, palm out. The beauty of these brightly colored, well-made robes contrasted sadly with the darkened, sullen faces of the boys, whose slanted small eyes peered out guardedly from misshapen heads. The boys' arms were too short, their fingers short and soft, their bodies blocky and inarticulate. Yet their movements were precise and delicate, and their sullen expressions had nothing to do with the present activity, to which they gave themselves wholeheartedly.

Both Harold and Ricky acted parts in the play, which was a simple tale of good and evil, death and resurrection. Harold had written a great deal of music, and with Ricky had devised an assortment of physical and musical tasks for the boys, demanding, but not too difficult to be achieved. It occurred to me that only an artist, Harold in this case, could have understood so well the quantities and kinds of labor involved in the production of art, and the absolutely essential requirement that the whole of it be serious. The play would soon be toured in the East to other facilities for retarded persons, and not only Harold and Ricky but the boys themselves would give workshops. The performance I was watching was the fifth dress rehearsal.

The music, though extremely simple, seemed to me to be praiseworthy Ashby, haunting and lovely. Harold was dressed in long white robes, a venerable beard, a conical hat. From time to time he went to the piano and added his own contribution to the many musical tasks performed by the others. Music underlay everything. The sun was made to rise by the music of the Mage's court. Peasant travelers knelt to pray in the woods at night, and the notes of xylophones and piano seemed to come from their lips. The moon rose and the stars came out, and it was as if they were dancers drawn out of hiding by recorders. The boys performed their musical and physical tasks with an earnestness that at first impressed me by its purity, but that I then saw was a curious testimony to their condition, an oasis of adequacy in an absolute desert of failure. They were not engaged in the art of the theater, and certainly were not creating illusions. The important thing for each one was that he had been entrusted with a task required by his mates, by the play, and by Harold and Ricky. These things— demand, responsibility, serious tasks, inclusion in public ceremony— had been absent utterly from the boys' lives, and they concentrated in a way that was gripping to watch. From time to time they glanced at Ricky and Harold. They were as grave as older infants, but their gravity was shadowed and anxious and lacked the grace of healthy infancy. And because of the deficiencies of the boys, certain things occurred that were remarkable to see. It was as if a realm had been revealed that one had not known existed, a place of great pain and great love, and of the shyest, most despairing hope, and of a vast willingness.

The boys' glances were pleas for encouragement and guidance. On one occasion a boy turned to Harold in perplexity, and Harold bent over him and whispered to him, putting his arm around the boy's shoulders. The boy's face underwent a transformation; it opened and brightened, and he looked at Harold with adoration, and leaned against him. The play had come to a halt while the others waited, but seeing Harold hug the boy, they came running, first one, then several, then all. Ricky joined them, and he and Harold together stretched their arms around the entire twelve, who were smiling now and twittering like little birds.

There were other incidents. Ricky was costumed as a shaggy ape, who wore a golden crown and a red cape, and carried a sceptre . . . an

ominous but oddly attractive figure. He menaced the kingdom of the
Mage. And as often as this play had been rehearsed, the ape's menac-
ing dance, to the accompaniment of drum and gong, piano and
one-string bass, all played by costumed performers who left their
places to become musicians, frightened one of the boys, who lowered
his eyes and ran to the dancing ape, crying. The boy seized him
around the waist without daring to look up. The ape knelt in front of
him and removed his mask . . . and the boy immediately placed the
fingertips of both hands on Ricky's face. Ricky spoke to him sooth-
ingly. Whatever he said caused the boy to lower his head bashfully, and
Ricky evidently felt that that approach could not succeed. He reposi-
tioned the boy, and had him stand near Harold during the dance of
the ape. Soon the play was in motion again. Four members of the
Mage's court surrounded the ape and, as it were, hurled the swelling,
lucid notes of Whitechapel bells at him. Each boy shook one bell as
high as he could reach. Each bell sounded one note. A lovely song of
four notes circled and recircled the head of the ape . . . and suddenly
the ringing notes became white birds, large gulls with extended
wings. The birds were made of papier-mâché, and came sweeping
into view out of the same black curtain from which the moon and
stars had emerged, and like them were mounted on sticks. Two performers, costumed in black, with black hoods covering their faces,
swept the four birds round and round the ape, who swooned.

When I walked with Harold later that day, he mentioned the various people who had worked with him on this play. The costume
designer was well-known. So too was the choreographer, who had
attended several of the earlier sessions. Both were friends from
Harold's heyday in music.

We talked of another incident. It occurred when Harold, in his
Mage's robes, and wearing his gray wig and long white beard, held
high in one hand a sparkling small glass ball. As he displayed it, he
spoke in an incantatory way of the power of the evil kingdom. I
noticed a strange perturbation among the boys, and saw that all,

without exception, had ceased to be performers and had turned to watch him. Some of the boys seemed pleasantly excited, but several watched the glass ball apprehensively. Ricky too had ceased to perform, and was looking here and there at different boys. He had been rescued from his enchantment as an ape, and his large-boned, loose-limbed body was clad now in spring-green tights. The Mage passed one hand before the other, and spread the fingers of both hands, showing first the palms and then the backs. The glass ball had vanished. Several of the retarded boys were smiling tentatively, but others, though they had seen this trick dozens of times, seemed scarcely to be breathing; they watched with open mouths, forlornly and anxiously. I thought of the disturbed children with whom I had worked. They had been attractive children, some startlingly so, but they had been far more drastically afflicted than were these mongoloids. They had possessed scarcely any self at all, scarcely any world, or much sense of where their bodies ended. The disappearance of this glass ball, that was causing such consternation, would have meant nothing to them; it could have come and gone, and neither the coming nor the going would have required a cause, or have implied one. There was a pleading, somewhat frightened look on many of the faces before me. But now the Mage's hands moved in the air a second time, and the glittering ball could be seen once more poised on the tips of his long fingers. The boys sighed, and the tension left their faces.

The finale of the play was entirely musical. Everyone played an instrument. Harold directed; and then he sat at the piano and brought everything to a close with music that—so it seemed to me—might have won praise in the concert hall.

The play was ended. At least for the performers it was. For me it went on a few minutes more, and those minutes have been unforgettable.

Harold removed his wig and beard, and he and Ricky, standing together, clapped their hands, applauding the boys.

"It went *beautifully!*" said Ricky. "It couldn't be better, boys!"

"Just perfect! Just wonderful!" said Harold, and there came a response that brought back to me the deeper joys I had known as a therapist, though I had never seen a sunrise like this. The retarded boys ran to them like little children, their faces utterly happy, and for the next few minutes I witnessed a scene of such jubilation and bliss as I could not have imagined might exist in the city of New York.

I waited at the lunch counter of a nearby drugstore. I felt as one feels at times of convalescence: fragile and transparent, yet purified and gathered. Whatever necessitous thing had been in me once, and had been answered by my work with children, lived in me still, in ways I didn't know. Images came to me of my second wife. I could see her sitting across from me in a light robe at late Sunday breakfast; and stepping out of the shower, wearing a bathing cap, squinting; and standing at the stove, her black hair vividly black against the yellow blouse I had given her, turning, grinning at me over her shoulder; and lying next to me in bed. And I remembered the faces of the children I had worked with, and the deep chagrin I had felt at times, finding myself day after day surrounded by those wrecks. The efforts of salvage I had just been watching had brought these things back to me, as had the joy and anguish of the children, and the method itself, which aroused the technical interest I had once felt in such things. But what mattered to me most was the evident spiritual meaning of the work in the lives of both men. I thought without pain of the long period of loneliness after the failure of my marriage, and of how, gradually, I had learned to be alone. Harold, I knew, had undergone something similar. When I had talked with him at the crowded party just the night before I had seen a residue of suffering in his face, and when he had said to me that he was using music therapeutically, I had envisioned the kind of thing I had heard in nursery schools, and I had thought of it as just another detail of his agony. But no one can predict the effects of genius. What I had just witnessed in the basement of the church, that calling out of souls from perdition, or of the unformed from their chaos of mere sensation, was not like anything I had ever seen before.

And it seemed to me now that Harold's genius had not abandoned him, and had not abandoned music, though perhaps, indeed, it had abandoned the civilization of music and had gone to live in a place (to put it this way) that was primordial, or magical, and that perhaps deserved to be called sacred.

I sat at the counter drinking coffee, filled with admiration of this man whom, really, I didn't know very well. That he had been able to attract to himself a person like Richard Rasmussen seemed to me still another impressive thing about him. Seeing them like this, in action together, I understood that I had come upon one of those rare relationships that increase the power of each member enormously, as when a husband and wife lend energy, hopefulness, and faith to each other, or as when parents lend courage and pride to a child, or siblings instill confidence in one another. The love of the two men was obvious; nor could I imagine it waning, there was such empathy and admiration in it. When Ricky had taken off his mask during the play and had knelt before the frightened boy, I had seen a deep, not entirely digested sorrow in his large-boned face. He had held the boy's arms and had looked at him without pity, but with a compassion of the kind that remains objective, or that continues some essential sacrifice and does not convert the suffering of another into a secret consolation of self. I knew already that this was unpaid work, that he had devised the project and supported it himself on the earnings of his practice with adults. I saw now that this compassionate objectivity permeated his relations with the children. Everything he did had the clean, simple lines that come of integrity and generosity.

Harold walked into the drugstore smiling and elated. It was late April. He wore a gray wool cardigan and a shirt without a tie. He inclined his head and greeted the middle-aged woman at the cash register, and then greeted the stout middle-aged sandwich man at the counter, both of whom clearly knew him and knew who he was.

The counter at which I sat was the same at which, years ago, I had sat with other students before classes and after lectures. I felt almost as if those exciting times had come again, I had so much to say to Harold. We went out immediately into the mild, sunny day, and began walking more or less aimlessly. Ricky would join us in an hour. I tried to tell Harold how moved I had been by what I had seen, and how brilliant it seemed to me as therapy. He explained certain remarks I had heard at their little conference, and spoke of some workshops Ricky would be holding soon. He wanted to know why I had left the field, and whether or not I missed it.

But all the while, as we talked, I could see that something else was on his mind, and I realized that what he wanted to know was my reaction to Ricky. I was glad to speak the praise I felt.

He listened to me with a lowered head, smiling shyly. "His mother is quite wonderful," he said. "Very like him. She's eighty-three, and still vigorous. She's going to India next week for the third time this year. She still has friends there, and the children of friends, and the grandchildren.

"She worked with Gandhi at two different periods," he said, "first at the Tolstoy Farm in Africa, and then in India on the staff of the paper. Her parents were Quakers, and she is, and Ricky is. . . ."

We went a few steps more, and he looked at me and said, "We've been so happy it almost frightens me"—and then hurriedly told me more of their work together. What I had seen was a small sampling.

We walked a block east and went past the Cedar Bar, and then on down to Washington Square Park, where renovations were under way, and then back to the Eighth Street Bookstore, and then up Fifth Avenue to where we had started. We looked in the windows of a used-book dealer, since it was here that Ricky was to join us.

It was a pleasant, old-fashioned, book-crowded place, of a good size, one of the oldest in the city and one of the few of its kind still left to us, a reminder of what the civilization of cities used to be. In the large windows on either side of the door were sets of Flaubert, Cooper, Dumas, Garland, Frazer. Mounted above them were large engravings in black and white of the biblical plagues, and color prints of French infantry and cavalry in red-and-blue uniforms. There were two photographs in frames, one of George Sand, the other of Chopin. Both frames incorporated autographs below the likenesses, notes each had written the other. These were propped on stacks of art books. In front of the stacks, close to the window, a Fra Angelico was held open by a stand, showing an enlarged detail of a painting: a chorus of angels in glorious robes, blowing golden horns.

Harold saw that I too was looking at the angels. His face came alight with wit. "They look like physicists, don't they?" he said. "Or like Italian Mozarts."

I supposed that he meant that they had such lucid, intelligent faces, faces of genius and great beauty. And he did mean this, but I was surprised by what he went on to say.

"I don't think that the God who invented mountains, and oceans, and whales, and hurricanes would have surrounded Himself with angels like these," he said. "He'd be attended by retarded angels, like the kids you just saw. . . ." And he sketched out for me a little story that I have never forgotten, and that has grown larger in my mind because I have thought of it so many times. What he said, more or less, was this:

The Retarded Angels are at a loss in heaven among all the lucid souls. They are unaware of their misshapen faces and small eyes, their stubby arms and soft fingers, but they are aware that many things go on without them, and they are often vacant, dull, and sulky. But then the Lord calls one to the throne, and the Angel's response is so quick that it's clear that he has responded to the intake of the Lord's breath preceding speech, or perhaps even to movements prior to that, a twitching of the neck before the Lord even turned to look for an Angel. The Angel kneels at the throne with his head thrust forward, and the Lord speaks a brief message to him, and tells him it must be taken all across the heavens. The Angel knows he must face terrible darkness, and dangerous winds, and solitude, but he nods gravely to the Lord, and is so intent on the words of the message that he neglects to speak at all, but gathers his entire being around the single sentence of the message. He leaps down into the darkness of the world, saying the words over and over to himself. And he goes that way through the upper skies, blinking in the wind and gritting his teeth against the cold. He must go through fearful places, and is subject to damage, but his only fear is of forgetting the message. Finally he arrives before the recipient and speaks the message aloud. He stares at the recipient with that sullen, serious face and says, "Can you say it?" and the recipient is puzzled, because the Angel seems to be saying *Are you able to? Do you possess the necessary powers of comprehension, memory, and speech?* And then he sees that the Angel is retarded, and he repeats the message to the Angel, who nods gravely and humorlessly, and without saying goodbye leaps into the darkness and goes back the way he had come, blinking in the wind again and gritting his teeth. His whole existence now is concentrated on the words he intends to say to the Lord: "I delivered the message." And finally he arrives in heaven and comes before the Lord and stands there waiting to be invited to speak. The Lord sees that his wings have been damaged and his garments torn, and the Lord says to him in a kindly voice, "Yes, my Angel?" And the Retarded Angel says, "I delivered it." And the Lord says, "You did well," and there comes over the Angel's face a brightness that even Fra Angelico couldn't depict. He rushes to the Lord and kneels beside the throne and puts one hand on the Lord's shoulder and one on His wrist and looks at Him in bliss.

"I think the Lord would love that look," Harold said. "I think he'd be astonished by it in the same way that, though He made the wind and the water, He's astonished by waves and delighted by them. And so He nods and strokes the Retarded Angel's face."

During all this story Harold glanced at me only once or twice and stood there gazing at the splendid robes, the lucid faces, and the massed golden trumpets of the angels.

"I don't believe in God," he said, "but those are the angels I'd paint if I could paint like Fra Angelico."

It was still light. We stood on the porch waiting for Harold. The curves and slopes of our mile-long road send two acoustic channels to the house, and twice we had heard the sound of a motor.

Ida and Liza understood quite clearly who was coming, but Jacob was confused.

"Do you remember that guy who came with those people at Christmastime?" said Liza. She was about to say more, but Ida broke in.

"Jacob, he was the one who played the piano when we sang Christmas carols."

"And he gave us those sleds that look like a chair on a ski," said Liza.

"Yeah!" shouted Jacob. "And he changed a regular ordinary egg to a chocolate egg!"

"Him," said Liza.

"Yaaay!"

The three dogs were standing in the road looking down the hill, barking vigorously, as if trying to outdo one another. Their movements grew more agitated and their barking louder. They began to rear as they barked . . . and a glossy red car, with exactly the look of a rental car, drove slowly into their midst, turned a right angle, and rolled to rest under the towering locust trees. Harold emerged from the car as Jacob and Liza, who had raced to it exuberantly, arrived there only to stand grinning side by side, looking up at him shyly while the still-barking dogs wove this way and that among all three.

I knew him at once, of course, yet for the briefest fraction of a moment I saw him as one might see a stranger, a man as yet unadorned by relation, a man in uncertain health, with (one would say) not many years to live, whose skin was oddly gray, but in whose face and brilliant eyes one saw a luminous and joyous quality, and whose prominent teeth were exposed in a shy smile, and whose close-cropped gray hair and sharp, high cheekbones could be those only of Harold Ashby, our own friend, whose arrival gladdened everyone.

Jacob ran to the house with Harold's small suitcase, and Ida ran beside him carrying the wine and ice cream he had brought. They both came running back a mere moment later.

Arching, and massaging the small of his back with both hands, Harold, after exchanging an embrace of greeting, looked this way and that at our brightly colored hills.

"What beautiful country it is," he said. "I've been admiring it all the way up. I passed several tour buses filled with blue-haired ladies out to see the maple leaves."

He wanted to stretch his legs. We walked around onto the broad, coarse lawn that flanked the house and that merged downhill with the undulating, tree-bounded pasture, still green with the rich, bronzed green of autumn. The valley and the broad expanse of hills lay spread out before us, and the children—and I too—smiled proudly to hear these things praised by our friend from the city.

Abruptly, after the smiles and hesitations of the first moments of meeting, a hubbub of conversation rose up. Jacob clamored to know if Harold had brought a chocolate egg; Ida and Liza reminded him of the sleds, which "really worked" and were "really neat"—and Harold smiled down at them.

Two bikes lay on the grass, and a yellow Frisbee, and a blue sweat shirt of Jacob's, and Jacob's sneakers, and a jump rope. Shouting, "Watch! Watch! I can ride a bike! Watch!" Jacob demonstrated his prowess, looking continually at Harold's face and not at all where he was going. Liza snorted and said, "Big deal."

We heard a muffled, rapid, resonant drumming. It came from the earth, and very rapidly grew louder. Ida glanced at me, brightening, and said, "Here they come!" The loud drumming grew louder still, and abruptly our two ponies, who had circled the house from the other side, burst into view on the broad lawn. They were going full tilt, holding their heads high, bunching and stretching and bunching again, their muscular haunches rounding in full curves and their noisy hooves striking the earth vehemently at the very points, as if to dig in. It was a running so exuberant, so playful and proud, that very often the children jumped and cheered for them, though the ponies had run like this at sundown every day for years. Their route varied, and was subject to improvisation, and to what seemed to be challenge and response, first one and then the other taking the lead, but their joyous and prodigal expense of energy had never changed. It was as if they were shouting and laughing and could not help doing so. Leaning suddenly at alarming angles they wheeled, came vertical again, and went back the way they had come, the loud drumming of their hooves becoming hollow and reverberant as they crossed an underground course of granitic ledge. They passed out of sight behind the house, then wheeled between the house and garden and came boisterously into view again. They swerved across the yard, not far from where we stood, and galloped straight down into the hilly pasture. The mare whinnied melodiously, and her large chestnut colt, with a long and amazing vibration of his nostrils, snorted back to her and then ducked his head between his forefeet. He heaved his massive rump high into the air and released a short, quick, two-footed kick in the direction of the clouds, then resumed his galloping without losing speed or falling behind his mother.

Ida clapped her hands and shouted gleefully. The ponies plunged on down the hill. They circled the clump of trees, and with an evident laboring of shoulder muscles came galloping back. Slowing perceptibly, but still galloping, they passed us. They crossed the yard in front of the house, went on across the road, and entered the orchard pasture where their sprint had begun, and where the sound of their hooves finally ceased.

The dogs, as always, had been stirred by this performance, but the golden retriever had been tumbled once by the gelding's hooves, and the Bernese mountain dog had been kicked a number of times, and now both, though they started off in pursuit, soon slowed and circled back to us. The canny, tireless, wolflike malamute, however, stopped for another reason. She had been chastised severely for harrying the ponies. She leaped at them, crouching, and went a few paces, then changed her course, glancing back at me guiltily. She threw herself on the ground and yawned, dropped her head abjectly on her paws, then got up and trotted briskly across the yard.

Everyone was smiling, as after any great show of prowess and benign vitality.

"They look like circus ponies," said Harold, "the way they tuck in their chins and point their toes. What a glorious run!"

Ida turned to me with a glowing face and said, "Tell him about the swallows, Dad."

She meant the sleek and powerful fork-tailed swallows who in varying numbers came back to our barn year after year. They were the swiftest of flyers, and all summer long, just before dark, after their hunting for insects was ended, they had sprinted as had the ponies, hurtling round and round the house at high speed in breathtaking undulant loops.

But the memory that dwelt in Ida's mind, and that brought such a glow to her face, was really of something else. We had sat side by side on the topmost wooden step of the unroofed front porch, in the greenest and sweetest of late summer evenings, and had watched the ponies speed by, and had watched the swallows circling the house, swooping out to the barn and back, around and around; and admiring all these things, we had fallen unaware into a bliss of contentment. I had said to her, "The swallows are like dolphins," and her face had brightened. She knew exactly what I meant. And because I saw that look of discovery on her face (she was glimpsing new uses of the process of abstraction; she was seeing another of the many ways in which accumulated experience acquired mental form and was discovering that the analytical mode could be a mode of praise), because I saw that look, I said to her, "Tell me what the dolphins and swallows and greyhounds and cheetahs and falcons have in common," and she grinned and said, "Oh, they're speedy, Dad!" And I said, "Yes, and they have in common that they make you say 'Oh'"—at which she smiled more brightly still, being well aware that she had just said "Oh!" We agreed that our ponies, delightful as they were, were not fast enough or splendid enough to be included in that company. "But they make us say 'Oh!'" she said. "We say it all the time"—and we talked of the "Oh!" of delight, or of admiration touched by love, and the "Oh!" of praise and tribute, or of admiration touched by awe.

All this was what she meant when she looked at me with that glowing face and said, "Tell him about the swallows, Dad."

I described the swallows to Harold (they had migrated several weeks ago); and saying that we had decided they looked like dolphins, I put my arm around Ida's shoulders, drew her to me, and kissed her temple.

Talking of such things, and in this mellow mood, we continued our tour (Jacob wobbling on the bicycle), letting Harold stretch his legs and relax from the strain of the two-day conference, at which he had been principal speaker and the subject of several interviews.

We went the way the ponies had come, but in the reverse order, going behind the house and then to the garden on the uphill side, where we leaned on the cedar rails and looked at the surviving greens, which were surprisingly numerous. We crossed the road, and went past the barn into the orchard pasture.

The ponies were standing quietly under an apple tree. They lifted their heads and looked at us. The fenced-off corn garden was bare except for a dozen orange pumpkins.

Ida picked up a stick, took aim, and threw. Three MacIntosh apples, dark red against the rich blue sky, had survived our picking and dangled from the topmost branches. She missed badly and stood there laughing while Liza and Jacob raced for the stick. The ponies, in the meantime, had been watching all this and came toward us with lazy, heaving motions, hanging their heads and moving their bodies as if in sections.

We went to the barn and Harold inhaled deeply at the door. "What an aroma!" he said. "It's like a drink of cider!"

Blades of daylight still glowed between the boards, though not with the molten brilliance I had seen before. I took him into the loft to see the apples, and we looked down at the press and barrels. He had begun to speak of Ricky, whose mother had died just three weeks ago, at the age of ninety-two. Her death had not been unexpected, yet its effect on Ricky had been severe. They had been close, and she had been remarkable. Even in her eighties she had organized food missions in several Third World countries, and in her seventies had helped with a land distribution program in India, living for two years at a village ashram. Harold had called me when she died, and had told me then that Ricky was suffering. I had invited them to come stay with us, thinking that a country interlude might be restful. But their situation in New York could scarcely be improved upon. They lived in a West Village brownstone that Ricky and his mother had owned together and that had been in the family for three generations. Ricky's mother had lived on the floor above their duplex, and the top floor had been occupied for many years by a close friend, a woman, who directed a concert choir.

We left the barn and went to the house. I said to Harold that Marshall would be arriving soon with the Chilean refugee. Harold was not political, but he glanced at me and said, "What a dreadful thing! What a loss in the world!" Soon, however, his thoughts went back to Ricky. He lowered his voice, though the children were still in the orchard. "If he weren't so strong and dutiful and could just collapse, collapse utterly, he'd get through it much faster. It's his time of life more than Mary's death. He's been working so hard, and gives so much. I really think he's been going through a breakdown, and now her dying has simply been too much."

⁓

While Jacob, Liza, and Ida bustled about setting the table, and I fetched things from the refrigerator, Harold, as if automatically and uncontrollably, went to the piano. He stood at the keyboard and ran his fingers up and down the keys, producing instantaneously little melodies characteristically his own.

"Not everyone has a piano in the kitchen," he said teasingly to Liza, who had gone over to watch his fingers.

She drew herself up and said, "This is the living room." She was grinning, and was delighted that he had remembered their little routine—which she herself (so I guessed) had almost forgotten.

I took him a bourbon and water, and found an ashtray for him. He carried them to the chair by the telephone in the cluttered front room, and while I stood at the stove cooking hamburger, broccoli, and leftover pasta for the children, and while the children finished setting the table and then traveled back and forth to the woodshed, he talked on the phone to Ricky.

Even if I had not known that Ricky was suffering a breakdown, I would have inferred from Harold's words that something serious had happened. He was obviously trying to engage him in practical tasks.

He said, "For my sake, Ricky, please. I'm not saying you're wrong, you're probably quite right, or *will* be right in a couple of weeks, but in the meantime it *does* make sense to take them. You agreed with this yourself. . . . I know, Rick, I know . . . but you're supposed to be resting, and resting means precisely that you *don't* meet those demands. I'll be home tomorrow night. Did you get the haddock? And the racks? . . . Good. Have you made the fumet? . . . But Ricky, you *must*. Don't let them sit there. . . . Yes. It would be so nice to come home to that. Really. I've been eating conference food. . . . Yes, it went splendidly. I'm bringing a tape for you. Ricky, do you remember Mrs. Johnson? I know you do. . . . Yes! Yes! We had a wonderful talk. She's going to write you. She admires you enormously. . . . Yes . . . exactly. . . . I said bring the clinic to New York and we'll think about it. I believe actually she wants to come back herself. . . . Well . . . yes . . . check, maybe we have some. . . . By all means, if we don't. That would be marvelous. . . . No, you must, you simply must. Tomorrow is Sunday, isn't it? . . . I know, darling, I know, but you mustn't be. Is Eleanor in town? . . . What about Jerry? Have you spoken with him? . . . But you don't have to do it that way. . . . Now Ricky, listen to me. What you want is reassurance, isn't that so? And some expression of sympathy, and perhaps even of love. And you know that Jerry actually does feel all those things for you. Call him and say to him directly, Jerry, I am going to spare you the details, but I have called to obtain expressions of reassurance, sympathy, and love. . . . Ha ha! . . . Yes. . . . Yes, Ricky. . . . Good! Call me back whenever you want to. Don't hesitate. Everyone here sends their love. It's turning cool now, but the day was quite warm. It's simply gorgeous. I wish you were here. We all do, but especially I. . . . Yes. Yes. Gladly. In that order: You are gifted and have helped many people, no one knows that better than I, and your own suffering and misfortune don't in any way diminish the wonderful things you've done for other people. And you know I mean this and am not making it up because you want to hear it. I am *saying* it because you want to hear it, but every word is true. . . . Sympathy . . . but of course . . . if you're the earthquake, I'm the seismograph, I can feel your tremors all the way up here. . . . Ah . . . yes . . . I love you too. . . . No, Ricky, it's not silly, not silly at all. . . . Don't try to talk. . . . We have time." There was silence for a while, and then Harold said softly, "I'm with you, dear. . . . You don't have to . . . let it come." Again there was silence. "I'm glad of that. You do sound better. I love you very much. Call me the very moment you want to, no matter when. . . . An impulse is a good reason, probably the best. . . . I'll ask him." There was silence for a full two minutes, during which time the chair didn't move. Then— "Ricky? Are you there? He was outside. They have crates and crates of apples in the barn. You wouldn't believe it. And he says *yes, of course.* They don't use the phone up here the way we do in the city. . . . No, they're not on a party line. Promise me, then. . . . Good. . . . I do, yes. Goodby, my love."

I could hear him hanging up the phone, but he sat there in silence for several minutes. When finally he did move, it was to go upstairs to Ida's room, to which we had taken his suitcase and which Ida had vacated. A moment later we heard his footsteps coming down the stairs, but heard also voices and piano music.

Harold was carrying his drink in one hand and a tape recorder in the other, from which there issued his own voice.

"Someone gave me this," he said, meaning the cassette. "There must have been a hundred of these things going."

He sat down with the children, who were already eating, and placed the machine among the plates.

"Is that you?" said Ida, who alone had understood what *conference* meant.

Harold nodded.

"What's that kid crying for?" said Jacob.

"The kid wasn't there with me," said Harold, "but the piano was. A wretched piano. The kid was on a tape like this one. I would talk a little—there was a whole room full of people, Jacob—then I would play the tape, then once in a while I'd play the piano. Somebody recorded all of it and gave me the cassette—this one."

"Oh," said Jacob.

"But what's he crying for?" said Liza.

"Mostly because he's terribly, terribly unhappy," said Harold. "He's not like a regular kid at all. Something's wrong with him."

"What's wrong with him?" said Jacob.

"He's nine years old," said Harold, "and he doesn't know how to talk."

"Hunh?!" Both Jacob and Liza were nonplussed.

"He can't play with other kids. He can't read or play games by himself. . . ."

"How come?" said Liza.

Harold shrugged. "Probably something went wrong inside him even before he was born."

"Can you fix him up?" said Jacob.

"A little. But it's very hard." To me Harold said, "Do you mind if I play some of this?"

He pressed the little lever, and his recorded voice emerged from the machine, speaking in the loudness and slower rhythm of public address. I knew from past conversations with him that he was improvising; that is, had not prepared a speech but was talking directly from his current engagement with the work.

The reduced, electronic voice was recognizably his. It was saying:
*. . . leave the child himself pretty much in control of things. He can terminate
the encounter. He can minimize it. This has to be demonstrated to him, since
there's no other way to allay his anxiety. Music can accomplish these things.
We're almost always responding, initially, to desperate infantile wailing, or else
to rage. But whatever else they are, crying and screaming are sound-structures,
they are made of notes, pitches, timbres, rhythms. When you play the structure
of the child's crying on the piano, but alter it ever so slightly, just enough to
make a skeletal little tune, you're enclosing a small piece of the real world in a
setting of his own most familiar emotion. Small as it is, that little piece of the
world is more than he has ever been able to handle. I don't believe that reality
can be put in a less threatening form than this. What you are initiating at this
point is, quite simply, experience. I think that his crying is* not *experience, but
when he responds to a music that resembles his crying, that is experience. I'd
like to play you some tapes made in the thirtieth week of sessions, and then
we'll compare them with tapes of the very first encounter. From a musical
standpoint, all of this reminds me very much of opera. And it's truly amazing
to discover that this most artificial and supposedly most arbitrary and conven-
tion-dependent of theater forms is—in essence—instantaneously accessible to
auditors who are not only uneducated but are scarcely even members of human
society. To us it's quite clear that the piano is imitating the crying of the boy.
We hear it almost as an echo, and there's no doubt in our minds. But after all,
a piano doesn't much resemble the human voice. Yet the autistic boy recognizes
the imitation. This means that he performs the same act of abstraction and the
same construction of symbolic form that we do. Which persuades me—and of
course I am not the only one—that the structuring and recognizing of symbolic
form is innate in us, and as a tendency is actually impossible to resist. Some of
you will be creating this kind of music for your own purposes. You can find
everything you need to know—and a vast world more—in opera. When you
listen to the great masters of the musical forms of emotion and fate, especially
Verdi—well, it's quite remarkable how clearly the emotions can be delineated.
Character, too. When Othello, for example, in the first act of that opera, inter-
feres in the sword fight between Montano and Cassio . . .*

Here Harold's voice, on the tape, very lightly, not really singing yet striking the notes with verve and accuracy, sketched the principal parts of that episode. I could imagine him standing before the conference audience, erect and alert, in an attitude of confidence, such as I had seen years ago when he had conducted his own work, his feet together, his bony shoulders squared, leaning forward slightly. . . .

The two men are dueling, said Harold on the tape, *everyone is rushing around calling for help*—Soccorso! Soccorso!—*and Othello enters.* . . .

Harold sang the long-drawn *Abbasso le spade!*

We could hear a ripple of enjoyment in the audience, scattered applause, and one pleased, good-humored voice calling *Bravo!* I glanced at Harold where he sat at the table in the straightback chair. His head was lowered and was propped on both hands.

Those great repeated notes of anger, his voice was saying on the tape, *that could become rage, but the anger is being measured, is being brought moment by moment under control, and finally the voice drops into emphatic command that no one would want to argue with, and there is anger stirring in the last syllable of the command, which is what makes it a threatening command, the command of a great and fearless warrior, but the rage has been controlled and civil peace is being restored. We've learned an awful lot about Othello in those six syllables, occurring when they do. And then the staggering emotions of love a few moments later.* . . .

Again Harold sang, first Othello's part and then Desdemona's, alternating. And then he said:

In Othello's voice we hear pent-up yearning, the yearning of many years releasing itself at long last into an absolute bliss of love, which structurally is both an overflowing and a mingling, and is such a passionate commitment of self in the past, the present, and the future as to be dangerously vulnerable, an extreme of love. He gasps: Ah! la gioia m'innonda . . . si fieramente—che ansante mi giacio—un bacio . . . Othello! Un bacio—ancora un bacio. . . .

The music staggers, his voice catches, he says 'I stagger'— each voice draws closer in quality to the other. We hear boylike tones in the voice of this great chieftain, and tones of maternal tenderness in the voice of Desdemona, who is young enough to be his daughter. The voices ascend the register, but softly, without shrillness, becoming more and more like a single voice, and they enter a realm of bliss that is quite beyond yearning but is sustained by vulnerable things: honor, and pride. . . .

Harold sat listening with fixed attention.

Liza and Jacob were becoming restive. Jacob, several times, had ostentatiously restrained himself from speaking, and several times had raised his hand for permission to speak, which had not been granted. He jumped up at last and ran to the refrigerator in the pantry and came back with an egg.

"Change it to a chocolate egg," he said, holding it out to Harold.

"That hen died," Harold said, pressing the lever that stopped the tape, "but I'll tell you what—I have a fifty-cent piece that dissolves in water."

Liza snorted skeptically, but she too went around to his side of the table and leaned against it, waiting.

As Harold reached into his pocket, Jacob said, "Is it a cookie?"

Harold offered him the coin, saying, "Bite it and find out."

Jacob plucked it from his fingers, and with a provocative loud chortling ran with it to the sink, dropped it into a cup, and filled the cup with water.

"It doesn't dissolve!" he shouted, coming back to us, laughing triumphantly and spilling water as he came. "It's just all one piece!"

"Oh, I'm not so sure," said Harold. He dipped his bony fingers into the cup, dried the coin with his handkerchief, and examined it. "Yes," he said. "Look. It's beginning to come apart."

Liza snorted again, but she too, as did Jacob, leaned in close to look at the coin. Ida never left my side. She watched everything with her soft smile and observant eyes.

Harold held the coin over the glass of bourbon and water. He covered it with his handkerchief, and tightened the handkerchief so that the outline of the coin could be seen. "Now," he said, "listen . . ." and he released the coin. Its little splash was audible, and we heard a faint *clink* as it settled on the bottom.

"Take away the handkerchief," he said to Jacob, who snatched it away instantly.

"Hunh?!" said Liza.

"Where is it?" howled Jacob. He peered openmouthed into the glass. He shook the handkerchief. He looked at Harold's hands and up his sleeves. And then he ran a few feet from the table and, laughing loudly, jumped up and down and whirled around. "Where did it go?!" he shouted, laughing at the same time. "How did you do it?!"

Ida had never stopped smiling. She laughed at Jacob's antics, and at Liza's surprise. To Harold she said, "I know how you did it."

He smiled at her and winked.

The night was dark now, and rapidly grew cold. Very likely there would be a freeze, since the wind had gone down.

The children laid kindling and small logs in the fireplace, over a mound of crinkled paper.

I recited to Harold a jingle I had heard from a whitehaired man on the coast.

> One log can't burn [he had said "bu'n"];
> Two logs won't burn;
> Three logs might burn;
> Four logs will burn;
> Five logs make a good fire ["fie-ah"]

"Neat!" said Liza, who had an ear for such things. "Is it true?"

"We just have four, Dad," Ida called.

She laid another stick, and lit the fire.

I went out to the garden, picking up on the way a shallow basket from the stack of baskets on the side porch.

❦

Ida had carried a nightgown and bathrobe, schoolbooks and a notebook, and her portable radio-cassette machine into Liza's room, but now it was decided that Liza too would give up her bed, and then it

was decided, by acclamation, that all three children would sleep in
their parents' bedroom; that our entire family, in fact, would sleep on
a raft of mattresses on the floor, as we had done last Christmas. The
children sped into action, fetching pajamas, blankets, and pillows.
They helped me carry a large mattress from the pile in the dormitory
and helped me lift the double mattress from our bed, which we placed
beside the other. Sheets and blankets and pillows were added, and our
raft was complete. Across the head of the raft was a wall of books;
another wall of books, half height under the windows, ran down one
side. My long worktable crossed the raft at its foot, and on the fourth
side, the eastern, uphill side of the house, were the empty double bed
and more windows.

The children tumbled immediately onto this irresistible soft floor
and tussled and rolled. I saw that they took it for granted—there was
no discussion—that Jacob would sleep next to Patricia.

I left them with the usual, "Wash your faces, brush your teeth"—
which they could do in the untidy upstairs bathroom. And I promised
to send Harold to them to say good night.

He was playing his cassette again, but turned it off when I entered
the room.

I had brought my notebook, and read him this entry:

> Jacob had been ill with strep throat for ten days, then improved
> dramatically with penicillin. *Instantly,* the very moment he felt
> better, he burst into song, and he sang and chanted every few
> minutes, as he normally does. He made up songs:
> *I'm so happy my medicine was invented!*
> *Oh, yes, my medicine is great!*
> *Oh, my medicine is great!*
> "Daddy! You know what? I had two wishes and one of them
> came true. I wished there would be a medicine that would make
> me well again right away. And I wished it wouldn't taste bad."

Harold smiled and said, "Yes."

I had meant to use this incident to develop an opinion: namely, that song was not "heightened expression" at all, but the ur-voice of humankind, the voice of our first utterances, of which "purposive speech" was an adaptation, and not the other way around. And I did hold this opinion, but I had no sooner heard Harold say *yes* than I realized that this was not mere opinion to me, but an article of faith. I wanted to know at once if he agreed with me, and in what sense, and with what qualifications, and soon we were talking with the buoyant intensity that to me has been one of the great pleasures of our friend-ship. I would willingly have prolonged that conversation for hours, and was much in need of it . . . but there came a rhythmic pounding on the floor above. I shouted to the children to be quiet and wait, and for a while there was silence and we talked on. Presently, however, we heard the sounds of a peculiar stride, a stride that was large and purpo-sive and yet was of no great weight. The footsteps drew closer . . . and in came Jacob. He was wearing his frayed red-knit pajamas. Grinning and swinging his arms he went straight to Harold, seized him by the hand, and said, "Upstairs, Mister man! Right this minute!"—and led him off. When I followed in a few minutes, thinking to rescue Harold, I found a most willing captive stretched on the edge of the mattress raft, his head supported by three pillows propped against the bookcase. He smiled up at me somewhat sheepishly, and said, "I've agreed to tell them a story. I hope it's all right."

"And Dad has agreed to get Harold's cigarettes," said Liza.

"A short, short, short, short story," said Jacob.

"And another drink?" said Harold, still smiling, holding up his glass. "And an ashtray?"

Seeing the looks of delight on all four faces I realized that I had no choice, and so I brought the requested articles, and sat on the floor and listened to Harold, who with an ashtray balanced on his chest, from which a ribbon of smoke rose swiftly, and the tall bourbon and water in one hand, began as requested a story of Houdini that was more or less a sequel to one that had enchanted the children last Christmas.

"What I ought to do," said Harold, "is tell you how he accomplished some of those wonderful tricks. People don't realize that Houdini's deceptions were continual. . . ."

"What does *continual* mean?" said Jacob. "I mean, I know what it means . . . but what does it mean?"

"Going on all the time," said Ida.

"Yes," said Harold. "Houdini wanted people to think that his tricks began at a certain point and came to a definite end, but it wasn't like that—they were going on all the time. Sometimes he would prepare things days in advance, or even weeks, and sometimes he still had to do things long after people thought the trick was ended. And some of his tricks depended on the great strength of his fingers, or the fact that he could untie knots with his toes. . . ."

"With his *toes?!*" said Jacob. "Wow!"

"Oh, yes," said Harold. "Sometimes when he'd be sitting around talking with people he'd throw a piece of string on the floor, and then using just his feet, he'd take off his shoes and socks and tie knots in the string with his toes, and then untie them, and tie them again.

"And some of his tricks, some of his best escapes," said Harold, "were done by hard hard work, and he *never* let anyone suspect *that*. Hard work is the opposite of magic. He had three men who helped him, who worked for him all the time, wonderfully smart men, who could make all kinds of machines and could take apart almost anything and put it together again. No one knew that they worked for him. They were secret. They were his secret geniuses. Now I'll tell you about one of Houdini's most famous escapes, and you see if you can figure out how he did it."

The children had started out all on the same mattress under the same red woolen blanket, but the warm air from the fireplace in the big room came up through the register in the floor and the children shifted positions in the pleasant warmth. Only Liza stayed under the blanket. She lay with her wide-open eyes focused somewhere above her in space, or not focused at all, and I could see in her demeanor both the energy of attention and the drifting sensitivity of dream, the same combination that I had seen so many times in her inventive and prolonged playing with her dolls.

Ida came and sat beside me where I leaned against the bed. She was wearing her long white flannel nightgown, and sat with her legs drawn up, holding them with clasped hands around her shins, her face resting sideways on her knees. Jacob lay between Harold and Liza, but at right angles to them both, with his head on Liza's belly and his feet on Harold's legs. He called to me, "Look Daddy! See what I have for a pillow? Liza!"

"Go on," said Liza to Harold, ignoring Jacob.

Harold explained to them Houdini's practice of issuing challenges. Any man who could tie him, or chain him, or lock him in a box would win a large prize of money.

"This happened in London," Harold said, "a big city, one of the biggest in the world, Jacob, far away over the ocean, in England. Houdini was performing in a theater there. He was very famous and every seat was taken every night. He offered a prize of ten thousand dollars to anyone who could trap him, and many people tried, they built boxes of all kinds, even of steel, but he escaped from everything."

"Superman could hold him. He could just grab him."

"Jacob, be quiet," said Liza, without moving at all, without even shifting her eyes. "Go on," she said.

Jacob folded his hands on his stomach and subsided again into his happy and perfect comfort. Ida glanced at me and smiled.

"Well, there was a man in London," said Harold, "not terribly old, but old, who thought he was the smartest man in the world, and who had always wanted to trap Houdini, and he saw that this was his chance. He was an expert maker of locks and safes. A safe is just a big box made of very thick steel, Jacob, with a special kind of lock. And this man had just made a super safe for a bank in London. It was the biggest and strongest in the world. It was as big as a small room. Its walls were a foot thick. You could only open it by turning a dial on the front of the door, and you had to know the secret numbers to turn it to. The dial couldn't be turned from the inside. There were no screws or bolts on the inside, just smooth walls, and a tight-fitting smooth round plate that was the back of the lock. The lock had been set into the door from the side, and when the door was closed there was no way at all to get to it.

"So the Locksmith went to the president of the bank and said, 'Let us challenge Houdini. There is no way he can escape. Our safe will become famous as the safe that made a fool out of the great magician. And after we've let him out, I'll laugh in his face and say, 'You lose, Houdini! Hand over ten thousand dollars!'

"'Well, but Houdini is a genius,' said the president. 'This could backfire. What if he escapes?'

"'A genius!' snorted the Locksmith. 'No man alive can escape from that safe. The steel is the hardest ever made. The walls are a foot thick and so is the door. If a man went in with a box of tools he could not break his way out. But Houdini will go in bare-handed; he will go in wearing only a bathing suit. And don't forget—if he stays longer than an hour he'll faint, and within a few minutes more he'll die for lack of air.'

"So the president of the bank agreed, and the Locksmith wrote a letter of challenge to Houdini, and Houdini accepted. . . ."

Harold drew deeply on his cigarette and quenched it in the ashtray balanced on his chest.

"Go on," said Liza, without glancing at him.

"Did they lock Houdini up?" said Jacob.

"Let me light a cigarette, kids. . . ."

A shaded lamp clamped to the bookcase behind Harold's head threw a cone of amber light close around us. The blue turbulence of exhaled smoke rolled in the air again, and a trickling thin column rose from the cigarette at rest.

"The big safe was brought to the theater by a moving company," Harold went on. "They set it up in the lobby. The theater was crowded again. After the show Houdini came to the front of the stage and said, 'Ladies and gentlemen, I'm sure you noticed the big safe in the lobby on your way in. The safe will be here on the stage tomorrow night. I will be locked inside it, and I will escape.'

"Just then a voice from the audience shouted, 'Yes, Houdini, you will be locked in the safe. But no, Houdini, you will not escape!'

"Everyone in the theater tried to see who was speaking. Houdini said, 'Who are you, sir?'

"'I am the one who wrote you the letter of challenge. I am the leading designer of locks and safes in all the world, and that safe in the lobby is my latest design. All London will be laughing at you, Houdini; you will have to be rescued. Your career will be ended.'

"Houdini smiled and said, 'Do you think so?'

"'Bring ten thousand dollars, Houdini,' said the Locksmith. 'And here is a word of advice. Don't stay too long in the safe. There is not enough air. You will die.'

"'I thank you for your advice,' said Houdini. 'And now I must insist that you be my guest tomorrow night. There will be a seat reserved for you, here, in the first row.'

"'I will be here, Houdini,' said the Locksmith. 'And we shall see who wins.'

"Well," said Harold, "you can imagine how crowded the theater was the next night."

"Did Houdini escape?" said Jacob, in an intent, actually worried tone.

"I'm going to tell you," said Harold.

"That's what the story is all about," said Ida. "You have to wait and see."

"Okay," said Jacob.

"Read," said Liza, forgetting that Harold wasn't reading from a book.

"Well," said Harold, "every seat was filled. People were standing in the aisles; it was so packed no one could move. . . ."

"Was that guy there?" said Jacob.

"Yes, he was sitting in the front row, in the seat Houdini saved for him. He sat with his arms crossed and his lips curled in a sneer. . . ."

Jacob glanced quickly across at Harold.

"The safe was so heavy," said Harold, "they had to put props under the stage to strengthen it. The safe rested on a thick carpet that covered the entire stage. The door of the safe was open. There were four tall thin posts around the safe, with wires running from one post to another, and I'll tell you in a minute what those were for.

"People began to clap and shout *Hou-di-ni! Hou-di-ni!* and they kept it up; then the orchestra started to play, and people stomped their feet, and finally . . . out came Houdini."

"Yaaay!" said Jacob, throwing up one arm.

"Yes," said Harold, "people were cheering. Everybody but the Locksmith, who sat there with his arms crossed. Houdini came out to the center of the stage. He stood right in front of the Locksmith and bowed.

"Houdini was wearing a silk dressing robe, a kind of bathrobe. He held up his hand for silence, and said to the audience that he had never faced a challenge as difficult as this one. He said that the safe had been designed by a very brilliant man, and he pointed to the Locksmith and bowed and introduced him to the audience. People applauded, but the Locksmith didn't look at them; he just sat there staring at Houdini with his arms crossed and a little smile on his lips.

"Houdini signaled, and a man came out from the side of the stage and handed him a bundle of money tied with string. Houdini held it up and said, 'If I fail to escape, I will give this prize of ten thousand dollars to the designer of the safe, and I will provide him with a bodyguard to escort him home.'

"People cheered. It was getting hot in the theater, there were so many people, and when they cheered it almost seemed to lift the roof.

"Houdini signaled again, and the same assistant walked in from the side carrying a little table. He placed it just to one side of the center, and Houdini put the money on it and bowed to the Locksmith and said, 'You asked me to bring the money. Here it is.'

"Now three well-dressed gentlemen came onto the stage. Houdini introduced them. The first was the president of the bank that owned the safe. The second was the editor of a famous newspaper in London. The third was a well-known doctor who worked at a London hospital. Houdini explained that two of them would examine the safe, and the doctor would examine him. He took off his bathrobe, and there were sounds of admiration, since he was extremely strong and muscular, and was wearing nothing under the robe but swimming shorts. There was a folding screen on the stage, and he stepped behind it with the doctor. The editor and the president of the bank examined the safe. They ran their hands over it, inside and out, and looked at the gigantic hinges, and checked the dial on the front. Then the doctor and Houdini came out from behind the screen, and the doctor spoke to the audience. 'I have examined Houdini,' he said, 'from top to toe. He is not hiding anything. There are no tiny screwdrivers clutched between his toes, no pieces of wire hidden in his hair. I have examined even his fingernails, which are cut short.'

"Houdini smiled. A man from the audience shouted, 'How do we know they aren't working for you, Houdini? Let somebody else come up there!'"

"'Of course,' said Houdini. 'Come up yourself.'

"But the man became embarrassed and wouldn't. Other people were shouting, 'Me! Me! I'll do it!' so Houdini picked three and they ran up on the stage and began examining the safe and looking at Houdini's hair. One of them in particular gave the safe a real going-over. He pounded on the walls and jumped up and down on the floor and kicked the door. And the safe never budged or jiggled. Even when he kicked it, it scarcely made a sound, the walls were so thick and the steel so strong.

"The orchestra played a fanfare—*da-da-da-DA, da-da-DA*—and Houdini stepped forward and said, 'I shall enter the safe.' If anyone in the entire theater had coughed or whispered, you would have heard it. That's how quiet it was. Houdini shook hands with the men on the stage. They all moved away to the side. Houdini raised one hand, then turned and walked into the safe. He faced the audience and folded his arms on his chest. He seemed to be concentrating fiercely. His eyes flashed. The bank president, the editor, and the doctor leaned against the huge door and pushed it shut. It closed with a dense, quiet *click*. The bank president twirled the dial. The other men tested the door. It was shut tight and locked. It could only be opened now by turning the dial, and of course Houdini could not reach the dial from the inside. Even if Houdini had begun screaming inside, no one could have heard him now.

"Two men came out from backstage and wrapped a huge, heavy chain around the safe and put a huge padlock on it. One of the men showed the key to the audience and put it in his pocket. The same two men pulled some curtains all the way around the safe. Do you remember those skinny tall poles I told you about? That's what they were for. They held up a wire that went around the safe. Curtains slid on the wire. Nothing could be seen on the stage now but those curtains. The safe was inside the curtains, and Houdini was inside the safe. All that remained in view was the table with the bundle of money. The orchestra began playing—*la-la-la-la-LA-la-la . . . la-la*— and people turned to one another in the audience and said, 'Oh, my, oh, my, do you think he'll get out?'

"Well he's Houdini isn't he?" said Jacob, with just a tremor of worry in his voice.

Liza was no longer lying on her back gazing at the ceiling. She lay on her side now, propping her head with one hand. She looked eagerly at Harold.

"I suppose he got out," said Jacob excitedly. He nodded vigorously and answered his own question, though not with entire conviction. "Of course. Of course."

"What happened?" said Ida.

"Well, people watched the stage and waited," said Harold. "And they talked to one another. And the orchestra played."

"Was that man still watching?" said Jacob.

"Yes, he was," said Harold.

"Was he worried?" said Jacob.

"Oh . . . I don't know," said Harold. "I don't know. But the minutes went by, and *some* people began to worry. I suppose they couldn't help thinking what it would be like to be locked up in a steel box, in the dark and the silence. All of a sudden a lot of people got worried, and a man said loudly, 'He can't get out! It's impossible!' and there was a murmur of voices all through the theater. Another man said, 'No, he can do it! He can do it, I tell you!' but he didn't sound so sure. The orchestra played again. People were getting up and standing on their seats to stretch their legs. Some were smiling and talking. A few were reading newspapers. But a great many now were very worried. Suddenly a woman screamed. Everyone jumped up. People shouted, 'What happened? What happened?' They were jumping up and down trying to see over one another's heads. Another woman screamed, 'He's dead! There's no air in there!' and a lot of men began to shout, 'Let him out! Open the safe! There's no air!'

Jacob now was kneeling beside Liza and looking full at Harold. His bare feet, which were tucked under him, were patting each other, and his toes were opening and closing rapidly. Ida caught my eye and, smiling, pointed to his feet. She leaned forward and said quietly, "Don't worry, Jacob," but her voice was obliterated by Jacob's own choked voice as he said to Harold, "Is he okay?" Liza, who had been his pillow, moved over and knelt beside him. She put her arm around him and whispered in his ear. They listened in that position, side by side, kneeling, sitting back on their heels, their spines erect and their heads held high.

"The orchestra leader jumped up on the stage," said Harold, "and beckoned to the doctor, who had been sitting in the audience. The doctor joined him and they signaled for quiet. 'Ladies and gentlemen,' the doctor said, 'there is enough air in the safe to last for an hour. Houdini has not been in there that long yet.'

"'Yes, he has!' someone shouted. 'More than an hour!'

"'I'm sorry to disagree with you,' said the doctor.

"'Your watch has stopped!' shouted the man.

"Checking his watch, the doctor got down off the stage, and so did the orchestra leader, and soon the orchestra began to play, but people wouldn't keep quiet; some kept shouting, 'Let him out!' and then a great many more began shouting, and then they all began to stamp their feet in unison, shouting, *'Let . . . him . . . out! Let . . . him . . . out!'* and it sounded as if the theater would fly apart. The orchestra leader ran up on the stage again and, signaling for quiet, said, 'Ladies and gentlemen, I have no choice but to do as you wish. I will ask the president of the bank to come up here and open the safe. He alone knows the combination.'

"The orchestra leader looked into the audience where the president had been sitting, and his mouth fell open—the seat was empty. He shouted, 'Ladies and gentlemen, we need your help. Did anyone see—' and several voices shouted, 'He's here! He's here! He fainted!'

"The doctor ran down and found him on the floor by his seat, where he had fainted from the heat and excitement. The doctor held smelling salts to his nose, and as soon as the president's eyes flickered, the doctor shook him and said, 'Sir! Sir! We have an emergency! We need the combination to that safe immediately. Do you have it written down?' 'Not . . . not written,' said the president, pointing to his head. 'Memory . . . memory . . .' but he groaned and closed his eyes. Now fortunately the doctor was a quick-witted man. He remembered the Locksmith, and he shouted up to the orchestra leader, who was still standing on the stage, 'Ask the Locksmith!' People heard him, and they shouted too, 'The Locksmith! The Locksmith!'

"The orchestra leader signaled for quiet. He leaned forward and spoke to the Locksmith, who was still sitting in the front row. 'Can you open the safe?' he said.

"The Locksmith folded his arms on his chest and smiled his little smile that didn't warm his eyes at all. His eyes flickered across to that bundle of money resting on the table.

"The orchestra leader said, 'Sir! Sir! If you are able to open the safe, would you please come up here immediately and do it?'

"The Locksmith cleared his throat and opened his mouth—but before a single word came out, a voice from the stage said, 'That won't be necessary!'"

Jacob was squirming uncontrollably.

"And from behind the curtains," said Harold, "out stepped Houdini."

Jacob shot bodily into the air, lifting both feet from the mattress and shaking both fists above his head. "Houdini! Houdini!" he shouted. "Yaaay! I *knew* it! I *knew* it!" He whirled around ecstatically, lifting first one knee and then the other.

Liza was smiling broadly. She turned to watch Jacob, who pounced on her, knocking her over. His excited fingers tickled her head, shoulders, and ribs while he bounced this way and that on top of her, yelling, "Houdini! Houdini! Yaaay!"

Liza laughed and fended off his hands, but soon she said, "Come on, Jacob, let's hear what happens."

Jacob, however, kept shouting and wriggling.

"Get off, Jacob!" she snapped. "Get off this minute! Jacob, I'll knock you into the middle of next year. . . ."

"Goody," said Jacob. "I'll be seven years old!"

"I'll scrunch you like a crumb, Jacob! I'll snangle you, whatever that means!" And then she said, in bright, questioning tones, "Don't you want to find out how he did it?" In an instant all was quiet.

"Well," said Harold, who had been watching Jacob with a somewhat patient smile, "you can imagine how people cheered. They made as much noise as Jacob—"

"More," said Jacob.

"Yes, much more, since there were many more of them."

"Right."

"And Houdini stood there for a moment panting for breath. All he was wearing was that bathing suit. His whole body was sweating. He was panting and seemed to be exhausted, but he drew deep breaths and began to recover. People cheered and cheered. An assistant ran out with Houdini's dressing robe and held it for him. Houdini raised one arm high and the theater became silent. People thought that he was going to speak, but he turned and walked to the curtain that went around the safe. He walked to both sides, pulling the curtain as he walked, and in a moment the curtain was open all the way—and there stood the safe. It was shut tight, the heavy chain was still wrapped around it, and the huge padlock was still locked on the chain."

"But . . ." said Liza. She was more baffled than anyone. She was deeply and perfectly baffled. Her eyebrows were drawn together and her lower lip was thrust out. Ida, however, seemed to be searching for an explanation. Her face wore a half smile of excited thought. As for Jacob, who was looking full at Harold again—he simply knelt there, rubbing his hands gleefully.

"People were cheering and laughing," Harold said. "They were looking at one another and shaking their heads and scratching their heads. The president of the bank had recovered by this time and was beginning to understand what had happened. 'Impossible,' he said. 'It's impossible.'

"Houdini invited the same men who had been on the stage before to come test the chain, and they did, but all three together couldn't budge it or spring open the padlock. The man with the key came out and opened the padlock, and the other men helped him unwrap the heavy chain. Then the president of the bank stepped up and began turning the dial on the safe door. He and the doctor opened the door wide . . . and there again were the smooth steel walls, shiny and unmarked and looking like a room of steel.

"Someone said, 'Look! There's something on the floor!' and one of the men rushed into the safe and came out reading a piece of paper.

'Read it to everyone,' said Houdini. The man came forward to the edge of the stage and read in a loud voice, 'You have built an excellent safe, Mister Locksmith. I congratulate you.'

"People laughed and cheered. Houdini went across the stage to where that bundle of money was resting on the table. An assistant ran out and Houdini tossed the money to him. Houdini came to the front then and raised both arms, thanking people for their applause, and then bowed deeply and left the stage.

"The Locksmith was furious. He was scowling terribly. He went rapidly up the aisle, but a laughing man reached out and caught his arm. 'Hey, Mister Locksmith!' he said. 'Do you know how he did it?'

"'Take your hand away!' said the Locksmith.

"The man stopped laughing and let go of his arm.

"'Yes, I know,' said the Locksmith, and turned away muttering, *'but I know too late!'* He went up the aisle and out of the theater, and Houdini never saw him again."

The children understood that Harold had finished his story.

"That was *great!*" cried Jacob. He threw his arms around Harold's neck and hugged him, began to sit in his lap, changed his mind, came to me and said, "Wasn't that *great,* Dad?" and hugged me, saying, "Oooo, Houdini!" and dropped into my lap.

"How did he *do* it?!" said Liza.

"Do you know how he did it?" said Ida.

"Alas," said Harold. "Yes." He glanced across at me happily and said, "That wasn't a good choice for a bedtime story, was it?"

"It was a *great* choice," said Liza. "Only you have to tell us how he did it."

"That's up to your father," said Harold. "You're supposed to go to sleep now, aren't you?"

We all went downstairs. The room was warm. Small flames still hovered and flickered above the reduced, charred logs.

Liza said, "One log can't burn, two logs . . . how does that go again?"

"Won't burn."

"Oh yeah. Three logs *might* burn . . ."

Ida joined her and they completed the jingle.

I made a pot of cocoa, and made fresh drinks for Harold and myself, and we sat at the long table in the warmth of the fire.

Jacob came around and put his mug of cocoa on the table in front of me, and climbed into my lap. He took my face in both hands and putting his own face close to mine said, "When is Mommy coming home?"

"Soon," I said. "Any minute."

"Goody," he said, and made himself comfortable. I could see that Liza, too, wanted to be held, and that she considered Harold's lap and decided against it, and I wondered what it was that in the children's eyes made him less embraceable than other people, even people for whom they cared far less than for him. The children wanted to be near him. They entered his aura readily but, once there, did not draw closer.

Jacob sat up in my lap abruptly and said to Harold, "What happened to that guy? You know—"

"The Locksmith?"

"Yeah. Him."

"He went away. Houdini never saw him again."

"Where did he go?"

"I don't know."

"What did he do?"

"I have no idea."

"He didn't just get to be a puff of smoke, did he?"

"He went and lived somewhere. He had a job somewhere. He was very, very good, you know."

"Oh," said Jacob. A moment later he said, "Did he have kids?"

"I don't think so," said Harold. "I think he lived by himself."

"Oh. . . ."

Before this exchange could be developed further, the dogs began to bark. Jacob cried, "Mommy!", leaped off my lap, and ran toward the front door. A moment later beams of light flashed across the front windows and went out.

But it wasn't Patricia. When Jacob saw the unfamiliar car he slowed his pace, looked back at me over his shoulder, and stood there waiting. He wore only his pajamas and was barefoot, but he seemed unaffected by the cold air and the moist grass.

Marshall called to us and waved. His white hair, so white as to appear almost phosphorescent, bobbed quickly before the car. He opened the other door and extended his arm solicitously, and I expected to see an elderly, crippled, or injured passenger, but a stately woman emerged who was none of these things. She took his arm, and he slowed his pace. She moved like a sleepwalker, yet there was strength in her bearing, and a self-possession that must have been so natural to her that nothing could shake it.

We gathered in the entrance hall, where Harold and the girls stood waiting for us, but even before our introductions were finished, the dogs barked again, Jacob rushed out, and this time came back clinging like a monkey to Patricia, his legs gripping her waist and both arms flung around her neck.

Marshall said to Liza, "How's my waterlogged child? Have you dried out yet?"—a reference to her week-long visit to his place in New Hampshire, where she had swum in the river from morning to night. While she stood there grinning he seized her and hugged her fondly, saying, "You're probably supposed to be in bed, but I'm awfully glad you're up."

Patricia saw at once the numbed suffering in the Chilean woman's face (it was Luisa Domic) and suppressed the happiness that had flared in her own, holding Jacob thus and finding Harold here among us.

There was some slight deficiency in Luisa's movements, as if her feet or lower back were weak; otherwise she was imposing and handsome, shapely on a large scale. She was perhaps forty-four or forty-five. Her hair was still black, though there were strands of gray in it. Her stricken eyes were large and dark, and her skin was pale. She seemed to be quivering from some dreadful, devitalizing blow, yet one could sense underlying habits of confidence and graciousness. One could not imagine that she lived without the love of a man, or that she had never borne children. She wore a sky-blue woolen skirt, a blue blouse of a lighter shade, and a lightweight cardigan sweater, also blue. The fabrics were expensive, yet nothing quite fit her, everything was somewhat rumpled, and it seemed likely that the outfit had been borrowed or purchased hastily, perhaps by someone else.

As we spoke our introductions she glanced at Patricia, who in stature and maternal presence somewhat resembled her, and a flicker of recognition lit her eyes. It was the kind of glance that women with children often exchange with one another, a glance of fellow feeling and shared work. But there was more to it than this. I remembered our neighbor here, widowed and in the early years of old age, a plain, reserved, hard-working, big-boned woman, known locally for her many kindnesses and small eccentricities, who had met Patricia only once but who on their second meeting, two years later, had embraced her warmly and had looked openly into her face. Whatever it was that Luisa saw in Patricia, her eyes came to life in a momentary touching and then subsided again. Patricia took her arm, held it close, and, inquiring whether she were hungry, or would like tea or broth or a warm bath, went with her from the hallway into the house. I sent the children up to bed. The explanation of Houdini's feat would have to wait until tomorrow. Harold, Marshall, and I followed the two women into the big room.

～

Luisa had been taking sedatives. She went to bed immediately in the downstairs guest room. The rest of us sat at the long table. Patricia had already eaten. She stayed only a moment and then went to the children. Marshall asked for herb tea and an orange and said brusquely, when I suggested something more, "I only eat when I'm hungry." Harold and I ate sandwiches. The gaiety that had filled the house just a short while ago was gone, chiefly because of the grief we had seen in Luisa's face, but also because Harold and Marshall were meeting for the first time and very rapidly were discovering the traits that had kept them apart for decades in New York.

Here were two men of the same generation, who lived in the same city (actually within a few blocks of each other), who were active in the cultural life of the city (Harold prominently), who shared several acquaintances, and who certainly recognized each other's faces—yet they had never met. Moreover, they were acquainted with each other's work. Harold had set many contemporary poems, and knew Marshall's own, at least the first two books, but he disliked their structural looseness, and disliked their populism, which he took to be inauthentic. He disregarded Marshall as a poet, much as Marshall disregarded the formalist poets of Harold's fashionable circles—of which circles he knew little, however, since they tended to be homosexual and monied. He could not imagine that Harold had made few friends in his own milieu, or that even in the heyday of his fame his life had been simple and he abstemious. Nor was Marshall musical. Nor did he care a bit or know a thing about psychology, but dismissed it with lofty Marxist scorn. Harold, on his side, was scarcely aware of Marshall's political writing. He knew that *Utopia and Human Labor* had been reviewed fairly widely and had been highly praised, but he detested politics, and tended to ignore such books.

So there they sat, on opposite sides of the table, looking at each other, saying the most innocuous things, and coming to quite accurate assessments of their incompatibility, the very same assessments, or roughly the same, that their mutual acquaintances and their one mutual friend (myself) had held for years and had consulted on many occasions in order to keep them comfortably apart.

Patricia sat down with us again and said quietly to Marshall, "Can you tell us what has happened to her?" Harold, too, leaned forward.

Marshall had finished his orange. He poured more tea from the pot I had put beside him, and said, "She may have lost her family. She doesn't know."

"Does she have children?" said Patricia. "Is that what you mean by 'family'?"

"I don't know," said Marshall. "I was told what I just told you. She doesn't want to talk about it, and I don't want to question her."

He sipped his tea while we looked at him in silence.

"I had another blowout after I called you," he said. "I thought the spare was okay, but it wasn't. We're hearing horrible things. It's much worse than anybody has been told. Much worse. Much, much worse."

He lowered his eyes to indicate that he did not want to be questioned.

"Our civilization is not what we think it is," he murmured.

Harold came upstairs when Patricia and I did, and we all three stood for a moment near the windows in the open attic of our two-part house. He kissed Patricia's cheek and said quietly, "It's good to see you, Patricia. I'm sorry we won't get a chance to visit. I'll be leaving after breakfast."

"Can't you stay longer?" she said. "Marshall and Luisa will be leaving after breakfast too."

"It isn't that. I promised to be home for supper," he said. "Ricky shouldn't be alone too much. . . ."

"That poor woman," he added softly. "She's in agony. . . ."

I heard the front door open and close, and saw Marshall crossing the yard with his long-bodied, flexible, loping gait, his tufted, thick white hair glowing in the moonlight. He wore the heavy brown sweater that he had worn in cool weather for fifteen years or more. While Patricia and Harold exchanged a few more words, I watched him. He walked with his hands in his pockets, his shoulders drawn back severely, and his head bowed and thrust forward. The events in Chile had disturbed him deeply, and I assumed that he was thinking of them. But knowing him as I did, I knew that a painful dialogue or, rather, assault of self upon self was also under way, and that it would goad him soon enough into an explosion of the temperamental egotism that had made everyone who knew him, myself included, exclaim at one time or another, "Marshall is impossible!" He seemed cut off from everything around him, even from the moonlight that lit the ground before him—but I had no sooner thought this than he stopped abruptly in the road and cocked his head. He stood there for several moments, and then he pressed his hands together, palm to palm, and brought them to his lips, bowing his head. He seemed to be murmuring some long and heartfelt prayer. He lowered his hands and cocked his head, and a moment later raised his hands once more and prayed, cocked his head . . . and finally stepped forward out of sight beyond the lights and darks of the trees that lined the road. I was smiling, and I felt a touch of the great affection I had once felt for him. He had been hooting at the owls, numerous in our woods, and had been listening to their answers. I thought of the many poems I had admired and that constituted, so it seemed to me, the permanent surprise of his character; and I repented of my effort to dismiss him as an ideologue who esteemed opinion before created things. His aid to the victims of the Chilean junta, Luisa's grief, Allende's murder, the moonlit road, the owls, the complex economic meanings of the coup—all these were continuous and whole within his cranky, strange character, and I understood, yet once again, that his broad engagement in the world really did command my undiminished respect. It was as if I were saying silently, "Well, Marshall—impossible Marshall—best of luck to you!"

<hr />

Ida and Liza were asleep on the mattress raft in our bedroom, and so was Jacob, who had declared that he would stay awake until Patricia, who had kissed him good night, could come back again and tell him a story. Ida lay on her back, snoring lightly. Liza lay silently on her side, with her knees drawn up and her hands tucked between her thighs. Jacob lay on his back, breathing as sweetly as an infant, his arms and legs flung wide and his soft, full face glowing with good health. Patricia could not look at this spectacle without smiling, nor could I. And when we lay down beside them in the twilight of the room, we succumbed at once to the charm of their presence. Patricia leaned over Jacob and, with a quiet chortle not unlike his own, stroked his face and kissed his forehead, while I, in the meantime, propped my head on one elbow and gazed vacantly at the three sleeping figures, subsiding almost happily into the underlying astonishment that is surely the very essence of parenthood.

But we had been waiting for this moment to talk to each other, and as we stretched and turned away from the children Patricia said to me in a whisper, "Something dreadful has happened to her. She must *know* that her family is gone. She's not worrying that something might have happened. It's beyond that, don't you think? It's grief. But it's more than that. It's beyond grief. . . ."

I said that I too had thought this. And I had wondered whether Luisa herself had not been tortured. I had watched her for signs of bodily pain but had not seen any.

Evidently this thought had not occurred to Patricia. She raised her head and seized her face with both hands, grimacing in a way that made me think she might cry. "Why would they torture her? What makes people *do* such things?" She lay back, clenching her jaw and frowning with combative determination.

"Do you think Marshall has told us all he knows?" she said.

We did not pursue this. Many times in the past we had turned for enlightenment to Marshall, who was vastly more knowledgeable than we. He had never come forth as we had wished, but had put us off with clever comments on our ignorance. He had written several long articles on Chile, had lived for a year in Santiago, and had talked with Allende himself on several occasions. No one's opinion could have been more helpful than his, but it would have been pointless to ask him Neither of us complained aloud of this, however. From the day of the coup Marshall had devoted all of his time and much of his meager savings to helping refugees like Luisa. We admired this, and the silence that came momentarily into our conversation was really an act of deference.

Several doctors and nurses had joined Patricia's group at the anti-nuclear conference. There were plans now to monitor the radioactivity around the coastal plant. One of the nurses had proposed that a private survey be made of the incidence of leukemia.

"She thinks there's more of it than there used to be," said Patricia, "but she isn't sure."

"And did you speak?"

"A little," she said. She had promised to try it. She was the leader of a faction that took seriously that most American nuclear materials were not industrial but military. This awareness had moved her group to a more radical politics than the conference as a whole had seemed willing to espouse.

My question, however, was about something else: namely, her promise to brave the terrible shyness that made speaking in public an ordeal for her, and raise some of the issues she had been studying. Even at home there were times when speaking was too hard for her and she would fall into silences that seemed perverse, or would blunder into shortcuts that were comical, as when she asked me once, at night, finding me in bed earlier than was my habit, "Where are you going? To sleep?"—which was all very strange, since in fact, in the darkness of our bedroom, or in such a moonlit dusk as filled it now, she was able not only to speak but to speak extremely well; and there were times, three or four in a year, when her conversation across the table in daylight or by lamplight was of a structuring so fine, so unhesitating and complete, that I would feel shaken at its end, as by a communion more full than one had any right to hope for.

And so, hearing the defensive note in her voice when she said, "A little," I said, "Any at all? Really?"

"Mostly Betsy did," she said.

"You met with her first?"

"Yes. We had lunch together."

I knew their relationship. Shyly and hesitantly Patricia had told her what to say, and Betsy, as on other occasions, had said it well.

We talked the logistics of the home then: Who would cook break-fast? What would be cooked? Which of our two cars would we offer Marshall to take to Quebec, since both were in better condition than his old VW?

While we talked in this way, I remembered that for several days we had been working up to a quarrel. I had had an irritable, resentful feeling, and had not known whether I was responding to subtle things I was observing in Patricia, or whether these things were aris-ing in me and causing reactions in her. And this quarrel of ours had kept drawing nearer, in spite of the fact that it lacked an issue. Then just last night, in a tentative, testing voice, Patricia had said, "I want to cut down even more on my cooking. There's so much else that's more important." She was doing no more than half, as it was. Now she suggested that we keep sandwich materials on hand and let the kids forage for themselves three nights a week. In part this had seemed reasonable to me, actually a good idea. But in part I had taken it as a withdrawal of support from my writing, which demanded more time than my character could give it, more than mortality itself would allow. That irritable feeling had kept nagging at me, without finding a voice. More than half our modest income came from my work (the rest was Patricia's inheritance), but this had nothing to do with what I felt. The truth was, I wanted her to care more about my writing than she did. I wanted her to care so much that it would stimulate me . . . even in those times when I myself cared scarcely at all.

But now as we lay there talking, I realized that the quarrel would not occur. The beauty of the day, the changing leaves, the quiet air and warm sunlight all had combined to make a momentarily unde-manding world, and because one did not have to struggle with it, one was free to look at it gratefully. And precisely because that world was so beautiful, so complete and perfect and motionless, one could not help feeling, *All this will go on without me. We all shall pass away, and our world will still exist.*

The breathing, warmth-radiating, occasionally stirring bodies beside us drew our attention once again. They were irresistible. They had grown so large! Their growth was somehow more astounding than the originally astounding fact of their tininess, and its collateral fact, apparent not long after birth, that they were indeed individuals.

I remembered Patricia stretched out naked on the bed nursing Ida, a mere few days old, also naked in our steam-heated apartment in New York. The sight of them had moved me strangely; it was grave and surprising, less maternal than merely creaturely, two furless animals, the tiny one shielded by the large, and the large in a repose so quiet as to have become the geography of the small. Our life together had changed my character; it calmed the berserk youth in me, and drew out the father. Now here were three children, a home, a way of life and the contact of other lives, all different in kind from the excitations of earlier loves, and especially of my love for my first wife. That love had begat chiefly feelings: intoxications I could never forget, and agonies I would be glad to forget. Patricia's plain, good-natured face never stirred me as had Rachel's sleek beauty, but there was far more world in it, a far broader presentness, and more future. It seemed to me, too, that her virtues were apparent in her face and bearing; they were aspects of her handsomeness: pride of an admirable kind, courage, and steadfastness, and especially kindliness. This last went beyond kindness; it was more primitive and continuous than kindness, and seemed to flow like a spring from some underlying source. These qualities illuminated many ordinary actions, especially her relations with the children, who were immovable presences in her being. Years had passed since any of ours had been crawling on the floor, yet occasionally I would see Patricia moving about the kitchen with a shuffling gait, not to step on little fingers, toes, or toys. Occasionally, too, at lunchtime or at supper, I would see her place her hand, unaware, full around one breast, as she had done when she had been nursing, testing its milk. Observations she had made stayed with me for years. We had visited friends to see their new baby, and watching its chortling enthusiasm, and its vigorous thrashing of torso, arms, and legs as its mother held it aloft, Patricia had said, "Look what he's doing! They can't do all those twisty, twirly things if they're lying alone in a crib! Only if someone holds them!" And I had realized that she alone had seen things from the baby's point of view, had seen experience and event, where we others had seen only a chortling infant. I had remembered at the time how she had turned with a smile to watch Ida, who lay beside her on the hospital bed, unnamed as yet, a mere two days old, and who with a look of grave attention on her tiny face was waving her arms and legs in soft, slow, continuous movements, and Patricia had said to me quietly, never ceasing to smile, "Look how she's stretching and swimming! She used to move like that inside me, those very same movements; then it got too cramped. Look at her! She's remembering."

Patricia's plain, yet sometimes handsome, and often downright noble face, so alive with goodness and generosity of spirit, moved me frequently to admiration, and often to gratitude to life itself, and in the ambience of these feelings the deeper emotions of love welled up, bringing with them a companionable erotic warmth.

We drew close and embraced. The heat of her large yet still shapely body under the frayed flannel nightgown aroused me just to the point of feeling that I would enjoy making love. But it was clear that she was even less desirous than I—was preoccupied and tired—and so we kissed and rolled apart. Almost immediately her soft snoring was added to the breathing of the children.

She slept in a position that was characteristic of her, and that seemed as odd to me as some I had noticed when the children were infants, in the most striking of which the sleeper faced the ceiling and pointed to something evidently situated there, one arm held up tirelessly, one tiny finger extended. Patricia lay on her back, her hands folded on her belly, her feet flat on the mattress, and both knees drawn high.

I listened to their breathing. Soon I could feel my consciousness begin its day's-end grazing like some animal in pasture, unless indeed consciousness were the pasture, and other creatures grazed there.

Luisa's grief was disturbing. And it was disturbing to me that my long friendship with Marshall was coming undone. I had cared for him a great deal. These presences, however, moved only briefly in the little field of my wakefulness. The cold nights and the early dark were achieving what even the most violent rains of summer had not, were pulling the two environments apart, making an outdoors and an indoors, an indifferent and potentially dangerous nature and a vast environment of human artifacts and care, a world of homes. All this, and now these benign recent days, had plunged me so deep in memory that it was as if the real fields and hills were a chrysalis that might at any moment burst and release the past itself.

For several days I had had glimpses, many times each day, of the dirt road, the overhanging trees, the streetlamps and lighted windows past which, tired and exhilarated, I had loped along in the brisk air toward home, tossing a football. Not far from that road there was a bulging, sloping field of buffalo grass, but the images of the road and the field were not connected in my memory; each was magnetized separately, the one, so it seemed, by happiness, the other, so it seemed, by desire, since at the top of that field was a house in which lived two sisters with adolescent breasts, complicitous, watchful eyes, and provocative gaits.

But the somnambulant quality of these sunny days was given less by images of remembering than by the dumb pressure of something that wanted persistently to come through into consciousness and could not. I had been stalking partridges just two days ago in the shaggy hilltop fields beyond the woods above us, and had flushed several out of the half-dead apple trees at the woods' edge. But I hadn't fired. It was midafternoon. The stillness and the sun were irresistible. I unloaded the shotgun and lay down by a stone wall that made me think of loaves from an oven, and was pulled under instantly. I slept for a long time, and then did not awaken all at once, but passed into a dream that was almost a waking dream, in which I imagined that I was coming into the entranceway of our present house, stamping my feet, and my father—who had visited here only once—leaned around through the

inside doorway angrily. He was talking on the phone. He covered the
mouthpiece and began to upbraid me, but I made some gestures of
apology. I noticed, in my dream, that I hadn't responded with false
pride, or with anger of my own, which on occasions in the past had
been severe. I felt a stirring of hope that excited me. A radiance and
buoyancy came into the dream, and everything took on a quality of
revelation. I put my arm around him and kissed his forehead, and he
blushed, and smiled happily. I was happy, too. The excitement I felt
now was the distinctive excitement that comes with new understanding, and with liberation from error. The dream changed into something like a chain of thought, or insight, and these insights stirred me
as deeply as had the images. I understood that *touching,* affectionate
touching, would ease our relationship of its angers, and would please
him far more than had the tokens of esteem he so often demanded. I
thought of times he had responded to affection with just this melting
surprise, blushing and smiling. But something was wrong. Something
was terribly askew. All that radiance and hope vanished abruptly, and a
sour, strange anxiety took their place. I became aware that I was not
awake, and promptly sat up in the cooling shadows of the wall, and
remembered that my father was dead, and had been dead for several
years. The ground was cold. The sun was low and the sky was white
with clouds. I could see my parents' faces, younger by far than I was
now, lively and good-looking. And I could see the grassy back yard
and the homely, pleasant porch I had enjoyed so much and had used
in so many ways, with its three broad steps and the lattice at one end
thatched densely with the leaves, vines, and blossoms of honeysuckle.
It was as if a curtain had been pulled aside from a window, and there
were all those things. I looked at them sorrowfully, not with joy at all,
yet they were bathed in a golden light and seemed utterly desirable.
Then they dwindled and faded. I could feel the process beginning, the
strangest of all physical sensations, an uncontrollable *otherness* within
the self, that was like pain, except that it was painless. I tried to slow
the process, and then tried to bring back at least an image of my parents' faces, but I couldn't, and my helplessness was so extreme that it

passed beyond any feeling of frustration to a kind of creaturely humbling, as by death. I picked up the gun and started back through the woods, which very rapidly were turning cold.

I thought of these things as I lay there beside Patricia and the children. And I remembered my mother's death and how I had held her in my arms, crying, and had kissed her forehead, which hadn't yet cooled. Patricia was pregnant then with Jacob. My father had died the following year, after Jacob was born. There was a photograph in the album they had given me that had taken on the status of a memory, it was so mysterious: my mother in a skirted bathing suit, just twenty-two, extremely pretty, with something innocent in her face, a leftover glow of childhood. Her legs were curled to the side and she leaned on one arm in shallow water on a sandy beach. She looked into the camera with a shy, pleased, trusting happiness. Her arms and legs were long, yet were handsomely rounded. Her abdomen, too, was slightly rounded, but I myself, in embryo, was the cause of that. This fading ochre and ivory image affected me strangely. Here was the woman herself, who later vanished into that beloved invention called *mother.* And here, invisibly, was the young man, my father, the mere youth holding the camera. Here also was I, before time had begun. . . .

Since my parents' deaths this image had come of its own into my thoughts, but I had paired it with another in a poem that was in fact a prayer of thanks and now the two were inseparable. No camera had recorded the second. I had heard the children's voices one August afternoon two years ago and had gone to my window in the upstairs room in time to see them striding along the road under the overhanging trees. They had been picking blackberries in the high field beyond the woods. Their faces and hands were stained. Ida carried a creamery pail, and all three were equipped with picking pails made from coffee cans, slotted and held at the waist with cords. All three were equipped, too, with staffs, crooked sticks picked up in the woods, and they planted and swung them as they strode along. They wore shorts of cut-off jeans and their bare legs were dirty and tan. Jacob's legs were painted with whorls and stars of bright-red Magic Marker. The stems of two long ferns were fastened under the cord that held his picking pail. The ferns crossed his chest and fluttered as he strode along beside Liza, his great love, who looked stalwart and vigorous. She wore a headband, Indian style, from which a fern arched backward rakishly, like a plume. The strap of a canteen slanted from shoulder to hip. She looked adventurous and dashing. Ida alone was unadorned. Her vivid, sensitive, ten-year-old face was thoughtful and earnest, as befitted the eldest of the expedition. Her movements were light, elfin light, but her legs were strong and they carried her along with such buoyancy that one expected her to bounce into a cartwheel at any moment, or take leave of the ground entirely. The children turned and came abreast through the wagon break in the low stone wall, and as they emerged from the shadows into the open sunlight of the yard, such happiness leaped through me as was almost frightening to feel. I wrote of that moment later, and of the photograph of my young mother, and those images, since that time, had belonged to each other.

Once again I looked at the sleeping children, who had grown so large, and who in their persons were all presentness, all immediacy, and were so compelling in that immediacy that one could scarcely believe in the past at all. I could feel the waning and dwindling of the process of thought, and then I was aware only of the four voices of breathing beside me . . . and I too fell asleep.

PART TWO

Our city friends slept hours later than we. I had taken some blueberries from the freezer the night before, and I went down and stirred them into a pancake batter, but the house remained silent, and remembering my own Sunday mornings in New York years ago—bagels and coffee and *The New York Times,* lasting well into the afternoon—I fixed a tray of breakfast things and went back upstairs. At the bedroom door I heard laughter, and sounds of exertion, and Liza's protesting voice: "Hey! You're on my side!"

Jacob was rotating with laughing fury on Patricia's back, trying to break her stance, while Liza tickled him and Ida tugged at Liza, Patricia all the while remaining firm on her hands and knees and laughing like another child.

The beautiful weather was holding. The chill of the night was gone. The sun had risen above the trees to the southeast, and the familiar colors of our autumn summer were spread large: the clear blue of the sky, the evergreen greens, the yellows, reds, and oranges of the hills.

In the bright light from the windows, we ate picnic style on a drawing board placed in the center of our raft: toasted cheese sandwiches, milk and coffee. Patricia heard the story of Houdini in three competing voices.

"He has to tell us how he did it," said Liza.

"He may not know," said Patricia.

"Yes he does, Mom," said Liza.

"Uh-unh," said Jacob, shaking his head. "He doesn't." We read aloud from Tolstoy's *Ivan the Fool,* a story the children had heard several times and loved, but we didn't get very far. Jacob went to the windows and looked out, and said, as Liza joined him, "Can't we play outside if we're quiet?" They spoke of an entertainment for our guests, and this seemed to involve costumes from the supply in the large trunk given us by friends in the theater, but I explained that our guests were leaving after breakfast. We heard footsteps just then, and the children went running down, clad still in pajamas and nightgowns. I followed them while Patricia dressed.

⟪

Luisa was not in her room. The door was open. I knocked on the jamb and called her name, and then looked in. She had used the bed, but there was no way to know how long she had been up. I went outside at once and circled the house, then crossed the road. The dogs were near the barn. They ran to me as I approached it. The early chill and freshness were still in the air, but the broad, mild radiance of the sun was settling down. Before I reached the barn I heard her strong, musical, desperately grieving voice, and its throat tones of agony stopped me in my tracks. She was crying, moaning, and talking. "Ay Dios, ayúdame! Socorro . . . Ay Dios! Dios! . . . Qué voy a hacer?"

Her voice came as if from underground, and was amplified by the barn. I knew that she must be standing or crouching under the barn, on the downhill side, where once there had been several stalls and which was now a walk-in storage space, cluttered with boards and broken barrels, bean poles, and chicken wire.

I went back to the house. Marshall was standing on the front porch, both hands around a cup of tea. He was worried. I told him what I had heard.

"I'm afraid to leave her alone," he said, "but I don't want to hound her either. . . ."

I suggested that we send the kids for her. They could shout from a distance, which would give her time to compose herself. "Good. Good," he said, and a moment later we were both giving them instructions. I didn't tell the children where she was, only that they should stand near the barn and call her name in unison.

"What shall we call?" said Ida.

They called Harold "Harold" and Marshall "Marshall"—it would have sounded very strange to hear them say "Mister Ashby," "Mister Berringer."

"Call 'Señora Domic,'" I said.

Marshall said, "Yes. Let me hear you say it: Señora Domic. . . ."

The grinning children repeated her name and then ran off to find her. I went back into the house. Patricia was setting the table. Coffee was under way. Two frying pans were heating, and the bowl of batter stood near them on the stove. Presently the children came in, and I could tell by the footsteps that Luisa was stopping at the bathroom.

Both Ida and Liza were aware of her unhappiness. I could see this as we took our places. Ida understood, too, that all of Luisa's actions were deflected by something that had happened, something powerful and recent, but invisible to others. She looked thoughtfully at Luisa from time to time.

Luisa obviously needed food. She was physically depleted. Patricia tried to interest her in eating, even tried to maneuver her into eating by speaking of the local origin of the things before us. The blueberries in the pancakes were from our own high fields, the eggs in the batter from our own hens, the butter, milk, and cream from cows that pastured just a mile away; the bacon had been butchered, cured, and smoked by a neighbor. And Luisa did sample these things, and did praise them, but she kept turning to Patricia, looking searchingly into her face.

Marshall praised everything and did his best to establish a flow of conversation.

Patricia asked Jacob if he would explain to Señora Domic how we made the maple syrup. As usual he had poured too much syrup on his pancakes. There was a pool of it on his plate.

"Yeah, sure," he said. "It's easy. You know those big trees right out there?" He pointed toward the front of the house.

"Jacob," said Liza, "there are millions of trees out there."

"The great big ones," he said.

"But you don't mean the pine trees," said Ida. "Those are the biggest."

"Ida," he said firmly, "let me tell it."

Luisa had brightened. She was smiling gently, looking from one child to another, and then her eyes rested on Jacob.

"You know those little things about this big?" he said, and turned to Patricia. Before she could speak, however, Liza said, "Spigots."

"Liza, let me tell it," said Jacob.

"Let Jacob, honey," said Patricia.

"Yeah, but who knows what he's talking about when he says little things about this big! They could be goose eggs!" said Liza.

"You can't hammer goose eggs in a tree!" shouted Jacob.

"Right!" said Harold. But he winked at Liza.

Marshall was Liza's partisan right along, and sat there smiling at her. We had spoken to him already about the car, and he had said that he would use his own. As for Luisa's staying with us—he had urged us to ask her, though relatives near Quebec City already had been contacted. Marshall planned to call them again before leaving.

Jacob described well enough the process of making maple syrup, though we were obliged to add that it was done at the very end of the winter, and that cold nights and warm days were essential to the running of the sap.

Luisa had begun to smile at Jacob more warmly. One saw what a handsome and vital woman she was. There was something luminous about her brow, or rather the entire setting of her eyes, and her eyes themselves were lucid, intelligent, and beautiful.

The telephone rang, and Liza, who had just carried some dishes to the sink, answered it.

She called to us. "For Harold Ashby . . . and Ricky Rasmussen gives his regards to everyone, especially Patricia, his favorite hostess"—and she said, in a quieter voice, speaking into the phone, "How was that?" for which she evidently received approval. I could see from where I sat that she was not only smiling but blushing.

"This will be the crossword puzzle," said Harold.

Smiling, he carried his cigarettes and coffee to the other room and set them on the little table by the phone. He seated himself, crossed his legs, lit a cigarette, and picked up the phone all in one easy flow of precise gestures that reminded me of the times I had seen him conducting.

"Greetings returned by everyone," he said. "How are you, Ricky? . . . Oh, that's good. I'm glad to hear it. . . . Of course. I knew the minute the phone rang. . . . No, I don't think there is a *Times.* Let me check if we can tie this up."

"May we monopolize the phone?" he called back to us. "Are you quite certain? Marshall? Luisa? Thank you, then." And to Ricky he said, "Read me the whole definition. . . . Seven? Well"—he sipped some coffee and drew some smoke into his chest, breathing it out as he spoke—"if the *o* is right, we wouldn't need another vowel. *Cyclops* would fit. . . ."

"We used to get the overseas *Herald Tribune.* We used to save the crossword puzzle for the children," said Luisa. "We thought it would improve their English, but we never found that to be the case. I believe the definitions are much too specialized."

"Crossword puzzles are almost unethical," said Marshall, frowning. "They have no relation to language."

"You are quite right," she said.

Yet we all were listening to Harold. The lure of the question-and-answer form was seducing us even at this remove. We heard him saying, "Maybe one of the adjacent . . . read me . . . go ahead. . . . Ah!

77

Of course! You're right! Figure means figure of speech. Now what do we have in that horizontal eight?"

The dishes were taken away. Even Jacob helped in this Whole Family task, the result of many plenary sessions, most of them futile. Marshall laid out a road map among the coffee cups and glanced at Patricia, who had sat down close to Luisa again and, so I judged, was about to open the question of her staying here with us.

It was at this moment that Ida came into the room carrying a basket of clothes for the washing machine in the cellar. Luisa looked up at her, and Ida smiled. It was like a circuit—the touch of a friendly glance and that flaring, happy smile. One would say that the circuit lay deeper in human life than individuality, and probably nurtured it.

But Luisa's glance was more than just approving. It was hungry. Ida was twelve. Childhood and girlhood were mingled in her. One could see her own future motherhood in the way she cared for Jacob, just as one could see, in the fellowship they shared, her lively attraction to the many childish things she had not outgrown. Luisa had looked at her repeatedly, really as if warming herself before a hearth. And now Ida entered the room in her sprightly, light-footed way, both arms around the large basket, and seeing Luisa look up at her and brighten faintly, she paused just inside the doorway and her face flared with happiness and goodwill.

The basket she carried was an Indian basket of fine ash strips, well-made and handsomely shaped. It was as old as she. I had rubbed it with linseed oil and now its patina was a soft onionskin brown.

Luisa commented on it. Ida carried it to the table and placed it on a chair, and Luisa examined it with both hands, questioning Ida and Patricia. Harold's voice, relaxed and intimate, could still be heard in the other room. Marshall looked up from the road map, and he too praised the workmanship of the basket.

Luisa's long-fingered hands were striking. They looked strong and deft, yet there were no signs of labor about them, such as one saw at a glance on Patricia's rough hands; they were straight and elegant, with soft, unblemished skin.

The Indian weaver, a neighbor, had found a suitable brown ash tree near the stream below the house, just beyond the millrace that once had fed a little shingle mill. He had come to the house with tools his father had owned before him. The oddly shaped tools were slight, and seemed delicate, yet had lasted two lifetimes.

Patricia explained to Luisa how an eight-foot length of trunk was squared and quartered, and the quarters quartered, and how the fine layers—growth rings, actually—were loosened in long strips by the rapid tapping of a light mallet. The strips could be split again. Those in this basket represented six months of a year's growth.

Ida stood by the basket listening. She looked from one face to another. Whoever glanced at her brightened and every glance touched off a happy response. Ida judged by our voices that we had finished and, raising her eyebrows, asked wordlessly if she might leave us. Luisa smiled her thanks, and nodded.

There now occurred a chain of events that altered many things.

The cellar stairs came up into the pantry. Ida opened and closed the pantry door, and opened the cellar door . . . and we were startled by a shriek of panic or terror, and a dreadful clattering on the cellar stairs. I knew at once that she had fallen. There were cement walls and a cement floor at the bottom of the stairs. I heard my own voice and heard Patricia's voice utter staccato cries of alarm. We both ran to her. But *ran* is scarcely the word. It was as if my body had been canceled. I reached her instantly. Behind me came Patricia. We both were calling "Ida! Ida!" before we came in sight of her.

Ida lay sprawled at the foot of the stairs, right in the corner of the cement walls. I screamed to her "Ida! Ida!" She answered me, and I felt a great subsiding of terror. The basket had saved her, the laundry had saved her. One arm was skinned. She began to cry, turning her eyes to mine and saying, "I'm okay, I'm okay."

As we bent over her, there came from the room above us earsplitting shrieks of a terror that far, far exceeded ours. Each scream used an entire breath, and both the scream and the gasping between screams had a quality of physical limit, as if one were hearing the rasping and tearing of tissue and membrane. The screams were bloodcurdling; the gasping had the harsh, grating quality of dry vomiting and was appalling. We ran back up. Luisa was staring wildly in our direction. She knelt on the floor with her knees spread and gripped the sides of her face with both hands. Her mouth and eyes were opened more widely than one would think possible. Her shrieking was frightening. One feared, rationally or not, that she would suffer damage, and we all ran to her, as one would run to staunch a heavy flow of blood.

But no one knew what to do. Patricia ran to the bathroom and came back with a warm wet towel. Marshall had already knelt in front of Luisa. He shook her by the shoulders, shouting, "Luisa! Luisa! It's Marshall! Can you hear me? Can you see me?" but she swept him aside with amazing force, not as if she were aware of him at all, but as if he were some object blocking whatever it was she was staring at in the corner of the room. I knelt beside her, shaking my head at Marshall, trying to convey to him that we should let her scream, she would find her own way out of it. But her terror didn't lessen, and the screaming went on. Patricia tried to put one arm around her and tried to touch the warm towel to her face, but Luisa pushed her away and held her off with a desperate thrashing of one arm, never taking her eyes from the apparition in the corner. Ida emerged from the pantry and stopped in the doorway, her head forward and her mouth open. Marshall, Patricia, and I all knelt on the floor, close to Luisa but not touching her. Marshall said, "Oh, God, I don't want to hit her! Should I hit her?" and Patricia said sharply, "Don't you dare!" I looked at Luisa's face as Ida came into sight. I hoped that this would affect her, but Luisa kept gasping and sending those appalling screams through the house. Jacob and Liza had been upstairs. They came to the doorway and stopped there. Jacob was frightened; he held Liza's arm. Harold had crossed the room just before they appeared, and now with an abruptness that startled all of us there came a jangling and crashing from the piano. Several moments passed before it became apparent that this wild sound, that seemed so bizarre an occurrence, was actually an imitation of Luisa's voice. Its notes were similar; it pulsed where her screams simply endured; it dropped to a lower register and pulsed more quietly while she gasped for air. I had seen Harold do exactly this with the disturbed children, and we had heard a sample of it just last night on the tapes, yet once again it was astonishing.

Luisa was braced in that kneeling position, holding the sides of her face and staring straight ahead. Her entire body shook when she screamed, and swelled like a bellows when she gasped for air. She caught her breath and screamed, caught her breath and screamed. One heard many notes in her voice, a hoarseness that conveyed the pain of her throat, notes of terror that were chilling to hear, and still others that expressed unbelief or outrage, but outrage so extreme, so astonished as to be a kind of vomiting of life, a retching of the soul. No instrument could have expressed all this as her voice expressed it, yet Harold contrived equivalents and accompanied her. Luisa gave no sign of hearing the music, yet it seemed that a calling and responding had begun. Where we others had been trying to calm her, to bring her back to normal, Harold's piano had gone out to her and found her where she was. Nor was he simply duplicating her voice, but receiving it and enfolding it in a structure that, however minimal, constituted a kind of music and could not be heard in her voice. It was this music, really, that achieved the human presence beside her in what one would have thought would be an absolute darkness of agony. That presence could do nothing, or little, about her agony, or about the outrage of soul; nevertheless it *was* a presence, and it said persistently, *I am with you, I am with you.*

Harold had been playing only two minutes when there came a small modulation in her screaming, a drop to a different register, a change in duration and loudness; and the piano responded to her instantly. For several moments now we did hear clearly the dialogue of Luisa's voice and Harold's piano, her desperate call and his response, her call again, and again his response, and then her voice dropped decisively into another mode, and the piano dropped, too, and was more musical than before, and though she did call out several times, it seemed that she was expecting the response of the music and was calmed when that expectation was fulfilled. Soon her body relaxed; she bowed her head, dropping her face into her hands, and knelt there weeping in an exhausted voice. Her crying was rational; she seemed present in her body again, safely on earth. The music no longer spoke to her phrase by phrase but, transposing elements of her sobbing voice, sang to her a full, very quiet song that she responded to at one moment almost as if she recognized it, and then she sat there weeping soundlessly. It was as if the sufferer and her guide had emerged from the underground into a little grove where sunlight shone among trees and bushes, and the sufferer sat with bowed head, grieving silently, and the guide sang gravely in his own solitude beside her.

Patricia had been kneeling close to Luisa all this time, with her hands in her lap, holding the moistened towel, which she now handed to Luisa, who had tried to clear her nose, and who without lifting her head had looked first to one side and then to the other.

I caught a glimpse of Ida's face in the doorway of the pantry, from which, in a moment, she turned away. Tears were glistening on her cheeks, and she touched the fingertips of one hand to her lips.

Patricia helped Luisa to her feet, and Luisa, her head still bowed, looked around as if to speak, but turned away. Patricia went with her to the guest room, holding her with one arm around her waist and bowing her head close to Luisa's own. Jacob and Liza followed them at a distance.

Half an hour elapsed before Patricia came back to the big room. She had helped Luisa into bed and had sat beside her holding her hand and stroking her face until she had fallen asleep.

Marshall and I, in the meantime, had gone to Harold where he sat at the piano, still lightly touching notes and isolated clusters of notes, still extending that chain or pathway of sound, as if unwilling for it to come to an end; but he did stop, when we spoke to him, and turned to us on the piano bench.

Marshall seemed shaken to his very bones. His moist dark-brown eyes had the passionate look of youth in them, and there was an adoring openness in his face. "My God!" he said to Harold. "I've never seen anything so moving. That was heroic! Simply heroic! It makes me want to cry."

As for me, I could say only, "Harold, that was wonderful." What I wanted most to praise I could not mention at all. It was this: that in the moments of Luisa's most frenzied screaming, when the rest of us had been reduced to helplessness and to panic and confusion, Harold had listened to her so closely that he had been able to construct that extraordinary musical imitation of her voice.

He said quietly what we all had come to know: "Something horrible has happened to her."

I heard Ida sobbing in the basement. She had gone down again to put the laundry in the machine. I went to her, stopping first in the bathroom to get peroxide and salve for her scraped arm. As I came out of the bathroom the telephone rang, and Harold, who was near it, said, "That's surely Ricky. May I?"

Marshall came to the door of the big room. "I'm going out," he said in a low voice. "I need to walk."

I could read my own feelings in his face. We all felt drained.

"We'll have to stay until she's rested," he said. "She's in agony."

Some minutes later, having looked after Ida and talked with her briefly, I went upstairs to Harold's room. He lay on Ida's bed, an ashtray on his chest, smoking.

I asked how Ricky was.

"Better," he said. "Much better. It's so odd. He hadn't gone to the third floor at all since Mary died, and then last night after I talked with him he went up and spent the entire evening. He said it was calming, not upsetting. He had been afraid of that." He paused and said, "She was an extraordinary woman. The apartment is so much like her it's uncanny. It would be an act of violence to change it. . . ."

"Can you use it the way it is?"

"That depends on Ricky. If it does have to be dismantled, someone else might do it. Eleanor might help with that. We'll wait and see.

"She's with him now," he added.

Eleanor was Eleanor Stalling, the director of the concert choir of that name. She had rented their top floor for years, and was like a family member.

"Is she resting?" Harold said.

I said that I thought she was sleeping.

"Poor woman," he murmured. "Has Marshall told you anything?"

"He seems not to know much."

He smiled his attractive, large-toothed smile as I left the room. "I want to just think for a while," he said. "I'll be down shortly."

Patricia and the children were waiting for me in the kitchen. The children wanted to know why Luisa had screamed like that, and Liza asked as well why Luisa hadn't been able to see us though her eyes had been opened wide.

Patricia said to her, "Sometimes when something terrible has happened people can't forget it. It comes back to them and they think they're seeing it again."

"But what happened?" said Ida.

"We don't know for sure," said Patricia. "She may have lost her family."

"Does she have kids?" said Jacob.

"I think so," said Patricia—and seeing that Jacob didn't know what she meant by "lost," she said, "They may have been killed."

"But *why?*" said Ida. "Who would kill kids?"

I explained to them that there had been a kind of war in Luisa's country just a few weeks ago, and that the army had killed the people who had been elected to run the country and now were running it themselves. And I said to them, "They've killed many people. . . ."

"Even kids?" said Liza.

"We just don't know," said Patricia.

Jacob said quickly, "Is there going to be a war here, Mommy?"

"No. Her country is far far away."

"And her kids are dead?" said Ida.

"Maybe not," Patricia said. "We just don't know. She's afraid they might be."

"Do you think they are?" said Ida.

"We don't know enough to think one thing or another," said Patricia.

I told the children that war made terrible confusion: people left their homes, families were separated, people used false names. . . .

"Maybe her kids are hiding," said Jacob.

"Yes," Patricia said, "maybe they are."

"Do you think they might be alive?" said Liza.

"Yes, they might be."

And I too nodded and said, "Yes, maybe they are."

The children looked at us soberly, but only Jacob spoke.

"Goody," he said.

Patricia said to them, "Play quietly now. If you go outside, don't play near the windows. She's sleeping."

I went to our room and lay down on the raft of mattresses, and Patricia joined me almost immediately, kicking off her loose boots and sitting down beside me, leaning on one arm.

"We should try hard to get her to stay here," she said. But there was no certainty in her voice, beyond that of the desire to help: Luisa would be met by a cousin who lived near Quebec City, and who had children. It was by no means clear that we had anything superior to offer. But we agreed to try.

She leaned close to me and said, "There's such horror in the world, and we're so lucky."

We had talked much of late about these things. Our country's complicity in the overthrow of Allende made one realize yet once again the degree to which we were not citizens at all, but hostages of a secret government. We had financed a murderous subversion, agree or not—and agree or not we would profit personally from the torments of Chileans.

I said, "There is, yes. And we are, yes."

She kissed me and looked at me gravely, then got up again and went downstairs.

I went down a few minutes later and went outside into the spacious, warm, brightly colored day, in which the terrors that people inflicted upon one another seemed so achingly discontinuous with the beauty and abundance of the natural world.

I walked downhill on our long dirt road, thinking that perhaps Marshall was walking there, but he had taken another route, and I didn't see him again until we gathered for lunch.

Luisa slept all morning, and was still sleeping at lunchtime, or in any event did not join us. Harold and Marshall and Patricia and I lingered at the table after we had eaten. Not one of us was quite willing to talk, yet we all—so it seemed—wanted to stay together. Liza and Jacob were playing together on the floor. They knelt facing each other in front of the bookcase and near the base of the floor lamp. This location had been magnetized by the elaborate play of the day before, and they had come back to it with a definite sense of return, as one goes back to a bed still warm and resumes a chain of thought, or even a dream. Several of Liza's dolls lay strewn about near the base of the lamp, together with some rubber animals, some plastic animals, some wooden animals, and a number of tiny cars and motorcycles. But many other things were laid out on one of the bookshelves, too: tiny chairs, a tiny bed, a table, some garden tools and cooking utensils— shapes of the world very pretty in themselves, and interesting; they had been appearing in abundance lately in the stores, just as poems in praise of animals or speaking farewells to animals had been appearing abundantly in magazines and books.

Liza stroked the long hair of one of her glamorous little dolls. I remembered how she had taken four of these dolls on our recent camping trip, and how, sitting in the doorway of the large tent, she had touched one finger to their faces, shoulders, and arms, talking to them softly all the while, and then had touched them again. The first touching had been suntan lotion, the second bug repellant. Jacob, too, played with the dolls, but he was seldom solicitous. Two swings, or trapezes, of red yarn and matchsticks dangled from the arm of the old cast-iron floor lamp. Liza held her doll on one of the matchstick bars and swung the doll back and forth, watching it dreamily. Jacob's trapeze was already broken. He touched a rubber dog to the remains of it, pulled it back, and hurled the dog with great élan all across the room. Their voices grew louder as their play became more physical. Soon they were putting on bits of costume, Liza a torn red hat with a veil, and some kind of fluffy plastic boa, also torn. Jacob put on a large drooping tam of black velvet.

"Hope you folks don't mind if we open up a little restaurant down here," said Liza. She spoke brashly, yet blushed at the same time, grinning shyly. She sat down at the far end of the table, and flounced impatiently in her chair. Jacob came back from the pantry and was now wearing a blue apron as well as the black velvet tam. He too was grinning with enjoyment.

"What do you want to eat, madame?" he said.

"Spaghetti and meatballs," said Liza, "and be quick about it."

"One pizzgetti coming up!"

"With meatballs, and don't shout."

"With meatballs, and don't shout! Yes siree, madame. . . ."

"No, Jacob, you don't say 'yes siree, *madame*'; 'yes siree' is *yes, sir* with an *ee* on the end; you only say it to a man."

"What do you say?"

"You say *madam!*"

"I *did!*"

"Oh, bring me the meatballs!"

"Comin' right up, honeychile!"

Jacob ripped up some newspaper and sprinkled the shreds on a serving tray. He tore several egg pouches out of a Styrofoam egg box and dropped those on the shredded paper. Liza drummed impatiently on the table while she watched all this.

"The service in this restaurant is terrible," she said. "What's that mess on the tray?"

"Pizzgetti and meatballs, madame."

"It looks like you stepped in it."

"It looks like *you* stepped in it!" said Jacob, and tilting the tray, he dumped the contents over her head. A moment later the tray was clattering on the floor and he was fleeing, chortling, yet looking back apprehensively.

"It slipped, madame!" he shouted. "I didn't mean to, madame! Ohhh oh. . . ."

"I'll meatball *you!*" said Liza. "You'll be a meatball when I get through with you!"

"Help!" he shouted.

"Hush! Hush!" we said to him.

"The meatball monster is after me!"

They ran twice around the table, which had been run around like this many thousands of times. We had stopped talking and sat there laughing. Ida appeared in the doorway. She had gone out to feed the ponies their grain, and now the moment he saw her Jacob ran to her calling, "Help, Ida! Help!" while Liza called, "Grab him, Ida! Hold him!"

It was Liza with whom Ida sided. Jacob twisted this way and that in his sister's hands, laughing. Harold walked quickly to the piano, where he called out to the girls, "Bring your prisoner over here!"—and in a moment he was touching the keys with his wide-ranging, hovering, complex touch.

"Listen to this," he said, and he played an extended, distinctive phrase. "That means chocolate bars. Chocolate bars. Now don't go running and looking, Jacob. I'm going to give you clues. In fact, I'm going to tell you where they're hidden."

"You hid chocolate bars?" said Jacob. "Where? Where are they? Yaaaay!"

"I'm going to tell you on the piano," said Harold. "Listen . . ." and he played again the phrase that stood for chocolate candy. "Now I'm going to hide the candy music in some other music. You give a yell when you hear it." He began to improvise, and played for a minute or so before playing the phrase again. Liza shouted quickly, "That's it!" and Ida joined her, but Jacob was confused. Harold played the candy phrase again for him, and then invented phrases meaning *under the big black chair, behind the sofa, in back of the phonograph, on the shelf by the fireplace windows.* He played these phrases several times, and said to worried Jacob, "No matter *who* finds the chocolate bars, there's one for each of you."

There now ensued a most closely attended little recital. One by one, and in many combinations, the various phrases entered and left the song, but none was joined by the candy phrase, and then finally the crucial phrase did appear, linked to one of the others, and Liza ran immediately to the high windows at the end of the room. She clambered on an easy chair, seized the chocolate bars, and held them high, shouting to Ida and Jacob, who had followed close behind her, "Got 'em!"

Marshall had watched all this from the table with Patricia and me. His own children were grown and living away from home. He smiled with wistful delight and said quietly, "Oh, I'll bet they learned more music in that five minutes than they could learn in a month at school. That was wonderful!"

We heard Luisa's voice behind us, and immediately everything was quiet. She came into the room as if in the depths of a trance. She seemed to have no contact at all with the place itself, but seemed to be moving in other surroundings. And yet it was as if a great awakening were taking place. She went to Harold, one hand extended, as if to touch him. He stood up and began to say something, but she interrupted him. She was smiling and seemed to be excited.

"That sounds so much like the music of Harold Ashby," she said, "but I've never heard it."

Harold was confused. "I was simply improvising," he said.

Now Luisa was confused.

All at once Harold understood why. He smiled nervously, and his eyes fluttered, as if about to turn upward into his head. "I *am* Harold Ashby," he said.

There now emerged from the woman before us another woman, perhaps not different, but vitalized and renewed. She said to him, with wide eyes, "*The* Harold Ashby? The composer?"

"Yes," he said.

"You are the one who wrote the *Concertante in C?*"

As she spoke the words of this question, she went closer to him and gripped his arms just below the shoulders. There was something fierce but also vulnerable and needy in her face.

He answered, "Yes."

She said, "You are really Harold Ashby? You are the one who wrote the Sonatas, and *For Travelers?*"

He nodded, ill at ease in her grip but touched by her intensity.

"And *Songs Without Breath?*" she went on. "And the lovely, lovely *Little Fugues?*"

To all of her questions he nodded, watching her closely.

She let go of his arms and put both hands to her face. "Of course!" she cried. "I recognize you! Yes! Oh! . . ."

She began to smile, and then smiled joyously. She took his hands in hers with movements that were both childlike and queenly, and this sudden vivacity seemed to be echoing with the past. One saw in her a largeness and fullness of being that led one to imagine bygone events of a lucky and nurturing kind, and associations of unusual quality with parents and grandparents, teachers and friends. Her large, almost black eyes were glowing. The white, white skin that had been dull seemed to come alive.

She suddenly remembered us, and looked over her shoulder. She hooked one arm around his and turned to us, saying, "Look who I have found! Oh I feel so idiotic! Here now I have been in the same house with him for hours, and certainly I heard the name Harold Ashby when you introduced us . . . and certainly I heard the name Harold at breakfast and said it myself; now I have just understood at last this is *Harold Ashby!*

"We *lived* on Harold Ashby! Oh, oh . . ." she said, glancing at him.

"My children are superb musicians, superb performers of Harold Ashby. Truly, there was a period of three years when anybody opening the door of our house could not fail to hear one Ashby or another, especially, of course, the Sonatas, and the *Duo Concertante,* since Dorotea and I both play piano, and Raoulito violin. . . ."

Impulsively, she sat down at the piano. I caught sight of Marshall. He was watching her with consternation.

She moved the bench a little closer than Harold's long arms had needed. She squared herself before the keyboard and straightened her back, and there exploded in the room an electrifying torrent of music, the "gorgeous explosions" (this phrase had been used in *The New York Times*) of Harold's first and most romantic period. I recognized the piano movement of the *Duo Concertante.* She played with power and stunning command.

She interrupted herself and spoke to an astonished Harold over her shoulder. "You cannot, of course, hear what I am hearing, and I regret that very much. I mean the violin—not perhaps the ideal violin you must have heard in your mind when you wrote this, but Raoulito's violin, which surely comes wonderfully close. He is sixteen, but he has been a mature musician for two years, at least. Dorotea is a year younger. They have played passionately since childhood, and have worked very very hard, and so their ages are no indication of their ability. Of course, they are my children as well as my protégés, and no doubt I am biased, but I am speaking also with realism. . . ."

By now there had appeared on all of our faces the same consternation I had seen on Marshall's. Even if by some miraculous chance her

children were still alive, this feverish animation denied the very existence of the dreadful seizure we had witnessed a few hours ago. No
one spoke, or knew quite what to do. The unreality of her words,
together with the sudden great vitality of her presence, brought one
to a pause.

She had addressed herself to Harold. His face, too, showed the
emotions we others felt, but she didn't notice. She turned back to the
piano, shook and squared herself . . . and once again a great torrent of
music filled the room. She was playing the *Serenade in G Minor*, his
most popular piece and one of three that summed up that first long
period of work.

I was not musical, and was long unused to live performance, and
therefore went again through all the naive reactions of my early
encounters with music. I was awed by the piano itself, that it should
be brought to such an astonishing presence among us, quivering and
detonating throughout the whole of its body. And since I could not
even imagine the pianistic technique that was producing those
sounds, I saw Luisa less as an artist than as a shaman of some kind, who
dwelt at the center of that loud sphere of passion and mind, and
whose substance was undergoing continually a miraculous transmuta-
tion into music.

Harold's face was rapt. He cocked his head like a bird. I could
almost believe that his large, slightly protruding ears were quivering.
Certainly a remarkable sharpening and magnification of hearing was
taking place, together with a great attachment of mind to the act of
hearing.

It was splendid to hear this, splendid in many ways. It reintroduced
Harold's fame and genius into my relations with him. Ricky, I supposed at Harold's request, had never played his work on their visits
here, and the fact was that years had gone by since I had attended a
performance of his things. Nor had I played his records for a long
time, since I had played them so frequently before that I was under the
impression—a very mistaken impression—that I knew them by heart.

The children were as electrified as I. Both girls were taking lessons, but they had never encountered a performance like this one. They could not have conceived, not even remotely, of such power and skill as this. Patricia was sitting at the table. Jacob climbed into her lap. Ida stood beside her with one hand on her shoulder. In a moment my lap too was occupied.

Marshall caught my eye from the end of the table. He was as surprised as we.

The ending of the *Serenade* is a slow and grave subsidence into silence, in some ways similar to the music of peace Harold had played for Luisa as she had recovered from her terror. The ending seems to appropriate to itself several moments of silence, phrases of silence, or a ghostly melody of silence.

She sat quietly at the piano. She closed the cover over the keyboard, and pressed the tips of all ten fingers upon it, and then stood up and turned to us.

Something had changed in her. Some sequence of inward events had reached completion. I became aware of the great reserves of pride within her, and I knew that we all were responding to something grand and severe in her bearing, that was womanly, attractive, and unaffected, and that yet was grave and proud.

Harold was the first to speak. He went to her and said "Luisa . . ." and paused. She smiled at him and inclined her head, and this apparently was the permission he wanted, for he then said "darling" and embraced her, pressing his cheek to hers.

"It was simply beautiful," he said softly, "simply beautiful."

"Oh," she said, "I'm terribly out of practice. There were dozens and dozens of errors . . ."

"Everyone has played that," Harold said to her, "none better . . . truly."

Her bright smile, a deeply pleased smile, a smile such as we had not seen on her face at all—such, indeed, as I would have thought would never again appear there—released us all from our silence, and we praised her in the timid, heartfelt way of admirers face to face with an artist of great power.

Except for Jacob. Understanding what was now permitted, he let it come out with its usual rush and amplification. He stepped up onto the chair from which Patricia had just arisen, stepped from there onto the big table, and shooting one fist toward the ceiling shouted hugely, "That was GREAT! Yaaay!!"

Luisa bent forward, smiling warmly, and blew him a kiss. He blew several back to her and shouted again, waving one arm above his head. Ida (whom, with Liza, I had taken twice to the opera in Boston) pulled him close and whispered in his ear. He glanced at her and grinned, looked at Luisa again, and shouted, "Bravo! Bravo!"

Marshall was strangely hushed. "That was magnificient!" he said to her quietly. "I haven't caught my breath yet." He was not aware, apparently, that the composer of that music was standing beside him, also looking at Luisa.

"You must be known," Harold said to her. "Should I know your name? I do know that you haven't recorded the *Serenade.* I could never forget that rendering."

"I used my maiden name professionally," she said, "Avila."

It was as if she had just arrived. We sat around the big table with coffee and tea, cheese, and crackers.

She had indeed had a concert career. She had played frequently in Chile, and had toured in the States to Dallas, Houston, and Los Angeles.

"When my gowns no longer fit me," she said, "I went home, but then I played anyway in Santiago and Valparaiso. I performed the *Second Sonata* very often, and also the *Imitations,* often the whole of it, but sometimes just a selection. And then of course I had to give up performing entirely."

She leaned forward, addressing every word to Harold. From time to time she remembered to include the rest of us, and then would turn and find our eyes with her own.

"My friends in the music world said to me that I would have to choose between having children and having a career," she said. "Perhaps in one sense they were right, but they were quite wrong, too. I did certainly perform again. And in any case, their criticism ignored completely the fact that I adored having children. I had two master students at the time, and it never occurred to me that I would enjoy inventing exercises for little fingers, but I did enjoy it."

Liza, Jacob, and Ida came and went while we sat at the table. All three were present at this point, and they listened attentively when Luisa mentioned her children. In some way they took her statements now as being refutations of their earlier fears. They were attaching belief and response to this present animated talk, and were forgetting the dreadful possibilities we had discussed that morning.

Luisa noticed the intensity of their attention, and smiled at them.

"If one thinks of careers," she said, "it is too late already for Liza and Ida. . . ."

She looked at them warmly, but without any softening of that statement. Her expression seemed to be saying, Yes, life is like that.

The girls were surprised to hear such a thing. Too late already? They had thought that all of life, and all the possibilities of life, lay before them. Besides, they were *taking* lessons.

Harold smiled and shrugged. "Maybe not," he said.

"That would be no reason, of course, to discontinue the study of music," said Luisa. "On the contrary, I cannot imagine life without music. Music is the very heart of life. And when you think what music gives to us, then it is quite proper that music should make such extreme demands. Perhaps if you feel there is a talent, and other factors seem right to you, you could make a beginning with Jacob. And I can tell you something I have found to be extremely important. You see, there are many people who imagine that if they practice and study two or three hours a day they are working hard at music. Raoulito was four years old when I began to teach him formally, and I arranged it so that Dorotea could play with her dolls in the very same room to enable her to hear us, and to hear my own playing, and then when she was four I began formally also with her. But of course from the very beginning there was music in their lives. They lived in a house of music. Even so, I wanted to *accustom* them to large quantities of work. I wanted them to take it for granted that one spent most of every day at one's instrument, even when friends were visiting. I wanted them not to think about it, not to be aware of it. I wanted them to say with surprise perhaps to some playmate, '*What?* You spent the whole afternoon away from your piano, or your violin?' But young children, of course, cannot sit still for very long. And they must not be asked to concentrate after they have grown weary, since the quality of attack falls away so badly. Our first lessons were only fifteen minutes long— one session in the morning and one in the afternoon. But from the very beginning I asked them to play *musique digestive* for fifteen minutes after every meal. And then in the evening, because I read to them at bedtime—and Alejandro did, too, when he could, and Mercedes would make them some warm chocolate—before all that, they played fifteen minutes of 'chocolate music.' So you see, from the very beginning, what with the lessons, and the digestion music, and the chocolate music, they were working very well, very keenly, for an hour and a half every day, and by the time they were eight years old that had become four hours, and then it became five hours, and then it became six hours, and on special occasions even more. Long before this, of course, Raoulito had surpassed my own experience with violin. He studied with Carlos Dietrich, and then was accepted by Henriquez, who is actually my cousin. Dorotea remained my own pupil. Truly, it was a house of music. The children had their own small studios, and we were obliged from the beginning to make them soundproof, or the cacophony would have been appalling. Between the ages of nine and eleven they made such leaps in technique as one could scarcely believe possible. And from the age of twelve they began to get really the glimpses of the intelligence and feelings of music . . . all that is so wonderful, so delicious, and so glorious in music, and that is so astonishing in Harold Ashby's music . . . our dear, dear Harold's music, that begins at times so gently and modestly, as if going nowhere, and suddenly is wrenching your heart. . . ."

She was smiling at him warmly, partly with the astonished discovery that never quite left her face the rest of that day, partly with open affection, as for an old, old friend, but also with an admiration so close to adoration that one felt that perhaps she herself had attempted composition and had failed at it, and that that failure had given her a still keener sense of its mysteries and demands.

She said, speaking again to Harold alone, "Raoulito composed a great deal when he was ten and eleven years old. Every piece he wrote was subtitled 'Chocolate Music,' and then when finally it was clear that there was enough for a collection, the collection as a whole was called *Chocolate Music,* or I suppose you would translate *Hot Cocoa Music.* The most precious gift I ever received at Christmastime was a hand-bound and beautifully copied edition of *Musico Chocolato.*

"But we were always giving musical gifts to each other. Alejandro is the only one who is not musical. He is not musical at all. He is a journalist and scholar. . . ."

She smiled and said, "My husband is Alejandro Domic. If you lived in Chile you would know his name." One felt that she was suppressing the words, *You would know my name too.*

Marshall nodded to her, with a pained look on his face. "I do know his name, of course," he said. "I've read his books." To us he said, "He's an important writer, important in the cultural and political life of Chile. He's a sociologist and activist."

"Yes," she said.

She went on talking to Harold. "His lack of musical talent is very strange," she said, "since his speaking voice is so beautiful and natural. But he cannot sing at all. Nevertheless, he adores music. He adores even to listen to us practicing. He attends the children's performances very faithfully, just as he did mine, amateur and professional both, from the time of our first encounter. I mean in Chile, of course, not when I was touring. He could not leave his work. Once when he was slightly ill he pretended to be more seriously ill—he confessed it to us many months later. The children were rehearsing for a concert very important to them and were using my piano in the music room. Alejandro lay in bed two days more just for the pleasure of listening. Of course he was writing, too, and did not put that aside, but combined the two great pleasures. We could not forget this. Really, it was a kind of praise one does not forget. And the following year he really was ill, and I asked him if this was a musical illness, and our doctor said to me that his fever was not in the least bit musical, and that he would of necessity be confined to his bed for several days. So the very next day we gave him a musical gift, and this was a concert entirely of the music of Harold Ashby.

"Yes, truly," she said. "I am not exaggerating. I am so happy to be able to tell you this. Oh, I still cannot quite believe my eyes, that you are actually here in the person." She reached across and touched his hand, smiling at him warmly.

"Since he had been ill," she went on, "he had been sleeping immediately after his dinner. We knew that he would awaken probably at three o'clock. We heard him ringing for Mercedes. She took him a tray of fruit juice, and a dish of melon, and on the tray there was a folded piece of paper on which I had written the program of the concert. It was called *A Concert of Works by Harold Ashby for Alejandro Domic.* Alejandro has saved that program. . . .

"Mercedes gave us the signal by ringing twice on the kitchen bell. This meant that he had read the program. The music room was exactly below our bedroom, and so we were not obliged to play with extra loudness. Our concert consisted of, first, the *Sonata in F for Four Hands,* and then the *Fantasy in A,* the 'Water-skimmers,' in Walter's arrangement for violin and piano, and then Number Three of the *Little Nocturnes,* which Dorotea played, and finally—which I played myself—the so beautiful and moving *Second Sonata,* which Alejandro loves as much as I.

"We ran upstairs then to face our audience and take our bows. We had dressed up in our formal clothes. Alejandro was sitting up in bed. He was smiling so lovingly, and yet the tears came down his face. Mercedes was sitting in a chair across the room, and she too was trying to dry her eyes. She adores Alejandro. We had intended to form a line, as on the stage, and join hands and bow, but he held out his arms so impatiently, and so we just went to him and were embraced instead. Raoulito stood beside him and Alejandro kept looking up at him, holding him by the hand."

All this, that was spoken with a strange combination of intimacy and formality, in an English learned from tutors and by traveling, was said so fully and directly and with such natural power that we listened to it scarcely moving. Jacob had climbed into Patricia's lap. What Luisa had said about the arduous studies of Raoulito and Dorotea, that had so astonished Liza, and especially Ida, was lost on him, yet something held him spellbound. He leaned toward Luisa from Patricia's lap, his eyes wide and his lips parted.

Luisa had begun by speaking to Patricia, and once had reached across the table and had taken her hand. But chiefly she was talking to Harold. When she said *dear Harold,* and spoke so ardently of his music and seemed to be thanking him for all that he had brought into her life, she became radiant, or one would describe her that way had it not been for something fixed in her gaze, and the slight touch of perspiration on her face. There was a velocity in her voice that one could not help but notice.

"We played two of those same pieces," she said to Harold, "in a fund-raising concert shortly after that, just a year ago—not even a year. We were raising money for medical supplies, and nutritionists and nurses to go into the *callampas* wherever possible. Those are what you would call slums, I suppose. It was out of the question to send doctors. Not many would have agreed to it. Colleagues of Alejandro's organized it. We were surprised at the range of people who took part. Raoulito and Dorotea did the *Fantasy in A,* and I the *Second Sonata.*

Other musicians performed, too. We had some De Falla and Poulenc, and some wonderful folk songs. . . ."

Her voice trailed off and she looked down at the table. In a moment a calm came over her, and her breathing slowed until it almost resembled the breathing of sleep.

Patricia asked her to sample a tea made of herbs she had grown and dried herself, and Luisa looked up and smiled. "Yes," she said quietly, "I would like to very much."

Patricia went to the stove, and Luisa once again turned to Harold.

"Everyone of course has heard that you have given up writing music," she said, dropping her head slightly to one side. "Forgive my raising this subject if it is bothersome to you, but you can see how important it is to me. Is it true? Does it mean really that the *oeuvre* of Harold Ashby is quite complete? Your interview with Marcus Horne was broadcast several times in Santiago, and so I am familiar with everything you said then. But that was several years ago." She paused and waited.

Harold was sitting erectly in his chair, both hands clasped before him on the table. He smiled that quick smile that signaled both distress and forthcomingness, and I could see the characteristic brief spasm of his eyes.

"Oh," he said, looking down for a moment, "it's complete, yes. I have that sense of it. I could be wrong, of course. If a new subject were to come to me I should be very happy, I think, but this is not something that weighs on me any longer. My work is complete."

I knew that he used "subject" in a special sense. He had said once that the whole of his production comprised just two subjects, and that the greatness of Mozart and Beethoven could be seen in the fact that they possessed four or five. I had never heard the interview Luisa had referred to, but apparently he had used the term then.

She looked at him impassively for a moment and then said, "I have always wondered about your idea of the subject. 'Subject' says nothing at all about the quantities that might be gathered into the one grouping or the other. And I am not sure that it speaks about quality. . . ."

"It doesn't do either of those things," said Harold.

"There's a tacit assumption of quality in the very use of the term," he added. "Otherwise, one doesn't talk. One doesn't even listen."

She laughed and said, "True."

The children, who had been interested before, now drifted away to pursuits of their own. Patricia came with a teapot and fresh cups. Luisa inhaled the aroma of this nameless concoction of five herbs and, with a glance at Patricia, praised it.

I took this occasion to say to Marshall that the piece Luisa had played was indeed one of Harold's. Marshall obviously had surmised as much, but had remained uncertain. He asked when it had been written.

"A long time ago," said Harold, turning to him. "It was in '62."

"Not so terribly long," said Luisa, "you are not ancient, after all.

"But then you are not well acquainted, really," she said. "I had assumed that everyone here was well acquainted."

"I've known our host and hostess for many years," said Marshall, "but I'm meeting Harold for the first time. I know his reputation . . . and some of his music—not nearly as much as I should."

I explained to Luisa that Marshall was a poet as well as a political theorist, and I mentioned the titles of two of his books. Marshall shrugged this away impatiently, and so I didn't carry it further.

Harold said to her, "Do you know my early work? *We Are Driven Into Pasture With a Blow?*"

Luisa brightened and said, "Oh yes, of course!"

"The text is a poem cycle of our host's," said Harold. "We didn't know each other then."

She laughed and clapped her hands, and turned to me. "Is it true?" she said. "Really? Then is *Ailanthus Tree* yours?"

I was happy to be able to say to her that it was, because she then said, "I love that one!"

An image or partial image of the tree itself, the friendly weed tree of New York that had grown outside my window, flashed in my mind. In times of inner peace it had seemed beautiful and had been a companion to me, but often I had looked at it with displeasure, a dusty, wretched weed of a thing.

"Oh, I have sung it so many times," she said. "For myself, my own pleasure—I am not a singer." And she raised one hand, averted her eyes for a moment, cleared her throat, and in a voice of melting maternal sweetness, a voice of generosity and tenderness, sang the song that begins:

> *How many times I've said goodbye,*
> *thinking of the crowds we're lost among as death . . .*

She sang the whole of it, ending with a smile and a restrained flourish of the head that offered the performance especially to Harold and to me.

There was enormous charm in her manner. It was a charm that was assured, yet was modest and almost affectionate, or, one would say, was disposed toward affection. Amidst all the murmurs of appreciation, I found myself wondering—and have wondered many times since then—what sort of man he had been, Alejandro Domic, who had won her.

❧

Again we all withdrew from one another. I urged Luisa to stay at least one more night. She agreed; and Harold, well aware of the importance this meeting had for her, said that he would delay his own departure until morning. The necessary phone calls were made. Patricia took the children to the barn to work on the cider press. And I, since I would be cook again that night, rummaged in the freezer and brought out a container of clam broth, and two packages of clams I had dug with a friend just a month before, and some chanterelles our whole family had gathered among the gray rocks and gray roots of a nearby beech grove, and some blackberries from behind the barn, and strawberries from the garden. As I came into the kitchen with these things I saw Luisa turning the corner to her room carrying a glass of water. A moment later I stepped outside, and on the front porch

encountered Marshall, who was standing there with his head drooping thoughtfully and his hands in his pockets. The sun was lowering
but the air was still warm and the sky clear. I wanted to walk, and
invited him to join me. He hesitated before answering.

"If you'd rather go alone," I said, "we can go different ways."

"It isn't that," he said, looking at me in a friendly way.

"I'm all wrung out. I don't know what I want."

We set off down the dirt road but soon turned aside onto a woods
road, not yet overgrown. Our feet began at once to stir a noisy
rustling in the brightly colored leaves.

The dogs came with us. The wolflike malamute trotted at my
heels. The Bernese mountain dog ranged erratically, and the aging
golden retriever preceded us by ten paces or so, stopping frequently to
look back. The leaves on the road were three inches deep, yet a great
many remained on the trees, and when the sun sent in slanting shafts
or masses of light there were dazzling towers of color all around us.
From time to time I saw the topmost leaves of birches and poplars, a
golden ochre, deliciously pale and glowing, swaying and flickering
against the light-filled sky with an effect as piercingly sweet as the
notes of flutes.

I asked Marshall what he had made of Luisa's seizure. He was going
along with both hands in his pockets. The weight of his forward-
thrust white-topped head tightened the two cords in his leathery
neck. He answered without looking at me.

"God knows what it means. Something horrible. I don't even want
to speculate."

He had not been told who she was, only that she was the wife of
Alejandro Domic.

"I felt like such a fool when I heard her play," he said. "She was
magnificent. Obviously she's known there. How could she not be
known?"

"How well known is Domic?"

Marshall turned to me with a contemptuous sneer that shocked me
and made me wonder why he wanted to be my friend at all. He

repeated in mocking tones the words *well known,* and then said, "Domic was famous. No one on the left was more conspicuous than he."

"Is he alive?"

"We know definitely that he was killed," he said.

"Does Luisa know?"

"She was informed. She was held for a while herself and then released."

"She was held?"

"Yes."

We walked along without talking. My face felt hot. I was confused. I asked him if he knew why Domic had been killed. He was silent, and then said, "If you knew the least thing about politics you'd know why. They've been killing their enemies. He was an enemy of fascism, an enemy of militarism, an enemy of imperialism, an enemy of nationalism itself, except that he loved Chile. He was a wonderful man, a scholar and journalist. No one was more capable than he of swaying the upper middle class and the professions—not that they could be swayed. But there are peasant groups and workmen's groups—not the trades or the petty entrepreneurs—who almost worshipped him. He was a marked man. Ideologically, he was to the left of Allende. There were serious differences between them, and yet they never quarreled, at least not publicly. But you wouldn't understand. It's complicated. There were half a dozen groups to the left of Allende. The important thing about Domic was that he was civilized. Allende trusted him. Everyone did. I met him several times. God knows, I may even have met Luisa. I don't think so, though."

"She talks as if he were still alive."

"I don't know what to make of it. It's horrible. I don't want to talk about it."

"What about the children?"

"You asked me that before! It's idiotic to repeat the question! Do you think I've received some kind of an update here in Maine? I said it's horrible. I'm being ripped up inside. Have mercy, for God's sake!"

We came to the stream, turned left, and went along beside it. The spur was badly overgrown, but there was still a path. The words formed in my throat—*Marshall, I ought to kick you in the stream!*—but I went along morosely. Perhaps, anyway, he was right. In a world of opinion and quarrelsome knowledge, he had given his life to real service, and I admired that enormously. Moreover, he was exhausted, and had been suffering emotionally.

Farther on the stream would pour down staggered falls and run swiftly through an ancient millrace, down falls again, and then would widen to form a pool; beyond the pool it would grow narrow once more and meander briefly through an alder bog and then through rushes and swale until finally, scarcely moving, and re-curved many times upon itself, it would join the large pond of which it was the inlet. All this would occur within less than a mile. There was extensive beaver work between the pool and the pond. I had come this way not long before, and loved this section of the woods. And there was something about the beavers that moved me. They were a social creature, were in fact a society, a responsible intelligence formed of woods, lakes, and streams and brought to its own perfection without regard to man. The beavers' dams and lodges, the pointed stumps and little piles of tooth-marked large chips, and their skid trails and felled food trees aroused in me the same sense of vastness and nonhuman time as did the Canada geese, who twice a year crossed our sky in noisy, hurrying formations. I had wanted to show all this to Marshall, but as we walked in silence along the stream my slow-burning anger made connection with so many previous angers that I wondered if our friendship had finally reached its end. I had had my fill of that quirksome arrogance, those harsh and contemptuous tones. This treatment was all the more painful in that it seemed to be the outcome of a far different exchange. During the writing of *Utopia and Human Labor* he had turned to me repeatedly for encouragement and for help against the violent irruptions of self-rejection that made so many things problematical for him. I had helped him editorially as well. The finished work was a triumph—but now just to the extent that it had been indeed a labor of self-transcendence, he began to alter his relations with the friends of his former life. I was not exempted from that process. To make matters worse, I wrote the first review of his book and thereby became the representative of the public for which he had hungered, and which, in truth, he did deserve, but which even now had not really been granted him. He began to posture in front of me, and to treat me with the most exasperating condescension.

And so I walked along, chewing on my anger and muttering to myself, "It's over! I've had enough!"

But then my anger spilled out anyway. We had reached the millrace when I stopped and blurted, "Marshall, why must you be so damned arrogant! And why do you have to bawl me out every time I ask you for information? And why must you be such a godawful, egocentric, self-righteous pain in the neck! Walk by yourself!"

"What did I do? What's the matter? What are you so touchy about? You're as bad as my son!" he called after me. "You're the one who's egocentric, not me!"

Marshall's son had left home to escape him. That had happened just a year ago; and yet this son, who was twenty-five and had been living with Marshall and Bonnie for economy's sake, had said to me recently at the home of friends, "There's nobody I'd rather take as a model than my dad. He's a hero."

Before I reached the house my anger ebbed away. And for some reason I kept seeing the widely reproduced photograph of agile, white-haired Marshall clambering over a hurricane fence at an anti-war demonstration, utterly fearless of the police waiting to club him, which they did. I found myself shaking my head helplessly. On my lips was an admiring, chastened smile, and in my throat were the words, "He's impossible."

~

I worked for an hour at my table in the bedroom. I had a shoebox of loose papers I had been carrying from the house to the cabin and back

to the house again. It was filled with notes of conversations with my
neighbors. I had made them over a period of years, not with any purpose but in a reflex of savoring; and then I had come to see that they
comprised a subject. What I had taken to be nostalgia wasn't that at
all. My neighbors' vanished life—the small farms, the crosscut saws
and axes, the teams of horses and oxen, the ten-cow herds, the modest
orchards, the sheep, hens, and kitchen gardens, the water-powered
mills—that life had *used* them powerfully and had rewarded them, not
by any means abundantly, but nevertheless along a spectrum of human
motives and not just in cash. They spoke of it in praise and with a certain pride. Most were mere employees now, and each was turned in
his isolation toward invisible powers in distant cities.

I heard voices, and went to the window, and saw Luisa and the
children standing at the edge of the yard, on the brow of the hill,
looking out across the valley toward the setting sun. The children
must have been telling her about our echo, because Jacob put his
hands to his mouth and shouted, "Hello!" and the echo came back,
"Hello!"

The children were grinning at Luisa. She spoke to them, bending
forward slightly. They listened attentively and then followed her
instructions, Ida taking a position on one side of her and Liza and
Jacob on the other.

Luisa stood up straight, put her hands at her mouth, and in her
musical, strong voice called, "Helloooo!" And the echo, overlapping
slightly, answered, *"Helloooo!"*

Luisa called, "Goodby!" And the echo called, *"Goodby!"*

"Hellooo!" she called again. *"Hellooo!"* it said.

"What, you again?" she asked. *". . . you again?"* it responded.

"Yes, me again!" *". . . me again!"*

"So goodby again!" *". . . goodby again!"*

"Hello again!" *"Hello again!"*

"What, you again?" *". . . you again?"*

"Yes, me again!" *". . . me again!"*

"So goodby again!" *". . . goodby again!"*

The children laughed and tried it themselves. Months later, when they referred to Luisa, it was never by name but either "that lady that played the piano" or "that lady that talked with the echo."

After the hubbub of shouting, Liza and Jacob took Luisa's hands again, and all three followed Ida, who walked a pace ahead, looking back. I saw them a few moments later standing near the rail fence of the garden on the other side of the house. The ponies were ambling toward them lazily, and Ida held out an apple to the large chestnut gelding, balancing it on the flat of her palm. The pony took the apple with complex movements of its lips, as if a dozen fingers were concealed within them. Instead of snatching away her hand, as she had used to do, Ida pressed the apple against the huge, rectangular teeth, assisting the pony, who with a thrust of his head and a vigorous bite, halved it, leaving a piece on Ida's hand.

Liza and Jacob kept glancing at Luisa, savoring her reactions to everything.

~

Toward evening Luisa suffered a serious loss of energy. She ate supper with her head bowed, avoiding our eyes. She had tried to sleep, but hadn't been able to. It was only when the children spoke to her that she brightened.

Halfway through the meal the children began to glance at one another and grin. Ida made a motion with her head, and all three began tapping rhythmically on the table, chanting, "Hou-di-ni . . . Hou-di-ni. . . ."

"How did he do it?" Ida said to Harold.

He looked at her blankly, then started and said, "Ah . . ." adding, "But this is not the best time, Ida. I'll come upstairs before you fall asleep."

This was my thought, too, and I was ready to quiet Jacob and Liza, who were begging him to tell them now, but I saw that Luisa, as before, had brightened somewhat, as if the children were a kind of sanctuary. Patricia noticed this too and, turning to Ida, said, "Explain to Luisa what you mean, honey."

"They locked him in a giant safe," shouted Jacob, "and he got out easy as could be!"

"No, not easy, Jacob," said Liza, "don't you remember? He was sweating. . . ."

And so Harold and the children, assisting and interrupting one another, sketched out for Luisa and Marshall a short version of Houdini's great escape.

"Well," said Harold, "I do know how he did it . . . but you won't like the solution. That was another of Houdini's great secrets. He knew that mysteries are far more appealing than explanations. People love to be mystified."

"They love to be unmystified, too," said Ida.

"Good for you," said Marshall. He gave no indication at all of remembering my outburst. I didn't know whether he was being generous or spiteful, but at least he wasn't sulking, and I was glad of that.

"You're quite right, of course," said Harold, "and that's probably more important in the long run. But after all, explanations are just the ordinary world of mechanics and treachery, whereas mysteries . . . well . . . mysteries are charming."

"How did he do it?" said Liza.

Harold laughed. Her peremptoriness was too innocent and queenly to be offensive. He folded his hands, leaned forward over them, and smiled at Liza. "I'm going to tell you, Liza," he said. "And I predict that the very first thing I say will make you say 'Hunh?'"

Liza snorted and tossed her head, but Harold said, "It's all based on mother love"—and Liza wrinkled up her face and, to the accompaniment of general laughter, said, *"Hunh?"*

Marshall, who was sitting beside her, put his arm around her and kissed the side of her head. "You don't often see predictions come true so fast," he said.

"It works like this," Harold said. "Mothers love their children, and because they love them they treat them well. And because the children are treated well, they trust their mothers. And because they grow up trusting their mothers, they have a tendency to trust other people too. And they have a tendency to tell the truth, since they grew up hearing it. So when that woman in the audience stood up and screamed, 'There's not enough air in there! He's going to die!' people thought she really was worried. It didn't occur to them that Houdini had paid her to do that."

"Hunh?" said Liza again.

"Well that's okay," said Jacob, who was quite confused and was looking from face to face.

"It's going to get worse," said Harold. "Do you remember how Houdini stepped out from behind the curtains, trying to catch his breath, and he was all covered with sweat? Well, that wasn't sweat at all, it was water, and he sprayed it on himself to make it look like sweat. As for the panting—he was just pretending."

Both Liza and Ida had begun to smile.

"But how did he get *out?*" said Ida.

"He had a tool, a special tool."

"I thought those guys searched him," said Ida; and Liza said, "What about the doctor?"

"Was Houdini paying him too?" said Ida.

"No, the doctor and the editor were well-known men. The tool was handed to him just before he stepped into the safe. Can you remember everything I told you? Do you remember a man in the audience shouted, 'How do we know they aren't working for you?' and Houdini said, 'Very well, come up yourself,' and then the man got embarrassed and wouldn't do it?"

"*That* guy was working for Houdini too?" said Liza.

"Yes. And his embarrassment was just an act. So Houdini picked three volunteers from the audience, and they went up on the stage and examined the safe. Do you remember? And then before he stepped into the safe, Houdini shook hands with them to thank them. The first two men were strangers, but the last man he shook hands with was a good friend of his, and he had a special little tool of hard steel attached to the ring he wore on one finger, and Houdini took it when they shook hands. So when that safe door was locked on him, he really *did* have something to work with."

Luisa had begun to enjoy the story, and was smiling at Harold. "It's like a detective story," she said. "We all know the crime, in fact we are the victims of it, and now it remains to be solved."

Jacob leaned forward and with a flourish of one hand said, "But how did he get *out?* That's the question." Everyone laughed; Jacob alone was not quite certain of what he had said, though he enjoyed its success and flushed with pleasure.

"Do you remember? The Locksmith had it figured out."

"'But I know too late!'" Liza quoted.

"Yes," said Harold. "He knew that even with a special tool Houdini never could have opened the mechanism from the inside. The steel was too hard, too thick. And so he realized that *something had been changed*. And then he realized that the safe had been standing in the lobby of the theater all night long, and all the next day, and it hadn't even been guarded."

"How come?" said Jacob.

"It was so big, so heavy, so strong. Nobody worried about it," said Harold. "And of course the Locksmith was right—something *had* been changed.

"Now," said Harold, "do you remember those three men who worked secretly for Houdini, the ones I called his secret geniuses? They had worked for him for many years. They were wonderful mechanics and were wonderfully smart. And really, you know, the big mistake the Locksmith made was to forget that there are a great many very smart people in this world."

"He thought he was the only one," said Liza.

"I'm afraid he did."

"But Houdini was smarter," said Jacob.

"No, probably not," said Harold, "though he was certainly very smart. And those three mechanics were very smart. They had already studied the safe very closely. And they knew all about safes anyway. The night that Houdini announced that he would escape from it, they locked the theater as soon as the audience left, and they rushed into the lobby and spread out a lot of tools on a canvas cloth and began working as fast as they could. They opened up that thick door of the safe and took out the entire mechanism of the lock. They put it in a box and left the theater and went to their hotel, where they had more tools and some special steel springs and other kinds of fittings of a special steel, a very soft steel, a weak steel. And they sat up all night drinking coffee and working as fast as they could, and then in the afternoon of the next day they went back to the theater and kept working, and finally, around suppertime, they'd made the safe look just the way it always looked, but all the hard steel parts of the locking mechanism had been replaced by soft steel, and it would now be possible, with a special tool and a lot of strength, to open the lock from the inside. By the time the moving company came to put the safe up on the stage, it was all set for Houdini."

"But what about that heavy chain around the safe?" said Ida.

"Ah," said Harold. "What do you think?"

"It was made of rubber bands!" said Jacob.

"No, Jacob," said Liza. "Don't you remember? That big guy leaned his whole weight on it."

"And then he patted it with his hand," said Harold, "or adjusted it a bit . . . and what he was really doing was releasing a little spring-loaded pin so that the chain would open at the slightest push."

"But wouldn't it make a noise falling on the floor?" said Ida.

"Not if there was a padded carpet under it and the orchestra was playing loudly enough," said Harold. "Houdini was out of that safe in a couple of minutes. He sat on the floor and read a book for almost an hour. Do you remember those tall thin posts that held up the wire for the curtain? Those posts were hollow. He had all kinds of things hidden in those posts, including enough water to spray himself with sweat.

"Right after the show that night his three secret geniuses went to work again and put back all the original parts of the safe. By the time the moving company came in the morning the safe was all ready to take to the bank."

Harold paused and looked at the children. "And that, alas, is what magic is all about," he said.

"Well, but it's quite wonderful, anyway," said Luisa.

"It's amazing how bold that man was," said Harold, "and how much it meant to him to create his own legend."

"I love your phrase," said Marshall, "*mechanics and treachery.* But there's a marvelous poetry in these things, too. There's nothing like it—a thoroughgoing mechanistic contraption posing as pure spirit."

"Yes, quite," said Harold.

Ida was smiling thoughtfully, obviously excited by this mingling of illusion and mechanics that resembled the play of children, yet drew upon the knowledge and skill of grown-up life. Liza understood the principle well enough, but she was frowning. As for Jacob—he probably glimpsed the principle of deception, but he was confused and it was clear that he would lapse again out of the world of causality into the world of legend, or of heart's desire. For him Houdini's powers were still intact, and he was not willing to let go of one single hero.

～

I had hoped that Luisa's excitement at meeting Harold would last longer and prove to be more sustaining, but now it seemed that that contact, too, led her to feelings and memories more painful than she could endure. I had the impression that she wanted to stay with us, in fact dreaded leaving us, yet everything that happened—except the animation of the children—was a source of pain.

She stood up and, breathing quietly, smoothed away the wrinkles in the light blue skirt and straightened the blue sweater that she wore unbuttoned over the lighter-colored blouse. She asked to be excused.

"Truly," she said, "I would much prefer to stay and talk with you, but I am so very, very tired."

We all stood near her to say our good nights. Luisa noticed that the children were whispering among themselves with a certain perturbation, and she asked them what was the matter. Ida glanced at me and then turned back to Luisa, but before she could speak, Jacob said to Luisa, "Can you stay up for just one minute and watch my play?"

I said to the children that Luisa had to rest. One glance at her face, however, told me that what the children were proposing did in fact offer her the most restful thing possible, not the play as such but the chance of sitting among us without being looked at and without being expected to speak.

"What sort of play are you talking about?" she said.

"My play!" said Jacob. "I wrote it."

"Ah! Well . . . of course," she said. "I would love to see it—if your parents will give their permission."

A few minutes later we adults were sitting on straight chairs in two rows in the darkness facing a small table set up near the fireplace. On the table there stood a rectangular frame on which white paper had been stretched tightly: a screen for shadow plays. We had all worked on it during the last Christmas holidays. Harold and Ricky had helped, but they had never seen the results of their work. We had made cutouts of animals, birds, trees, and flowers, and had written a play for the children to perform on New Year's Eve, as one of several such contributions at an annual gathering of friends in Vermont. Tonight's play was something new, however, and Jacob had written it—that is, had talked it over with Ida and Liza.

We could hear the children whispering and could see them moving in the darkness behind the screen. Liza got down on her hands and knees near the baseboard, and then a floor lamp came on, its light subdued by a towel draped over the shade. Ida stepped round in front of the table, carrying her recorder. She was dressed in a pleated tunic that once had been a bedsheet and that was gathered by a necktie sash. Her long, light-brown hair was pulled back in a ponytail. She played a simple tune, then said unhurriedly, "Our program is in two parts. Part One is a play written, directed, and narrated by Jacob: *The Mystery of the Splatted Pie.*"

The light went out.

In the darkness we heard the croaking of a bullfrog. Ida walked around behind the screen, passing Jacob, who came to the front. Now we could hear a cricket's *chirr,* and then a second frog, as if in the distance, answering the first. There came a twittering of birds, and in the dim light before the screen we could see a fluttering motion. The rectangle of the screen burst into brightness. On it, in black silhouettes, were the shapes of trees and bushes and a small house. Both Marshall and Luisa murmured aloud, Marshall saying, "Ahh . . . very nice," and Luisa, "Lovely." Two little birds fluttered before the screen, dangling from threads tied to sticks. The birds were drawn up and their twittering silenced, and Jacob, who stood to one side of the screen, cleared his throat and put one hand on his stomach. He was dressed in a striped smock and fur hat, the significance of which I couldn't guess.

"Okay folks," he said, "The Mystery of the Splatted Pie. Well. Hum. Once upon a time there was an old shack in the woods and three robbers lived in it, and they were planning on stealing a pie—"

A whisper from Liza broke in: *"Slow down, Jacob!"*

"Hunh? Oh, yeah. So they were going to do it on Monday, but everything got mixed up . . ."

Ida's and Liza's voices (agreeing emphatically): "Yeahhh!"

". . . and finally it was Monday," said Jacob, "and they went off to do the evil deed. End of Act One. Intermission. Okay. Here's a riddle."

The screen went dark, the shaded floor lamp came on, and Jacob said, "What's the answer to this?" He raised the pitch of his voice and spoke carefully. *"Those we found, we left behind. Those we couldn't find, we took with us."*

"Oh, I know that one," said Marshall. "That's really an old one; that's the riddle of Heraclitus. The answer is *fleas,* or *lice.*"

"Uh . . . yeah . . . that's right. How'd you know that?" said Jacob. "Well . . . okay, folks. End of intermission."

Liza could be seen again on her hands and knees fumbling at the baseboard. The screen flashed into brightness. The silhouettes now were of a large house, a large willow tree, and many flowers. The same two birds twittered briefly and stopped.

"Part Two of *The Mystery of the Splatted Pie!*" announced Jacob. "Ahem. Yes. Part Two. So the robbers . . . oh, yeah. I said that in Part One. Okay. The robbers had to drive a mile to get here. Why they picked this night is because they knew the family had gone out for supper. And why they knew is because they have a party line and they heard the people talking. They went in the house and one of the robbers went to get the pie and when he came back he slipped and the pie splatted in his face. So then there was no more pie. So then they went home. And they went to bed and lived happily ever after. The end."

He bowed and walked around into the shadows, obviously enjoying the noisy applause and indulgent laughter. The screen was dark again. Ida and Liza picked it up and carried it across the room, and as they did so Jacob came running to Patricia and jumped into her lap, whispering loudly, "Wasn't that great, Mommy! Did you like it? Did you like it, Daddy?"

Luisa turned round to him, smiling, and said, "A delightful play, Jacob."

"Thanks," he said—and then, because Luisa held out one arm to him, and because Patricia nudged him, he slid off her lap and hugged Luisa, who smiled and touched her cheek to his. He climbed into Patricia's lap again and sat there contentedly, his head pressed back against her breast, his feet dangling, and the fingers of his hands interlaced and resting on Patricia's large, interlaced hands, which rested on his belly.

Ida came in front of the table and turned on the floor lamp. She played briefly on her recorder, and said, "The second part of our program: *Travels in Space.*"

Liza, who had been standing back from the table, now stepped up to it and placed a small doll and a red coffee can on it. Her thick, long black hair that was so often tousled had been brushed. She wore a quilted floor-length skirt of a handsome dark red, and a short-sleeved black velvet bodice. If I had not been already a doting father, the sight of her would have turned me into one. Her frame was larger than Ida's, and her limbs more rounded. The quilted skirt took a feminine curve at her hips, and her well-formed arms and rounded white neck, emerging from the black velvet, were quite simply alluring. It was as if an imagery of the woman she might one day be flickered like lights over the child she was, with her unconscious vitality, her generosity and hopefulness, and the unaffected seriousness that characterized everything she did.

Marshall, who sat in the front row, on the other side of Harold, turned around and leaned toward Patricia and me. "She looks *beautiful!*" he whispered.

Seeing her standing there, I realized that one of the attractive features of that age was the relative largeness of the head in relation to the shoulders. This very proportion characterized Patricia and was attractive in her. She was like a nine-year-old equipped with hips and made large.

Liza said, "Ladies and gentlemen, allow me to introduce Maria Crespi." She indicated the doll with a gesture of her hand and, bending slightly toward it, said, "Good evening, Maria, it's nice to see you. Will you tell us your occupation?"

The wide-eyed doll seemed to be standing at attention. She was somewhat scratched and nicked. She had mounds of black porcelain hair and was dressed in a white and yellow porcelain gown with many flounces at the hips. Liza leaned close to catch her answer.

"Maria says she is a doll," said Liza.

One could hear, in everything that Liza said, the artificial phrasing of a script. But exactly this—her naive surrender to the text—freed her own child-voice of all duties of relation, and one could listen to it almost as pure music.

"And do you have any hobbies, Maria?" said Liza, once again bending close.

"Really? In *outer* space? Why, that's amazing, Maria!

"Maria says she likes to travel in outer space. But Maria, how do you do it? Do you have a rocket ship? What? *With* you? You don't mean this little coffee can, do you?"

Liza held up the red coffee can and tapped its bottom and sides, saying, "It's just an ordinary coffee can, Maria. What did you say? The *inside?* Ahhh . . . yes. . . ."

Liza turned the can and held it so that we all could look into it. The interior of the can was painted black. A small, creamy phosphorescent moon and tiny phosphorescent stars glowed in the darkness. I glanced at Harold. It was he who had shown Liza the trick last Christmas, and had written the text for her, and then had never had a chance to see it. I remembered him sitting at the table, Liza leaning close beside him. Both were looking into the red coffee can, and Harold was manipulating a long, fine-pointed watercolor brush.

"Yes, of course!" said Liza. "There's the moon! And there's the constellation Orion, and the Big Dipper, and the North Star. . . .

"What now, Maria? Are you going to show us? Okay, here goes."

Liza clapped the can over Maria Crespi, who was perhaps two thirds its height.

"Wait a minute," she said, "I forgot to ask you if it's dangerous, and do you ever have trouble coming back. . . . Maria! Do you hear me? Maria!"

She lifted the can. There was no Maria.

"Oh, my!" said Liza. "Well, there's nothing to do but wait."

She inverted the can and called immediately, "Maria, are you back yet? Are you down there?"

She lifted the can and looked, but still there was no Maria. Liza waited with her hand on top of the inverted can. "Are you back yet? Are you down there? Can you hear me? Ah! I think I hear something. . . ." She bent close, saying, "Yes! I *do* hear something! I hear somebody breathing!"

She lifted the can, and there stood wide-eyed Maria Crespi, scratched and nicked.

Jacob shouted, "Hi, Maria!"

"Ah!" said Liza. "You *are* back. Welcome home, Maria. What did you see in space? The moon and stars? And the earth . . . and then the earth got smaller and smaller . . . and it got to be just another faraway star in the darkness? Oh my! I bet you're glad to be back! We're certainly glad to see you! Thank you very much, Maria. What?"

Liza bent close to the doll, and then stood erect and faced us, and said, "Maria says, 'You're welcome.'"

She bowed and turned, picking up Maria and the coffee can.

Harold swung round to me, grinning, and nodded once, emphatically.

Both Ida and Liza would be leaving for school early in the morning. If the weather were good, they would walk down our mile-long road to meet the school bus. They said their brief and bashful goodbyes to our guests before going up to bed, Ida still wearing her pleated tunic and Liza her long skirt and black velvet bodice.

Luisa embraced them both. To Ida she said, "You play the recorder with excellent, spontaneous feeling. Best of all, you let each note get ripe, and that's a very good sign."

Ida blushed and smiled. Her lips formed the words *thank you,* but very little voice came out.

To Liza, Luisa said, "I shall never forget Maria Crespi, who jumped up to heaven through a coffee can."

Liza said, "Aren't you ever coming back?"

"Oh, I do hope that I shall," said Luisa.

"You won't be so very far away," said Patricia. "It would be wonderful if you would come. It's a day's drive."

"I would love to," said Luisa, "and I promise to write you as soon as I arrive."

Harold, too, embraced the girls, promising to see them at Christmas. He had spoken already with Liza about Maria Crespi, and when their eyes met now it was with a special warmth and pleasure.

Marshall, alone, planned to get up early. "I won't say goodby now," he said, "I'll say it in the morning, at breakfast. I want to do it in a special way, a way of saying both goodby and thank you for the wonderful show."

When Marshall spoke in this light, caressing manner one could see the charm that had attracted so many young women to him. He had been divorced for fifteen years, and in that time, until settling down with Bonnie, he had known scarcely a woman over thirty, and Bonnie herself, when they had met, had been a mere thirty-five. His white hair was so thick and so brilliantly white that it seemed vital, and therefore youthful. His large eyebrows were jet black, and his dark brown eyes had a youthful, passionate look to them. Even Luisa, who had seemed to dislike him, was smiling at him now.

Jacob, who would not be going to school, and would be joining us for breakfast, had been a silent and sleepy observer of all this, leaning back against Patricia, who rested her hands on his shoulders.

All three children, and Marshall, too, went up to bed. The telephone rang, and Ida called for Harold. Patricia and I walked with Luisa to her room. We knew that we would meet again at breakfast, but the emotions of parting were affecting us all.

We stood just inside the door of the guest room. Patricia had already carried a pitcher of water and a glass to the bedside table. She offered Luisa an extra sweater or jacket, since the weather in Quebec would be colder than ours, but Luisa said, "Ah, no, I am well enough provided for.

"You have been so kind to me," she said, "and the feeling of friendship is so strong here. I feel as if I know you both far better than I really do. It has been so strange for me . . . meeting Harold. And to think," she said to me, "that I have been singing a poem of yours for so many years. It is like a dream, really, entirely a dream."

"Luisa," Patricia said, "don't be offended if we ask you one more time . . . but will you please stay a while? Say yes, Luisa."

"You could not offend me. You are a person I trust completely. But no, I'll leave you tomorrow, as we planned. But I will definitely write to you from Quebec."

She reached out and rested her hand on Patricia's arm, saying, "I will not let this friendship go to waste, I promise you."

Luisa took her by the shoulders, leaned forward and pressed her own cheek to Patricia's, and did the same to me.

"I will say good night to you now," she said.

❮

Ida and Liza ate their breakfasts at about six forty-five. When the weather was bad, Patricia drove them down our road to meet the school bus, but today was another of the days (it proved to be the last) that prompted the old to search their memories for an autumn of comparable beauty. There was a chill of night still in the air, and the sky did not yet have the luminous brightness of the fully risen sun, yet it seemed likely that by the time the girls finally reached school they would be carrying their sweaters.

While I scrambled some eggs for them, and made toast, and Patricia packed their lunches in brown paper bags, Marshall, who wore jogging shoes and an ancient, patched-up sweat suit of a faded gray, said to them, "Now sit together over there so you can watch me while you eat. I'm going to dance for you. I do this every morning, but usually nobody watches. Today it's for you, to thank you for Maria Crespi and the Splatted Pie. I'll bet you never saw an old man dance before. Here goes. . . ."

Delighted smiles had already come to their faces, still smooth and pale from sleep. They ate without speaking or taking their eyes from Marshall, who with slow, flowing movements crouched and straightened, pivoted and glided, moving his arms continually in slow flexions and extensions that were like a somnolent underwater swimming, and that had about them also something calligraphic. He winked at the girls. "I'm dancing in Chinese," he said. "How do you like that? Yeah, this dance was invented in China, it's called t'ai chi. Some people think it's just exercise, but it's not, it's a dance, and if you want to see it done really well by some wonderful old Chinese gentlemen, just walk through the little park in Chinatown early in the morning sometime."

The girls were ready to go before he had finished. He said to them, "I'll walk you down and jog back, and then I'll dance again, I'll dance for the dogs. Come on."

While Patricia packed lunches for our departing guests, I went outside and waved to the girls from the front porch. They waved back, and looked up at Marshall, grinning. Each carried her lunch. Marshall smiled at me over their heads, and all three, joined by the frisking, excited dogs, stepped off down the road, Marshall bouncing lightly on the balls of his feet, as if he wanted to break into a run. The anger and resentment I had felt toward him yesterday seemed remote to me now. It was good to see my children going off so happily with my old friend, good to see them so affectionately cared for.

By the time Harold and Luisa came in for breakfast Marshall had already had his morning walk, morning run, extended t'ai chi, and a shower. But the lighthearted lucidity of his early hours gave way gradually to a characteristically impatient and somewhat cranky sobriety. We were all uneasy at breakfast, actually unhappy. Luisa's face, at one moment, had a look of haunted grief, and at another seemed unnaturally calm. She looked up from time to time at Harold, and he returned her gaze with a sympathetic openness, but neither could find much to say. While we sat there we heard a strange, excited, highpitched barking, as if a multitude of dogs were running toward the house. The barking changed rapidly in pitch and loudness.

Patricia jumped up. "Luisa!" she said. "You have to see this! It's something special. Come."

She put her arm around Luisa's shoulders and went beside her out to the yard in front of the house. We all went out and clustered there not far from the locust trees, tilting our heads. We had heard only the high notes indoors. Now the deeper, rasping, *honking* notes could be heard, a raucous, protesting, arguing, egotistic, *intelligent* sound. The large, wavering V of the geese's formation came toward us swiftly in a vigorous flickering of wings. It came in over the wooded slopes to the north, from exactly where the North Star hung in the sky at night. Soon the geese were over our heads, not terribly high, jabbering noisily, their wings beating hurriedly. The wave of their honking passed over us. At a slight distance the undulations within the V were striking, each bird rising as on shallow slopes and settling buoyantly in the currents of the air; and from this angle their powerful wingbeats took on the plunging and pulling motion of oars. Very rapidly they passed into the distance, their jabbering diminishing and losing its low notes, and their wings once again flickering in the light blue of the sky, and then they were gone and everything was quiet. Or rather, our local sounds were heard again, our voices commenting on the geese (not with the excitement of the first occasion, years ago, but as older people do), a chain saw in the woods, and the intermittent diesel motor of a skidder.

Luisa stood there looking up, one hand against the side of her face. Her sweater and skirt were almost the color of the sky she was looking at. It was only when Patricia, who delighted in the geese, turned to her with a questioning smile, that Luisa smiled too, and said, "An extraordinary sight."

Half an hour later we all stood in the yard again, close to the cars and directly beneath the towering locust trees. The day was noticeably brighter and the sun warmer. I put Luisa's suitcase under the hood of

Marshall's VW Beetle and put the lunches in each car. Harold tossed his small satchel onto the back seat of the shiny red rental car, and we all faced one another. Before we had really begun our farewells, however, the front door of the house opened and Jacob staggered out, rubbing his eyes. He was wearing his frayed and faded knit pajamas, and was barefoot. Luisa smiled and said, "Ah, here is Jacob! I am glad he is awake at last and I can say goodby to him."

Jacob clung to Patricia with one arm. He answered everyone politely, in spite of his partly unawakened state. To Marshall, who said, "It was nice to see you, Jacob," he said, "Thanks." To Harold he said, "Thanks for the Houdini. It was great." I thought that he was going to say to Luisa, "Thanks for the piano music," or something of that sort, but he said, "Thanks for watching my play." She knelt and he went to her and put his arms around her neck while she hugged him.

"It was a great pleasure to watch your play," she said, still kneeling and holding him by the waist at arm's length. "I hope you'll do another for me sometime."

"Okay, I'll write another one," Jacob said. "When do you want to see it?"

"Come at Christmas," said Patricia. "That would be wonderful. Or at Thanksgiving. Or just anytime."

"I would love to and I'll write to you immediately," Luisa said. She embraced us both, and turned to Harold, who had been watching her and waiting. She held out both her hands and he took them. They looked at each other almost like lovers, certainly like people who had shared many things, and things not easily spoken of. His eyes were grave.

She said to him, "It would be impossible to tell you what a great happiness it has been to me to meet you. If there were time, I should love to play everything of yours for the piano and hear your comments."

"Luisa," he said—he held out a piece of paper—"take this. This is my address and phone number in New York. We have lots of space. We can give you an entire floor if you come to see us. There's a

Steinway up there and a Bechstein down below, and I would love to hear you play, not only my things but anything at all. Your playing of the *Serenade* was simply thrilling."

She took the piece of paper from him. She smiled at him and leaned forward and pressed her cheek against his, while he put one arm around her and one hand on her shoulder.

We had already spoken with Marshall about his staying with us on the way back, and he had said that he would. He shook hands with Harold and said a few words. Then he said, "We're in different spheres, somehow. They don't seem to overlap much, but I wish they did. Do you think we might get together sometime?"

"Call me, by all means," said Harold. "Please."

Both seemed to be sincere, and yet I doubted that that meeting would ever take place.

Marshall carried a small overnight bag in one hand. He threw it on the back seat of the old cream-colored VW, and stood by the door, waiting to open it for Luisa.

Luisa looked around at the sun-brightened reds and yellows of the trees, and at the green expanse of grass on which, not far from the house, the ponies were grazing. Beyond the ponies lay the valley and the colored hills, and above everything, drawing one's gaze continually, there stretched the luminous pale blue summery sky. A few locust leaves floated downward swiftly, wobbling with small motions. Wherever one looked a leaf, or many, could be seen falling, rocking in the air. "It's so very, very beautiful," she said.

She and Marshall left first, and before the car had rolled out of sight she leaned from the window and waved and blew a kiss, obviously directed to Jacob, who stopped waving for a moment and blew one back to her.

Harold, too, leaned across the empty front seat of the rental car and waved goodbye . . . and the rural quiet closed around us. We turned back to the house. Patricia sighed deeply, saying quietly, "Ah . . . God. . . ."

From our house to Quebec City was a drive of six hours.

We dismantled the mattress raft, and I worked all morning at the table in the bedroom while Patricia and Jacob finished waxing the catchment barrel of the cider press. After lunch I took Jacob to a playmate's house. We had delayed entering him in public school, and we felt lucky to have found a boy his own age only half an hour away. I went then to the farm of a neighbor and friend, Hazel Currier, from whom we had bought a sheep. I had promised to do the slaughtering, not only of ours but of two more for Hazel's own freezer, but a bear had broken into the outlying stable just before daybreak and had attacked her daughter's riding horse. The panic-stricken horse had crashed through the rotten wall.

I took my place in a crew of people spread across the small unfenced pasture into which the injured horse had run. The horse stood between the woodlot and our advancing line, stamping its forefeet and moving from side to side, watching sixty-five-year-old Hazel, who walked ahead of us in her mechanic's pants and faded flannel shirt, calling to the horse in her crisp, intelligent voice. A trail halter and a short length of rope lay across her left shoulder. She held out the grain bucket with both hands, rattling the grain and calling to the horse.

The large, decrepit, slowly disintegrating farm lay across the spine of a high ridge, one of the handsomest sites in the entire county. The broad, winding river could be seen on one side, and on the other our own large stream. One could see where they joined, and could see the first bridge beyond that juncture, under which the now massive river flowed. Several ponds and lakes appeared on both sides of the ridge, silvery in the sunlight, and there were hills everywhere, blazing with autumn colors. Just to *be* there would have been exhilarating, and usually was, but I was confused, and heavy spirited. Images of Luisa came to me repeatedly, and I could hear again the music of Harold's that she had played, and could hear her singing my own poem of loss. I thought, too, of something Harold had said to me shortly after he had arrived. I had not realized, at the time, how profound a meaning it actually had, but his words, and his look as he spoke them, hadn't left my mind. He had said to me, "I've been very happy lately, and I don't know why"—and that was all; but those words, and that moment, had acquired the status of a philosophic or spiritual meaning.

"He prob'ly won't bolt," Hazel said, "he's clevuh, and he'll want the grain, but if he gets loose from here . . . I don't know . . . I don't want 'im on the road. . . ."

The horse snorted vigorously, tossed its head, and trotted right up to her. The raking bear-claw wound on its haunch was a bad one. There was dried blood around it, and I could see flesh, curdled and dark red.

"Good boy, Danny," said Hazel. The horse put its muzzle in the bucket, and Hazel talked to it while it ate. "I suppose bein' scared makes you hungry. That's quite a gash you've got back there, but we'll patch it up and you'll be good as new."

She let the horse eat, then set the bucket on the grass and made him wait until she had put the halter over his head. Her movements were unhurried and accustomed. She snapped the short lead onto the halter and stood beside him, talking in her kindly, soothing way while he finished the grain. "Well, I hate to say it, Danny," she said, "but that bear prob'ly did have in mind eatin' a right good piece o' you, so we'll call Gerry Morin. Yes, that's what we'll do. I don't like doin' it, bears got a right to this earth too, but we can't let 'im scratch you up like this. Go ahead and finish, that's a good boy, then we'll go down t' corral and put some salve on those cuts."

It was unusual for a bear to do this, especially in this well-fed season, but she remembered how it had happened similarly nearly forty years ago, except that the bear then had also killed and eaten two sheep and left the pelts rolled up, as they do.

Hazel's middle-aged son and her smiling young son-in-law, who wore a beaded band around his matted, thick red hair, had gone with tools to the little stable and were prying off the broken boards.

I walked with Hazel downhill toward the house and the corral, and the horse ambled on the other side of her with its muzzle close to her shoulder. We agreed to do the sheep a week from today, after the cidering. "There's no hurry," she said, "as long as the bears don't get 'em, but I don't suppose they will. I'll have to call Morin, there's no help for it."

Morin was a bear hunter, or rather executioner, since his method was to set out a carcass and shoot from a tree. A bear could undo a family's finances in a single night, expecially if cows were its prey. Hazel opined that this bear had come from the dump. The odor of the horse beside us was pleasant. I could feel the warmth of the sun radiating from its dark brown side.

"The coons bother you this year?" she said.

"We didn't use the rotenone after all," I said (it had been she who had recommended dusting the tassels of the corn, as a repellant). "We planted squash among the corn."

"Yes," she said, "I'm told that works quite well. It scratches their bellies and they don't like it. Of course, with those dogs you shouldn't have trouble. . . ."

We were nearing the large, weatherbeaten house. It was of a kind almost extinct, and that never will be built again, it was so prodigal in its use of wood and labor, and so generous and convivial in its proportions and size. It was a house that took for granted three generations staying together. It had the same robust, outgoing, *citizenly* quality of the old farms, with their orchards and pastures, barns and sheds, coops and pens and kitchen gardens. Hazel and her first husband had bought it, and with enormous hard work had built it up. He had died and her second husband had left her. She struggled now just to pay the taxes and keep the roof in repair. There wasn't a nickel left over for paint or new clapboards. She bred dogs and goats in the big barn attached at right angles to the house; she kept chickens, two pigs, some turkeys, some sheep. And she was the sole support of several people who for various reasons had attached themselves to her.

We came into the sunlit workyard in back of the house. The house was set close to a small dirt road and lay in a shade cast by three gigantic maples and two even larger pines, all surely more than a century old, but here in back everything was bright and sunny. There were tall asters near the house, some of which still had blooms. A cluster of tansies stood near the kitchen door, their small button heads darkening from yellow to an ochre or dusty orange, but still bright. An axe was embedded in a large drum of rock maple beside a loose pile of split and fitted stovewood. Pale, clean chips and splinters lay scattered near the drum. Two faded cotton dresses, some socks, two pairs of the gray mechanic's pants that one saw everywhere and that Hazel herself almost always wore, a pair of blue jeans of her daughter's—all these dangled from a short line. A glance at them told how poor their owners were. An old, round wicker basket lay on the ground under the laundry line. Off to one side, where the sun would last the longest, Hazel's father slept in his wheelchair.

"We put Dad in the sun," she said, "but of course he's sound asleep now."

He was not slumped or twisted in the wheelchair, but had fallen forward like a rag doll, his face on his knees and his arms out of sight. An ebony cane with a silver head leaned against the chair. When he died it would pass to the eldest man of the town, which he himself presently was, at ninety-eight. When he had first been pointed out to me, I had been told how, twenty-five years ago, he had saved the life of his wife, then already in poor health, by throwing himself under the front wheels of their car. The car had slipped out of gear at the dump while he was walking with a box of garbage, and was rolling toward a steep bank at the bottom of which lay water deep enough to drown in.

"He's been speaking of late about the French place," Hazel said. This was the tumbledown house at the entrance of the little field in which I had built my studio cabin.

"There's not much left of it," I said.

"Ayeh . . . well, he remembers it. He lived there several years as a boy. And of course your place, which to him is the Blanchard place. He lived there, too, and his sister lived there for ten years before Heikenen bought it. She married a Blanchard, you know."

"You came over with your aunt a couple of years ago," I reminded her, "not long before she died. Your dad was with you. He was walking then."

"Oh, yes. He had the cane with him that day. Old Ben Mitchell had died. Flossie had brought it over. He'd had it about two weeks. Yes, I remember it very well. Patricia served us the most delicious blueberry muffins. And she had some mint tea made the way I make it. In fact, I believe I told her how."

Partly to ease the oppression in my chest, partly to please Hazel and do a kindness to old Dana, I suggested that I take him for an outing. If I had been offering a service to Hazel herself she would have demurred, gently but unswayably. This offer, however, she accepted, and while I held the horse, she shook her father's shoulder, calling to him in a loud voice, "Dad! Would you like to go for a drive, Dad? It's a beautiful day. Wake up, Dad, you're going for a drive!" She looked aside at me and said, "That'll get through. He'll come round. Dad! You're going for a drive, Dad!"

The skin of her father's small, bald, speckled head was so dry that it looked dusty. A few pale hairs lay across it like dried grass or broken filaments of spider web. It did not seem to be a head at all, but a stone or dried gourd lying on a heap of rags. But there began to be a small stirring, as when some tiny forest creature moves furtively under a pile of leaves. The cords of the neck tightened, the head came up an inch, rotated with a tentative motion and moved forward; there was a tightening or stiffening of the back and spine under the loose flannel shirt, and the torso, too, came up an inch, and hands emerged from beneath it.

"You're going for a drive, Dad!" shouted Hazel.

The first look of consciousness on Dana's face was a look of anxiety, but then he relaxed and his face took on its characteristic mixed expression of dependency, sweetness, gratitude, and hopeful expectation.

His blind eye was closed, and was closed so tightly that one might have thought the upper and lower lids had melted and joined; but the other eye, a bright blue, looked at me out of a triangular aperture of soft skin. He cleared his throat slowly and laboriously and in a faint, far-away, questioning voice said, "Yes?"

"You're going for a drive, Dad," she repeated.

Shortly later he and I were driving up and down the sunny hills, following roads he had driven years ago with horses, collecting cream. It had been astonishing to see him emerge from sleep and reassemble the faculties of consciousness and then laboriously organize them into attention, memory, and speech. But this process didn't end. The triangular blue eye saw distant things very clearly; and it was as if these landmarks of his life, that lay all around us, were physical parts of memory itself, and real remnants of the competence he had once possessed. He would point to an overgrown field and say, "That's the Porter farm. I used to reach that barn around four in the morning," or, "That's the Mitchell place, or 'twas. They had fotty caows. This used to be all clear, and there was a set o' buildings right up in there. I thought we could look at the pond awhile, but it's all growed up. My brother and I used to cut ice down there. I had to use it in summer, you know, to pack the cans, and then blankets went on top." He smiled at me and said, "I had four brothers and two sisters and a mother and father; now I'm all that's left."

The ebony cane leaned against the seat between his legs. He liked to hold it and rest his hands on it. His fingers no longer came out straight from the knuckles, which were large and knobby, but were twisted to one side like the tines of a bent rake. His speckled temples and cheeks were sunken. He had put in his dentures. A crumpled handkerchief lay in his lap, and he lifted it frequently, his hand trembling and moving slowly, and pressed it against the blind eye.

Some neighbors were coming out of their drive and pulled their car alongside mine. Both greeted him, but the woman seemed to know him better. "Well hello Dana!" she called, leaning across her husband. "How've you been doin'?"

"I'm doin' poorly," he said, smiling with pleasure, "but better than I was. I don't sleep so good nights, and there's pain in my right knee I'm takin' medicine for. Do you know, I woke up last night. I was dreamin', and in my dream I was tellin' 'em how old I was." He laughed in a droll way, and the man and wife, of Hazel's generation, smiled at him. "I told 'em the truth," he said. "I said t' them, 'In February I'll be ninety-nine, and next February I'll be a hundred.'"

"Oh, you'll make a hundred, all right, Dana, and some to spare," said the woman.

Her husband said, "How's the town look to you, Dana?"

"Well, it looks all right," he said, and his face grew brighter still; it became actually merry. "But I don't see no money floatin' round," he said.

The way he said it made one think of dollar bills falling like leaves, or drifting like leaves in the streams. He chuckled, and so did his neighbors, and the woman said, "No, we've never been noted for that."

We drove on, and stopped again. He pointed to a massive, long hill, his finger trembling, and in his soft slow voice said, "You see that black growth right up in there, right above that birch? I was born up there, right on the line. The house was in Dower and the barn was in Weld. But we didn't git settled till we bought the old Tibbets place right there in the intervale."

In his slow, soft voice he placed one word neatly after another, as a man places one foot after another, walking slowly. "We had twelve caows and about eighty sheep," he said. "We had five hundred hens and sixty apple trees. But there warn't much money comin' in. The old creamery failed, so my dad went round t' the farmers and asked if they'd let us haul their cream. They said they would. 'Twas March. My dad took ill, and my brother was shearing sheep, so my dad said to me, 'Would you rather haul milk or shear?' and I said it didn't make no difference, both o' them was work. So that's when I started. I was sixteen years old. I hauled milk for sixty years."

I had heard him say all this before. I nodded and smiled at him.

"Sixty years," he repeated. "That's a long time. I believe I've gone more miles on a milk route than any man in the world. I don't know how many hosses I wore out. I had one hoss had thutty-two mates. I wore out several Fords, a Dodge, a Reo, three Chivvies. I changed to trucks when they wanted whole milk instead of just cream, but I still used teams on the back roads. Hosses could often get through mud and snow that a truck'd git stuck in."

I took him to our place, and on up the road to the little field that held both my cabin studio and the remains of the house he had lived in. He smiled the same delighted smile all afternoon. It was a smile of reverie, and yet his attention to the things around him never flagged.

In midafternoon I took him home. On the way (having noticed my own sighing) I realized that he did not sigh, I had never heard him sigh, and I took this to be an effect of his sweetness and great age. And then I remembered that Luisa had never sighed.

As we drove down our road (I intended to drive on and fetch Jacob) we saw two small, brightly colored figures in the distance: Ida and Liza coming home from school. Both wore blue jeans, Ida a yellow T-shirt, and Liza a red one. They were carrying their sweaters and walked zigzag up the road with lolling, pensive gaits.

By this time Marshall and Luisa had emerged from the timberland between here and the Canadian border, had passed through the farming and maple country of southern Quebec, and had reached the city. I learned later that Luisa had asked Marshall to stop for purchases at a pharmacy, and then they had taken rooms at a small hotel. They intended to telephone her relatives, who owned a farm in the Gaspé, but Luisa had asked that they delay the call while she rested for an hour.

Shortly before supper our telephone rang. The children were riding their bikes in the front yard. Patricia had just come in from the garden with some pots of parsley and was setting them on the windowsill in the cluttered front room. I was heating leftovers for supper.

Patricia went to the phone. I heard her saying, "Yes. Yes, it is. . . .
Yes, we will." And then, "Hello, Marshall. Is everything all right? Are
you in Quebec? How was the trip? Marshall . . . is something wrong?"
A note of alarm came into her voice. "Can't you talk? What happened? . . . Marshall! You've already said it, you can't take it back! Tell
me. . . . Oh my God! Oh my God! Oh my God!"

She sank into the chair by the phone. "Yes," she said, in a drained
voice. She began to ask him something, but evidently he was rushed
and was extremely upset. "It doesn't matter, Marshall. Whenever. It
must be terrible for you. Call us if we can help . . . That's all right.
Goodby, Marshall."

She seemed too weak to get up from the chair. She handed me the
phone and looked at me with stricken eyes.

"She's dead," she said. "She killed herself." And then she said, "Oh
God!" burst into tears, put both hands to her face, and ran upstairs.

I sat beside her on the bed. She lay with her face in the pillow,
crying.

We heard the children downstairs.

Patricia turned over quickly. "I don't want them to know," she said.
"There's nothing to be gained by telling them."

I agreed that it would be pointless to tell them.

She began to wipe her eyes with the backs of her hands. Jacob was
calling for her already. She went to the upstairs bathroom and splashed
water repeatedly on her face.

Ida and Patricia set the table. Jacob and Liza were playing on the
grass near the open side door, and the dogs were playing near them.
The sun was low but still warm, the blue of the sky was at its deepest,
and there was such a richness of color everywhere that it was as if
the world were thrumming with music, or vibrating with just-ended
singing voices. It was not the season alone that did this, but the death
that had just touched us closely yet not with paralyzing grief. I
remembered how on other occasions of death—in boyhood, in early
manhood, and twice since then—a great current had seemed to pass
through everything, as if with a thrumming of music, and I had

turned back with a heavy heart to a world revitalized, made luminous, and beautiful beyond description.

Jacob's and Liza's voices came in at the open door. He was lying on the grass and she was sitting on his belly. They had been shouting and laughing, but now suddenly were playing a game in which she was supposed to imitate everything he did.

"Whoops, Johnny! Whoops, Johnny!" He spread the fingers of one hand, and with the forefinger of the other went up and down, tracing the outline of thumb and fingers, saying, "Whoops, Johnny, Johnny! Whoops, Johnny! Whoops, Johnny, Johnny!" In a moment they were laughing and tussling, but I watched them as if they were shadows or mere memories, having by this time withdrawn to my thoughts or, rather, simply to an appalled amazement at the political deaths that had multiplied over the earth under this same beautiful sun.

In principle I knew what had happened to Luisa's husband and children, but when the facts of the coup became known they were shocking beyond anyone's surmise. It was not from Marshall that we learned of these things, but from his lover, Bonnie, who also told me that while Marshall had waited in his room at the hotel in Quebec, Luisa had filled the bathtub with water, had lain down in it dressed in her blue skirt and blouse, and with deep strokes of a razor blade had cut the arteries in her wrists and elbows. She had been dead for an hour by the time Marshall and the manager went in for her.

The truth of what had happened in Chile became known only slowly as refugees and the survivors of torture and imprisonment told their stories. Bonnie, who had worked for years with an organization devoted to the rescue of such victims, sent us copies of depositions, and of the articles based on them that began to appear in newspapers and magazines. We learned that in the single year before the Fascist coup two attempts had been made to kill Alejandro Domic. Marshall himself had not been aware of this, and perhaps even Luisa had not. Domic and a handful of colleagues who had supported Allende and constitutional government, and who had made themselves conspicuous by organizing medical and educational programs in the slums, were murdered in the first hours of the coup and their bodies were taken by truck to the National Stadium, where they were left in a basement corridor with other bodies awaiting an order for disposal. Several thousand people were held as prisoners in this sports arena. Many were killed by firing squads. Many were tortured. Among those who were first tortured and then killed were Luisa's children. The torturer was a Brazilian soldier who did not know who Domic was, or why he was wanted, and could not have identified the body, which lay with others not one hundred feet away. Luisa, who had been forced to watch, did not know herself where her husband was, and said wildly improbable things in an effort to save the children. She was released through the intervention of a civilian who was present when the children were killed, and who might have saved them. This man, who had been a member of Domic's faculty at the University of Chile, in Santiago, and who had taught special courses at the Technical University, as had Domic, was an economist and later obtained a high post under the dictatorship. Luisa knew him socially. He identified the body of Domic, and led Luisa to it personally, then denied her access to any of the bodies for burial. The first of the two following depositions was taken in Paris, the second in Mexico City.

. . . Toward the end of August the Chamber of Deputies officially called on the Armed Forces to compel the President "to govern within the law." Those were the words of the resolution. To us it was like a signal. We knew the coup would come soon. But we couldn't guess the viciousness of it. We couldn't guess the mass killing, the torture, the burning of books and closing of schools, just as in Nazi Germany. And we couldn't guess that fascism, real, authentic fascism, was only a few days away from us. There was much, much that we didn't know. Six weeks before the coup we had heard of an attempted coup, a so-called aborted coup. But that was not a failure at all, but was staged by the conspirators to find out which officers and troops would remain loyal to the constitution and perhaps impede the coup. And they did find out. The night before they killed Allende and bombed the Moneda, they killed 200 officers and more than 2,000 troops. . . . Some of the Leftists had tried to arm themselves. The people in the MIR, especially. They organized the shanty towns. Ránquil was well organized. But they had no arms. It was pathetic. Domic and I and a few others tried to undo all that, as there was no hope there at all. We knew that millions of dollars had come down to the armed services from the United States, and they were not buying battleships but automatic weapons, short-range artillery, armored trucks, helicopters. We tried to tell them at Ránquil, and at the Technical University, where there was a strong movement in support of Allende, that they should not consider themselves armed because they had thirty rifles and twelve target pistols. We went around in the days before the coup . . . we wanted to prevent massacres, but we were wrong, look what happened, they killed and killed, and almost none of their victims were armed. They killed in shanty towns if you were organized. They shot you if you belonged to a union, or read the Marxist newspapers, or belonged to the Student Feder-ation, or were a Mapuche Indian, or if you came from Bolivia. We were crazy to think we could prevent massacres. When the coup broke out in the morning a number of students and mem-bers of the faculty who were loyal to Allende rushed over to the Technical University to see what their comrades were going to do. Other people went there, too—Victor Jara, the singer and songwriter, who had done much for the workers—and Domic went there, or tried to get there, as I say, to prevent a massacre. I had gone to Ránquil, too far to reach, things were moving so fast, and I managed to escape only because the soldiers got there ahead of me, and I was not as important as Domic. Domic never reached the Technico. He was intercepted and killed. In my opinion he had probably been followed for days. He had helped organize evening classes at the Technico for workers. And the Rightists hated his books. He was a marked man. . . .

We took lockers and tables [at the Technical University], anything to make a barricade. I couldn't believe that we had a chance, but there was nothing else to do. It was over quickly. Our barricades were nothing. They used heavy artillery. They killed maybe 500 of us. They took all the rest as prisoners. Many who were only wounded were dead by the time they moved us to the stadium, because they made us lie face down all day, until six o'clock at night. If you moved even slightly to help a comrade who was bleeding, they shot you. We were taken to the National Stadium. There were bodies in the basement corridor. I recognized my good friend, Jorge Ruiz. His father had become a printer and belonged to the union. Jorge had gained a scholarship and earned a small amount of money helping me in the lab. He wrote for the student paper. I recognized two others as well, Alejandro Domic, who taught at night at the Technico and was well known as a writer. Enrique Moreno was an editor and publisher. His body was mutilated. I recognized these three as they marched us by. We heard gunfire above us, automatic weapons, up on the playing field. Then they marched us onto the playing field ourselves. There were bodies on the field that had just been shot and were bleeding. I thought that our turn was next, but they told us to go up into the bleachers and sit down. They put spotlights on us and fired at random. Several were killed that way. Victor Jara was with us. Everyone knew him because of his songs. He realized that some of the soldiers killing us were frenzied and could be touched off very easily. He went among us quietly, saying, "Comrades, keep calm." An officer shouted at him and then paused and started playing an imaginary guitar, grinning at him, as if saying, That's you, isn't it? Jara nodded. The officer called four soldiers and they took Jara to one of the tables at the edge of the field, and held his hands on it. The officer took a hatchet that was lying there and was already bloody, and with a few hard strokes cut off Jara's fingers on both hands. Jara lay on the ground curled up. His whole

body was shaking. The officer kicked him and said things,
something, I don't know, "Why don't you sing, Jara?" Jara's
body got smaller. He was using his elbows to get up. He came
stumbling toward us, holding up his bleeding hands. He stood
there swaying and somehow didn't fall again. He shouted,
"Comrades!" and began shouting a song he had performed
many times, one we all knew, a revolutionary song. We all sang
back to him. How could anybody not respond to him? Many
jumped up and we sang as loud as we could, forgetting everything. The soldiers became enraged. They shot Jara to shreds
and turned their guns into the stands. Whether you lived or
died depended on how many people were in front of you. I was
hit five times. I tried to pretend I was dead, but they discovered I
was alive. A number of us were taken inside. I had two bullets in
one leg and one in the other. I was in agony, but there was
worse to come. I thought, *This has to end sometime, why are they
doing this? What purpose can it serve?* We learned later that many
of the soldiers hated us and wanted to destroy us because they
had been told we had put their names on execution lists and
planned to kill them. They were shown the lists, which of
course had been invented by the junta themselves. Step by step
the junta were doing all the things that had been done in the
military coup in Brazil nine years before. We learned about this
later. While these horrors were actually happening, all I could
think was, *Oh, God, why? Why?*

There were basement rooms used as cells and used for interrogation. Groups of soldiers were passing in and out continually,
moving prisoners. There were more bodies in the corridor. A
few civilians were present, talking to higher officers. I recognized a lecturer from the Technico. He was looking at Domic's
body. I had worked there for years in the materials lab. I was
really in charge of it, though I was not a teacher and never could
be, without degrees. I had gone as far as I could. I recognized
this professor. He did not use the lab, but many times I had

helped him get ready for lectures when he was using films or charts. He knew me well. He was a conservative and hated Allende, but I thought, *My God, he's not a killer, he's not a butcher.* I was only about twenty feet from him. The legs of my pants were bloody and there was blood in my shoes. My shirt was bloody where the bullets had gone into my arm and shoulder. I called his name and he turned around and saw me. I said, *My God, help me! Don't let them kill me!* He nodded, but his eyes never touched mine. Yet I think he did save my life. I heard gunfire close by. They took me into the room it came from, and I saw that what I dreaded most was actually going to happen. There was a table. Several soldiers were placed here and there in the room. The man at the table was a Brazilian soldier. He became well known in Santiago. He had been trained in Panama by North Americans. Everything there I saw in one glance. A young girl had just been shot. She was fifteen or sixteen years old. She lay on the floor with her face up and her arms spread out. Her hands were all bloody. On the table there were several objects, a bar, a heavy mallet, pliers for pulling out fingernails, an electric prod, a butcher's knife with a curved blade. The Brazilian was just standing there. A Chilean officer stood near him. Two Chilean soldiers held a teenage boy by the arms. He was kneeling near the table. One of his hands was smashed like the girl's. His face had been cut and was bleeding. He was coming to and moaning. A woman was screaming. She too was on her knees. There was a soldier on each side of her holding her arms, and one in back holding her by the hair with both hands. The boy regained consciousness and said, "No, Mama, no." The Brazilian began looking at the things on the table, then he looked in my direction, but he looked over my head, and the Chilean officer looked over my head, too, and nodded. I turned around. A high-ranking officer stood in the doorway, and the professor from the Technico stood beside him. The officer in the room took his pistol out of the holster and went around behind the table and went behind the boy and shot him in the head. They took the woman out of the room. She had vomited and was gagging. I was taken up to the table. The bodies were still there. I tried to step over the boy, but they made me walk on him. I watched the Brazilian to see what instrument he would pick up. I turned around and called again to the professor, but he wasn't there. The Brazilian picked up the iron mallet. He looked into my eyes, and I became terrified and said goodby to my life. The soldiers beside me held my right hand on the table, and I braced myself, but he swung the mallet against my teeth. I couldn't see anything. Then I felt the mallet hit my hand and I passed out. They dumped water on me. He had the knife in his hand and cut my belt and my pants, and they pulled my pants off, and I thought *Oh, my God, kill me! Kill me!* He looked at my legs to find the bullet wounds. He used the electric prod on me. Then he took the bar and pounded my legs where the bullets had gone in. I passed out several times. This was called interrogation, but he never asked me a single question. The Chilean officer, the one who shot the boy, said to me several times, "You are really a Mapuche Indian, aren't you? You are really a Mapuche Marxist." I saw the professor standing there again, but I passed out many times. I wanted to be dead. I was trying to die. He must have said something, "Don't kill him," I don't know what. When I came to I was in a truck with lots of others. I ended up on Quiriquina Island. I had no medical attention until they amputated my leg and hand. I thought they would kill me after all, because we were expected to work there, building our own prison, and I couldn't work. But they didn't kill me. And then after several months they released me. . . .

Domic's body and the bodies of the children were interred in the wall of the National Cemetery, with an unknown number of others. Luisa's home was looted. Her belongings and financial holdings were impounded. These were the facts which we saw only as a look of haunted grief when she appeared at our door with Marshall. Though Liza, and Jacob, and Ida had witnessed Luisa's seizure, and though they had been told that Luisa's children might be dead, they could not imagine the kinds of things that had actually happened. Luisa's look of grief, that had affected all of us, had been to them an appearance without sufficient cause, and without category, and they had scarcely responded to it, though it had indeed registered on Ida, as I learned much later. Nor did the children notice, at supper, after we had learned of Luisa's death, that Patricia had been crying, or that both she and I were subdued and distracted. They talked busily among themselves and glanced repeatedly toward the open door, beyond which the setting sun threw a softened radiance over the green grass and the fire colors of the hills. A lazy movement of sun-warmed air passed along our table.

The children ate rapidly and rushed out. All three were barefoot. The dogs came running, and Ida and Liza responded to them, but Jacob ignored them and did something he had used to do often between the ages of one and four, and that we had often watched with delight: he danced. He lowered his head, ignoring everything, bent his knees slightly, stretched both arms to the sides, and turned slowly, bending and straightening, and leaping and stepping. In a moment he had moved away several yards from the others. And this dancing was so very exactly what Ida and Liza wanted to do—was what anyone would want to do on such a day—that they watched him only a moment and then began leaping and cavorting themselves. Whatever Ida had noticed about us, and whatever she had felt, could not compete with the great irruption of joy within her. She shouted, "Mom! Dad! Come on! Take off your shoes!"

We didn't respond, and Liza shouted too. "Come on! It's great!"

Nothing could have been less like our feelings at that moment than this happiness of the children. The thought of joining them was absurd. But it was equally absurd to sit there like lumps while they praised this glorious day that was left to us by jumping around on the grass. Patricia glanced at me. Ida and Liza called again and came to get us, obviously wanting the whole family to be together, and so we took off our shoes and joined them. Soon we all were spread across the grassy yard, each one several paces from the nearest other. I danced mechanically, or rather, I couldn't dance, couldn't generate the spirit of music, even a mourning music, but simply moved my arms and legs, turning away continually to the hills. A glossy, large crow was flapping slowly in an undeviating straight line up the whole length of the valley, its plumage brilliant when it passed maples and poplars, but invisible against the shadowed spruce and fir, and it seemed to be flickering on and off. Patricia began to move vehemently, lifting her arms and legs as if in anger, and as she turned, I caught a glimpse of her bunched and tense face. Her cheeks were wet again and her mouth was opened wide. Abruptly, she ran into the house.

The frantic barking of the dogs grew louder. They hadn't been fed yet and were confused by all this movement. They became more and more excited and ran from one person to another, the two younger dogs nipping at each other's feet and throwing their bodies against each other in vigorous sideswipes. A white rubber ball lay there on the grass. I threw it toward the front of the house, and the dogs turned and raced after it, converging as they neared it. All three were growling and barking, the aging retriever very loudly and in desperately complaining tones. The other two let him pick up the ball, and all three strained and crouched with the effort of turning at high speed. Just at this moment the black pony and the brown one trotted out briskly from beyond the house, quite close to the dogs. They pulled up short, lifting their knees sharply, and all five animals, wheeling in unison, came prancing toward us in a momentarily perfect flank. Ida shouted and clapped her hands. Liza turned to see what was happening, and she shouted too.

Jacob alone was unaware of all this. He whirled and jumped and kept throwing out his arms, first one and then the other. Even after the girls had ceased their own capering and were sitting on the edge of the small side porch petting the dogs, he kept whirling and leaping on the weather-softened grass, looking down in concentration and talking to himself, or chanting.

～

I called Harold the next day to tell him of Luisa's death. I knew by his response to my first words that he had guessed what my subsequent words would be.

He said quietly, "I was terribly afraid that that would happen."

"Yes . . ."

"I don't think anything could have prevented it," he said.

There was little to say that each of us did not already know. I asked him about Ricky.

"We've made an extraordinary discovery," he said.

They had known, he told me, that Ricky's mother, Mary, had kept a diary, but they hadn't guessed what they would find, though it should have been obvious.

"She started when she was just eighteen," Harold said, "and kept going until four days before her death. There are seventy-five volumes, and they aren't small. . . .

"It's a godsend for Ricky," he said, "a wonderful, wonderful stroke of luck. . . .

"We're leaving the apartment just as it is. When you all come down, that's where you'll stay . . . at least we hope so."

Luisa, I learned later, was buried in Canada, which had offered asylum to refugees from the junta.

～

Two years after the events I have described, I drove with Ida one Friday night to our nearest city, forty miles away. I was treating her to a film she had wanted to see. Patricia had gone to Boston for the weekend, and had taken Jacob and Liza, and Ida was disappointed at having been left behind. Driving home later, over the dark hills and over bridges already dangerous with ice—it was late October, and there had been rain—we talked together of what we had seen. The film had told of an accident at a nuclear plant, almost a meltdown. But we had seen, as well, so much corruption, so much cowardice and trivial greed, and such a desolation of technology and superfluous artifact as to bring a numbness on the soul. We had driven a good distance when she said to me, "Did this really happen, Dad?" She was fourteen now.

"Yes," I said. "Not in this way, but it happened."

If the questions of young children are the questions of metaphysics, those of adolescents are of ethics and polity.

"Why do they build them," she said, "if they're so dangerous?"

I tried to tell her that laboring men and women had always been injured and killed for the profit of others, in mines and factories, on the oceans and in forests. The unprecedented thing was that entire populations were now subject to accident, and that the earth itself was being poisoned.

I could hear the bafflement in my voice as I talked to her, and I wondered if she noticed it. I wondered, too, if she guessed to what degree I was measuring the truth to her. I thought but did not say, *Ida, you could walk all day in the city of New York and just look at the crowds, and walk for several weeks like that, then do the same in Chicago, and Los Angeles, and San Francisco . . . and all the people you would have seen—that many people—were murdered deliberately in just two countries. . . .*

The road was level only by ponds and lakes. The trees were bare, and from time to time we could see water. A tiny frog, utterly alone, as if without environment, crossed the black asphalt in our headlight beams, leaping with pathetic ineffectuality in high gothic arches. A barn and silo sped by, a good-sized house with sheds, but most of the houses were small and poor. Some were little more than shacks. There were many "mobile homes" that never had been mobile at all.

For an hour, while we traveled uphill and down, always by dark masses of trees, Ida's every utterance was a question.

She asked, "What did Ian say about nuclear wastes?"

She sat across from me in the front seat, leaning back against the locked door. Whenever I glanced at her I found her eyes on mine.

Ian was a physicist, a good friend, who lived in England. He had stayed with us recently, and Ida had listened to his conversation.

"There's no way to contain it safely."

"But then what do they *do?*"

"They put it in temporary containers and hold it in temporary sites. Some of it gets moved around."

"How?"

"Trucks. Trains."

"What if there was a wreck?"

"There have been."

"Were people killed?"

"You mean from radiation?"

"Yes."

"I don't know. It takes years to tell. And people don't admit the accidents. It's hard to learn of them."

Again there was silence. We turned into the valley of the large river. There were several handsome fields at the turn, and by habit, as the headlights swept them, I looked for deer. It was the kind of moonless night on which they often came down from the hills.

"Look, Ida! Quick!"

Two does stood quite close to the road. They raised their long necks, and with their huge ears erect peered wide-eyed into the light. They were as motionless and tense as the hieroglyphic animals on some Egyptian stele.

"When the people die," she said, "the ones who know where the wastes are buried"—she modified her question. "How long does it have to go on?"

"Thousands of years for some of it."

"*Thousands?*"

"Yes."

We drove for a while in silence, but as we neared our own village she said, "Do we live in an evacuation zone?"

"At the edge of one. Maybe just beyond it." And fearing that she was imbibing, or constructing, a disastrous and unbalanced view of mankind, I said to her, "Ida, darling . . . not all the world is like the people who want to run the world. Really, Ida, the things you find the most of are kindliness and sanity—"

She interrupted me, smiling softly, and said gently, her eyes on mine, "I know, Dad."

I slowed the car as we came to the darkened houses of Dower. Huge maples and pines were scattered among them, and our broad, rocky stream passed through their midst, pouring noisily down a six-foot ledge behind the store.

We drove through the silent village, and up the floodplain of Dower stream. There were fields on both sides of us, but the hillside pastures long since had gone back to trees. Soon we were climbing our long dirt road, and then our three hungry dogs, their eyes shining hugely in the light and their barking audible over the noise of the motor, came leaping and sprinting down the hill to greet us. I let them rear and paw the windows while I sat with Ida facing the dark house.

Some drastic subject, more extreme than those we had been talking of, lay just under our words, deflecting everything. We both were aware of it. And I know that if I had spoken my thoughts, she would have heard a voice more puzzled than her own. *There is no hope for mankind,* that voice would have said. *Our world is doomed.* And then it would have countered its own assertion: *No, no . . . mankind is great, and endlessly surprising. . . .*

Ida sat with her head bowed, an expression of earnest thoughtfulness on her brow, chewing her lower lip.

Into the imagery of my own doubts and longings there came now, as there had come frequently during the last two years, memories of Luisa in her brief hours at our home. I could see her bending over the enamored Jacob, smiling and resting one hand on his shoulder; and sitting at the piano enveloping us all in that magical turbulence of music; and looking so openly into Patricia's eyes, saying, "I will not let this friendship go to waste."

Ida turned to me and said, "Do you and Mom ever hear from that lady—you know—who came here with Marshall? Luisa?"

She was speaking carefully, so as not to reproach me for having lied. She had asked me this question before.

I said to her, "Ida, Luisa is dead."

Evidently she had suspected this. Yet there were notes of dismay in her voice. "She is?" she said.

I told her what had happened, and we went into the house.

I woke up several times during the night and listened anxiously to the silence. And then I awakened with a feeling that some disturbance had occurred. The room was filled with a cold, even light, and the house was silent. I became aware that the wind was striking the house violently, and shaking it. The wind was pouring in strongly over the valley, beating this way and that against the angles of the hills, and hitting the house with a rushing, pressing roar. The tops of the pines were bending and thrashing. But now, abruptly, another sound penetrated this roaring, a sound as fragile and sensitive as a breath, but it didn't stop, and it seemed to be inhabited, miraculously, by presences greater than itself. It was the sound of Ida's flute. She was practicing in her room. I lay there and listened to it as if it had been her voice. The simple melody and her dutiful care for it expressed such childish faith that I was flooded with love for her and hope for her, but only for a moment, and there occurred within me a paroxysm of emotions so balanced in their contradictions that nothing could be expressed. If I hadn't been enraged, I would have been crying bitterly: If I hadn't been grieving, I would have been raging bitterly. I thought of Ida, Liza, and Jacob; but I was thinking, too, of mankind as a whole, and of civilization, and the natural world. Memories began to crowd my consciousness. I remembered summer nights of my boyhood during the Depression, how we had hurried in talkative, excited little bands down the narrow alleys and tree-shaded streets of our small town, and I could hear the quiet voices of adults singing and talking on unlighted porches. I remembered how vast and incorruptible the night sky had seemed to me, and how vast the ocean. And I could see Luisa standing like a sleepwalker in our hallway downstairs.

The music of the flute went on. I prayed a prayer of the kind that had come to my lips in recent months, and this one, too, seemed absurd to me, yet I spoke it: *Protect her, Lord . . . if You exist . . . if You will . . . .*

She corrected herself and repeated certain passages.

I lay there after the flute had ended. When I went down at last to breakfast, Ida heard me on the stairs and joined me, though she had eaten earlier.

It was Saturday. She came with me in the car, and got out at the little house at the bottom of the hill, where her friend lived. She intended to spend the afternoon.

At the post office I found in our box the book I had been expecting for several weeks. I made more coffee and, without moving from the breakfast table, read the sixty poems of *Canciones de los Muertos,* by the Chilean exile Roberto Palma, in Marshall's translation. The last poem was addressed to Victor Jara. . . .

But every person in the book was a victim. It was a book of the dead.

I called Marshall at lunchtime to express my gratitude and praise his work. He thanked me and said, "I'm glad you like it." He paused. "I'm glad you called. We should be more in touch."

I could hear another voice and could hear Marshall speaking briefly aside; then: "Bonnie sends her love. I should have written you. I've thought of you often. . . ."

We spoke of Luisa Domic, and Marshall asked about Harold. We spoke of the book again. Marshall had worked from Palma's own manuscripts, and the English version had appeared within weeks of the Spanish.

After talking with him I went out of the house and set off through the woods, under the impression that I wanted to think, and arrange my thoughts, but in fact an independent process of memory and emotion had already begun and was joining things I might not have thought to join, and I went back to the worktable in the upstairs bedroom and began the account that is now ended. Almost daily, during the writing of it, I walked through the woods to relieve the monotony of sitting. My turning point, when I walked to the east, was the massive outcrop of ledge on a hill above our broad river. From the ledge I could see the white spires and dark roofs of the nearby town. Between the town and ledge the latticework of the old railroad bridge crossed from one high bank to the other, emerging from trees and plunging into trees. When I walked in the other direction, downhill to the west, a shorter walk, I turned habitually just beyond the crumbling millrace that I had walked to with Marshall, where the widening stream, meandering among alders, becomes the inlet to the pond, and the domain of the beavers begins. Months ago I began thinking of these places as cenotaphs. Our rocks and rivers, streams and ponds, that we had used to think of as being settled in geologic time, have achieved a mortality at last in technology and human time, and it is not presumptuous now to invoke them as our memorials—as I have done for Luisa—nor preposterous to think of us as theirs.

It was immediately after reading Roberto Palma's *Songs of the Dead* that I began writing this book, which I want to close now as the other book was opened by Marshall, who dedicated his labors to the memory of Alejandro, Luisa, Raoul, and Dorotea Domic.

SHAWNO

[finches and morning. euphoria. shawno.]

We could hear our children's voices in the darkness on the sweet-smelling hill by my friend's house, and could hear the barking of Angus, his dog. At nine o'clock Patricia put our three into the car and went home. My friend's wife and son said goodnight shortly afterward. By then he and I had gone back to the roomy, decrepit, smoke-discolored, homey, extremely pleasant farmhouse kitchen and were finishing the wine we had had at dinner. It was late August. Our northern New England nights would soon make frost, but the cool of the night was still enjoyable. He opened a bottle of *mezcal* he had brought from Mexico, and we talked of the writings of friends, and of the friends themselves, and of our youthful days in New York. He had written a paper on Mahler. We listened to the Eighth and Ninth symphonies, and the unfinished Tenth, which moved him deeply. We talked again. When we parted, the stars, still yellow and numerous in most of the sky, had paled and grown fewer in the east. I set out to walk the four miles home.

I was euphoric, as happens at times, even without *mezcal*. For a short distance, since there was no one to disturb (the town road is a dead-end road and I was at the end of it) I shouted and sang. But the echoes of my voice sobered me and a dog began to bark. The night air was moist and cool. I became aware that something was calling for my attention, calling insistently, and then I realized that it was the stream, and so I listened for a while to its noisy bubbling. The lower stars were blocked by densely wooded hills. A dozen or fifteen old houses lay ahead of me, still darkened for sleep.

Angus came with me. He is a pointy-nosed, black-and white mongrel in whom border collie predominates, and therefore is bright-eyed and quick-footed, and is amazingly interested in human affairs. He pattered along beside me, turning his head every few seconds to look at me, and it was as if he were keeping up continually a companionable cheerful jabbering. I spoke to him at one point and he barked lightly and jumped toward my face, hoping to kiss me.

Abruptly he sat down. We had come to the edge of what he imagined to be his territory, though in fact we had crossed his line several paces back. He sat there and cocked his head, watching me as I walked away. I had taken only twenty steps when on my right, with jarring suddenness, came the explosive deep barking of the German shepherd tied before the one new house in the valley. Angus sprang up, braced his legs, and hurled his own challenge, which was high-pitched and somewhat frantic, and immediately there came a barking that seemed limitless. I could hear it speeding away into the far distance, dog after dog repeating the challenge. Certainly it passed beyond our village, very likely beyond our state. I was in a corridor of barking dogs.

A soft projectile of some sort spurted from the shadows to my right and came to rest not far from my feet, where it turned out to be a chubby little pug. It was bouncing with excitement, and was giving vent through its open mouth to a continuous siren of indignation. The cluttered porch it had been guarding flared with light. Two elderly spinsters lived here. They rose with the sun, or before it, as did many of the older folk. The clapboards of their house had been a mustard color, the trim of the windows white, but that had been thirty years ago. The barn beside the house had fallen down, the apple trees had decayed, the mound of sheep manure was grassed over. The pug stopped barking and began to wheeze excitedly. It reared up and tapped its tiny paws against my shin, and looked at me out of bulging eyes that seemed adoring and shy. I patted him and scratched his ears. Twenty paces on I was startled by a barking more savage than that of the shepherd, a murderous, demented screaming that aroused real fear and detestation. He was chained to a dying apple tree before a collapsing gray house on the left side of the road. The hard-packed yard was crowded with wheelless cars. The dog was a Doberman. He leaped at me fiercely, leaped again and again, and was jerked back violently by the chain, as by the hand of a violent master.

Overlapping these disturbing sounds there came the melodious deep tones of the long-legged black hound tied before his own little house in the strange compound farther on: a mobile home, half of a barn, some small sheds, a corral, all huddled before the large trees that bordered the stream. Nothing was finished. There was an air of disconsolate ambition everywhere, failure, and disconsolate endurance. The hound itself seemed disconsolate. He was not tugging at his chain. He had not even braced his feet. He followed me with his eyes, barking his bark that was almost a baying and was actually beautiful. His head was cocked and he seemed to be listening to the other dogs.

What a racket! What a strange, almost musical hullabaloo! I myself was the cause of it, but it wouldn't end when I passed. The sun would be up, the dogs would keep barking, the birds would twitter and chirp, and that wave of noise, of energy and intention, would follow the sun right across the land.

More lights came on. The sun hadn't risen yet, but the night was gone. It was the morning dusk, fresh and cool. Birds had been calling right along, but now there were more. At intervals I could hear roosters. There were only three. The valley had been noisy once with crowing, and the asphalt road had been an earthen road, packed by wagon wheels and shaded by many elms. The elms were stumps now, huge ones.

Even so, it was beautiful. There were maples and pines beside the road, a few cows were still milked, a few fields were still hayed, a few eggs were still gathered, a few pigs transformed to pork, a few sheep to mutton.

Swallows were darting about. They perched in long rows on the electric wires.

A car passed me from behind, the first.

And Brandy, the Kimbers' gray-and-ginger mutt, trotted up from the stream and joined me. His hair was bristly, his legs short. He was muscular, energetic, stunted, bearded and mustachioed, like some old campaigner out of the hills of Spain. He went beside me a little way, cheerfully but without affection. There was no affection in him, but gregarious good cheer and selfish, robust curiosity. He left me to consort with a fluffy collie, who wasn't chained but wouldn't leave its yard. I passed another German shepherd, a chained husky, an aged cocker spaniel who barked from the doorstep and wouldn't even rise to do it. I came to a small house set back from the road by a small yard. A huge maple overspread the yard. Beneath the maple there stood a blue tractor, a large orange skidder, a pickup truck, two cars, a rowboat, a child's wagon, several bikes. A large, lugubrious Saint Bernard, who all summer had suffered from the heat, was chained to the tree, and she barked at me perfunctorily in a voice not unlike the hound's, almost a baying, but it wasn't a challenge bark at all, or much of one. She wanted to be petted, she wanted to lie down and be scratched, she wanted anything but to hurl a challenge; nevertheless, she barked; it would be shameful not to. I came to a boxer, tied; a purebred border collie, tied; a rabbit hound, tied; several mongrels, not tied, but clustered and apparently waiting for their breakfasts. One, a black, squat hound, had a lame foot and a blind eye, mementos of a terrible midwinter fight with a fox in defense of newborn pups, who froze to death anyway. She barked vociferously, but then ambled out to apologize and be petted. How fabulous our hands must seem to these fingerless creatures! What pleased surprises we bring to their foreheads, their throats and backs and bellies, touching as no dog can touch another dog. . . .

At almost every house there was a dog. At absolutely every house with a garden there was a dog. One must have one to raise food, or the woodchucks take it all. A second car passed me.

The turn to my own road was close now. In the crook of the turn there was a trailer, a so-called mobile home, covered with a second roof of wood. There were three small sheds around it, and a large garden out back, handsome now with the dark greens of potato plants and the lighter greens of bush beans. Near the garden were stakes and boxes for horseshoe pitching. A few steps away, at the edge of the stream, there were chairs, benches, and a picnic table. Two battered cars and a battered truck crowded the dooryard, in which there was also a tripod, taller than the trailer, made of strong young maples from the nearby woods. From its apex dangled a block and chain. Bantam hens were scratching the dirt.

The house was silent. All had watched TV until late at night and were still asleep, among them my seven-year-old daughter's newfound friend. The uproar of dogs was considerable here. Six were in residence, more or less. The young German shepherd was chained. The handsome boxer was free; in fact all the others were free, and with one exception ran to upbraid me and greet me. The exception, the incredibly pretty, positively magnetizing exception was Princess, the malamute, who did not bark or move. She lay at her royal ease atop a grassy mound that once had been an elm, her handsome wolflike head erect and one paw crossed demurely and arrogantly over the other. Her slanted almond-shaped eyes were placed close together and gave her an almost human oriental-slavic air. It was as if she knew she were being admired. She followed me impassively with those provocative eyes, disdaining to respond. How strange she was! She knew me well. If I went near her she'd suddenly melt. She'd sit up and lift one paw tremblingly as high as her head in a gesture of adulation and entreaty. She'd lay her head to one side and let it fall closer and closer to her shoulder in a surrender irresistible in its abject charm—"I am yours, yours utterly"—as if pulling the weight of a lover down on top of her. She ends on her back at such times, belly exposed, hind legs opened wide, lips pulled back voluptuously and front paws tucked under in the air. Especially in the winter, when she alone of the six dogs is allowed into the lamplight of the little home, she indulges in such tricks. The place is overheated. There are times when everyone seems glassy with contentment, and times when bad humor, apparently passing over into bad character, seems hopeless and destructive, and there are quarrels as fierce as the fights of cats. But peace comes again, usually by the intervention of Betsy, the mother, who is mild and benign. She has lost her front teeth and can't afford dentures, yet never hesitates to smile. The children drink soda pop and watch TV, while Verne, who is deep-voiced and patriarchal, with the broad back and muscular huge belly of a Sumo wrestler, sits at the kitchen table sipping beer from a can, measuring gunpowder on a little balance scale, loading and crimping shotgun shells and glancing at the program on the tube. He is opinionated, vain, and egotistical, to the point of foolish pomposity, but he is good-natured and earnest and is easily carried away into animation, and then the posturing vanishes. He issues an order, directs a booming word to one of the kids or dogs, but especially to Princess, who draws effusions one wouldn't think were in him. "Well, Princess!" he roars, "ain't you the charmer! Ain't you my baby! Ain't you now! Oh, you want your belly scratched? Well, we all do, Princess! We all do! But you're the one that gits it, ain't you! Oh, yes you are! oh, yes!"

This morning I didn't stop to caress the malamute. At the turn in the road I heard a far-off barking that made me smile and want to be home. I crossed the cement bridge and turned into a small dirt road. There wouldn't be a house now for a mile, and then there would be ours and the road would end.

Day had begun. There was color in the sky. The moisture in the air was thinning.

The land was flat and paralleled the stream, which was to my right now. Here and there along its banks, in May, after the flood has gone down and the soil has warmed, we gather the just-emerging coils of the ferns called fiddleheads. Occasionally I have fished here, not really hopefully (the trout are few), but because the stream is so exciting. Once, however, while I knelt on the bank baiting my hook, I glanced into the water, deep at that point, and saw gliding heavily downstream a fish that seemed too big to be a trout. What a passion of helplessness I felt! I would have jumped on it if I could have. I learned later that ice had broken the dam to a private fishpond in the hills and this prize and many others had escaped down tributaries to the main stream and the river.

To my left, beyond a miniature bog of alders and swale lay a handsome small pond. Its outlet joined the stream fifty yards on, flowing under a bridge of stout pine stringers and heavy planks. The game warden had been here several times with dynamite, but the beavers had rebuilt their dam across the outlet, and once again the pond was eighteen inches higher than the stream. It was not unusual to see them. They had cut their half-tunnels under all these banks, creating concave, overhanging edges. I had stood here with the children one night, downstream from the bridge, at the water's edge, looking for beavers, and two had passed under our feet. It was a windless mellow night of full moon. I saw the glint of moonlight on the beaver's fur as he emerged from his channel under the bank, and then I saw his head quietly break the water. The dark shape of a second beaver, following him, glided like a phantom among the wavering images of the moon and trees.

I couldn't hear the barking on the hill anymore. I was hungry now and felt sleepy, but here between the pond and the stream the morning air was endlessly refreshing and I entered that pleasant state of being wholly relaxed, utterly drained of muscular energy, yet suffused by awareness, interest, and approval—the mild, benign energies of momentary happiness.

Five or six bright yellow streamers—so they seemed to be—approached me and sped by, dipping and rising. They were finches. The pattern of their flight was of long smooth waves, in the troughs of which they would flutter their wings to ascend the coming slope, but fold them before the top and soar curvingly over the crest. Sleek as torpedoes or little fish, they would glide downward again into the next trough and there extend their wings and flutter them.

A glossy red-winged blackbird emerged from a clump of alders and glided to a large gray stump.

Beyond the bridge the road began to climb. On both sides vigorous ferns, green but no longer the vivid green of summer, crowded the sunny space before the trees. The coolness of night still poured from the woods, mingling with the warmer air of the road.

Abruptly I heard and saw him, and though no creature is more familiar to me, more likely to be taken for granted, I was thrilled to see him again, and gladdened, more than gladdened, filled for a moment with the complex happiness of our relationship, which is both less than human and utterly human. Certainly I was made happy by his show of love for me. But my admiration of him is undiminished, and I felt it again, as always. He is the handsomest of dogs, muscular and large, with tufted golden fur. The sound of his feet was audible on the hard-packed, pebble-strewn road. I leaned forward and called to him and clapped my hands, and he accelerated, arching his throat and running with more gusto. He ran with a powerful driving stride that was almost that of a greyhound, and as he neared me he drew back his lips, arched his throat still more and let out a volley of ecstatic little *yips*. This sound was so puppyish, and his ensuing behavior so utterly without dignity, so close to fawning slavishness, that one might have contemned him for it, except that it was extreme, so extreme that there was no hint of fawning, and certainly not of cringing, but the very opposite: great confidence and security, into which there rose up explosively an ecstasy he couldn't contain and couldn't express rapidly enough to diminish, so that for a while he seemed actually to be in pain. I had to help him, had to let him lick my face protractedly and press his paws into my shoulders. And, as sometimes happens in such early-morning solitudes, there came over me a sense of the briefness of life, and of my kinship with all these other creatures who would soon be dead, and I almost spoke aloud to my dog: how much it matters to be alive together! how marvelous and brief our lives are! and how good it is, dear one that you are, to have the wonderful strange passion of your spirit in my life!

As he wound around me and pressed his body against mine, I remembered another greeting when I had seen blood on his teeth and feet. He was three then, in his prime. I had been away for several weeks—our first parting—and he had been baffled. When I came back I had reached this very place in the road, in my car, also in summer, when I saw him hurtling toward me. His first sounds were pathetic, a mixed barking, whimpering, and gulping for breath. I had to get out of the car to prevent him from injuring himself. I had to kneel in the road and let him kiss me and wind around me. He was crying; I had to console him. And then he was laughing, and dancing on his hind legs, and I laughed too, except that it was then that I noticed the blood. He had been in the house, Patricia told me later, and had heard the car. He had torn open the screen door with his teeth and claws, had chewed away some protective slats and had driven his body through the opening.

He danced around me now on his hind legs, licking my face. I knew that I could terminate this ecstasy by throwing a stone for him, which I did, hard and low, so that he wouldn't overtake it and break his teeth. A few moments later he laid it at my feet and looked into my face excitedly.

Patricia and the children were still sleeping. I ate breakfast alone, or rather with Shawno, who waited by my chair.

I had hoped to spend the morning writing, but my eyes were closing irresistibly. I pulled up bush beans in the garden, and carried tall spikes of bolted lettuce to the compost pile. There is a rough rail fence around the garden to keep the ponies out. Shawno lay beneath it and watched me. I cleared a few weeds and from time to time got rid of stones by flinging them absently into the woods. I pulled out the brittle pea vines from their chicken-wire trellis, rolled up the wire, and took it to the barn. After two hours of this I went to bed. Shawno had gone in already and was enjoying a second breakfast with the children. I had forgotten about him, but as I left the garden I saw by the fence, where the grass had been flattened by his body, a little heap of stones. He had chased and brought back every one I had tried to get rid of.

[his parents.
incidents in the park.]

When Patricia was pregnant with Ida we were living on Riverside Drive in New York. One bright October day we saw a crowd of people at the low stone wall of the park. Many were murmuring in admiration and a few almost shouted with delight. Down below, on the grassy flat, two dogs were racing. The first belonged to an acquaintance in our building. She was tawny and short-haired with the lines of a greyhound, except for a larger head and more massive shoulders. She was in heat and was leading the other in fantastic, playful sprints, throwing her haunches against him gaily and changing direction at great speed. The male, a Belgian shepherd with golden fur, was young and in a state of transport. He ran stiff-legged, arching his neck over her body with an eagerness that seemed ruthless, except that his ears were laid back shyly. The dogs' speed was dazzling; both were beauties, and the exclamations continued as long as they remained in sight.

Shawno was the largest of the issue of those memorable nuptials. He arrived in our apartment when Ida was twelve weeks old. She looked down from her perch in Patricia's arms and saw him wobbling this way and that, and with a chortle that was almost a scream reached for him with both hands. Soon she was bawling the astonished, gasping wails of extreme alarm (his needle-point bites), and he was yelping piteously in the monkeylike grip with which she had seized his ear and was holding him at arm's length, out of mind, while she turned her tearful face to her mother.

These new beginnings, and especially my marriage with Patricia (it was my third marriage), occurring late in my maturity, ended a period of severe unhappiness. And I found that loving the child, holding and dandling her, playing little games with her, watching her sleep, and above all watching her nurse at Patricia's breast, awakened memories of my childhood I would never have guessed were still intact.

Something similar happened with the dog. I began a regimen of early morning running, as if he were an athlete and I his trainer, and I had trotted behind him through the weathers of several months before I realized that my happiness at these times was composed in part of recovered memories of the daybreak runnings of my youth, times so full of hope and satisfaction as to seem to me, now, paradisaical.

The dog developed precociously. At eighteen months he was jumping seven-foot walls, chasing sticks I threw for him. He was a delight to watch, powerful and beautiful, with a quality of spirit that was like the nonchalant gaiety of human youth. He became a personage in the park and acquired a band of children, who left their games to play with him, and invented new games to include him. It was not only his prowess that attracted them, but the extraordinary love he showed them. The truth was, he was simply smitten with the human race. I was crossing upper Broadway with him once; he was leashed; the crossing was crowded. There came toward us an old gentleman holding a four-year-old boy by the hand. The boy's face and the dog's were on a level, and as they passed the two faces turned to each other in mutual delight, and Shawno bestowed a kiss that began at one ear, went all the way across and ended at the other. I glanced back. The boy, too, was glancing back, grinning widely. In fact, the boy and Shawno were looking back at each other. This incident is paired for all time with another that I witnessed in New York and that perhaps could not have occurred in any other city. It was in the subway at rush hour. The corridors were booming with the grinding roar of the trains and the pounding of thousands of almost running feet. Three corridors came together in a Y and two of them were streaming with people packed far tighter than soldiers in military formation. The columns were approaching each other rapidly. There was room to pass, but just barely, or not quite. The columns collided. That is, their inside corners did, and each of these was occupied by an apparently irascible man. Each hurled one, exactly one, furious roundhouse blow at the other, and both were swept away in their columns—a memorable fight.

I would never have known certain people in New York if it hadn't been for the dog; worse, it would never have occurred to me that knowing them was desirable, or possible, whereas in fact it was delightful. The people I mean were children. What could I have done without the dog? As it was, I changed my hours in order to meet them, and they—a group of eight or so—waited for us devotedly after school. Most were Puerto Rican. The youngest was only seven, the eldest eleven. They would spread themselves in a circle with the dog in the center and throw a ball back and forth, shouting as he leaped and tried to snatch it from the air. When he succeeded, which was often, one saw the merriest and most musical of chases, the boys arranged behind the dog according to speed of foot, the dog holding the ball high, displaying it provocatively, looking back over his shoulder and trotting stiff-legged just fast enough to elude the foremost boy, winding that laughing, shouting, almost singing line of children this way and that through the park. Invariably the boys asked me to make him leap, and I would throw the ball over fences and walls. Perhaps in emulation of the dog—and certainly because I myself wanted to do more than watch—we began a game of leaping, or rather of flying through the air, the boys diving headfirst from the steep stone wall by the stairs, holding out their arms like wings . . . and I would catch them at the armpits and set them on the ground. Most were too heavy to dive from very high, but one, a bold and wiry seven-year-old, launched himself from heights that made a few bystanders turn away in horror. He held out his arms like sparrows' wings, and lifted his head, his face shining with bliss. I would catch him and he would dart away to try it again, apparently unaware of the awe and the smiles of admiration on the faces of his friends. I discovered later that some of our audience came on purpose at this time to watch the children and the dog. One elderly white-haired man I have never forgotten. He was Jewish and spoke with a German accent, wore a felt hat and expensive coats. He came to the playground regularly and stood with his hands behind his back, his head dropped forward, nodding and chuckling, and smiling unweariedly. His face was wonderful. It was intelligent and kindly, was still strong, still handsome, and it possessed a quality I have come to associate with genius, an apparent unity of feeling, an alacrity and wholeness of response. Whatever he was feeling suffused his face; he didn't have attitudes toward his feelings, and counter-attitudes toward his attitudes. The dog delighted him. He deferred to the headlong, boisterous children, who when Shawno would appear would shout happily and in unison, and Shawno would go to them, bounding exuberantly, but it wouldn't be long before the old gentleman would call him, and Shawno would leave the children, not bounding now but sweeping his tail in such extreme motions that his hind legs performed a little dance from side to side independently of his front legs. The old gentleman would lean over him, speak to him, and pet him, and the dog would press against his legs and look into his face. We usually talked for a few minutes before I went home. When I asked him about his work and life he waved away the questions with gestures that were humorous and pleading yet were impressive in their authority. One day I recognized his face in a photograph in the *Times,* alas, on the obituary page. He was an eminent refugee scholar, a sociologist. I discovered, reading the description of his career, that I had studied briefly with his son at Columbia. By this time we had moved to the remote farmhouse in the country and our second child had been born.

[past lives. streams.
ferocity and family concern.]

Our house had been occupied by Finns, as had many others near us. The hill, actually a ridge, sloped away on two sides, one forested and the other, to the south, open pasture with the remnants of an orchard. At the bottom of these fields was a stream, and in a bend of the stream, a sauna. It was here that the old Finn who had built the house had bathed his invalid wife, carrying her back and forth every day until her final illness. From this same small pool he had carried water in buckets to the garden a few strides away. The sauna was damaged beyond repair, but we let it stand; and we brought back the garden, which now was one of three. For the few years that country living sustained the glow of romance, this garden was my favorite, and I carried water to it in buckets, as had the old man. Just beyond the sauna a wooded slope rose steeply. Raccoons and deer entered our field here, and it was here that the ponies and dog all came to drink.

There were other relics of those vanished lives: handmade apple boxes with leather hinges cut from old boots; in all the sheds door handles made of sapling crotches; a split round apple ladder with flakes of spruce bark on the sides and rungs made of rock maple saplings; ten-foot Finnish skis that had been cut by hand and bent at the tips with steam from a kettle. There were hills wherever one looked, and there had been farms on all the hills. Some of the Finns had skied to market, and had cruised their woodlots on skis. Some of their children had skied to school.

The hills and ridges are so numerous that in the spring, while the snow is melting, the sound of water can be heard everywhere. It pours and tumbles; there is a continual roaring; and when the thaw is well advanced the large stream in the valley makes the frightening sounds of flood, hurling chunks of ice ahead of it, crowding violently into the curves, and hurtling over falls so deep in spume that the rocks are out of sight. Later, in the hot weather, one hears the braided sounds and folded sounds of quiet water. The orange gashes and abrasions on the trunks of trees are darkening. More trees are dead. The banks of the streams, however beautiful, and however teeming with new life, are strewn with debris in many stages of decay.

The streams have become presences in my life. For a while they were passions. There are few that I haven't fished and walked to their source. These have been solitary excursions, except for the single time that I took the dog. His innocent trotting at the water's edge disturbed the trout. Still worse was his drinking and wading in the stream. I called him out. He stood on the bank and braced his legs and shook himself. Rather, he was seized by a violent shaking, a shaking so swift and powerful as to seem like a vibration. It shook his head from side to side, then letting his head come to rest took his shoulders and shook them, then his ribs, and in a swift, continuous wave passed violently to his haunches, which it shook with especial vigor, and then entered his tail and shook the entire length of it, and at last, from the very tip, sprang free, leaving behind, at the center of the now-subsided aura of sparkling waterdrops, an invigorated and happy dog. It was at this moment of perfected well-being that one of those darting slim shadows caught his eye. He dove into the water headfirst, and thrust his snout to the very bottom, where he rooted this way and that. He emerged and looked in amazement from side to side. The trout had vanished without trace. The dog had no notion even of the direction of its flight. He thrust down his head again and turned over stones, then came up, smooth and muscular, with his streaming fur clinging to him, and stood there peering down, poised in the electric stillness of the hunter that seems to be a waiting but is actually a fascination. Years later, after my own passion for trout had cooled, I would see him poised like that in the shallows of the swimming hole, ignoring the splashing, shouting children, looking down, still mesmerized, still ready—so he thought—to pounce.

During most of the thaw there is little point in going into the woods. Long after the fields have cleared and their brown is touched with green, there'll be pools and streaks of granular snow, not only in the low-lying places in the woods, but on shadowed slopes and behind rocks. For a while the topmost foot of soil is too watery to be called mud. The road to our house becomes impassable, and for days, or one week, or two, or three, we park at the bottom of the road and walk home wearing rubber boots and carrying the groceries and perhaps the youngest children in knapsacks and our arms. This was once a corduroy road, and it never fails that some of the logs have risen again to the surface.

Spring in the north is almost violent: after the period of desolation, when the snow has gone and everything that once was growing seems to have been bleached and crushed, and the soil itself seems to have been killed by winter, there comes, accompanied by the roaring of the streams, a prickling of the tree buds that had formed in the cold, and a prickling of little stems on the forest floor, and a tentative, small stirring of bird life. This vitalizing process, once begun, becomes bolder, more lavish, and larger, and soon there is green everywhere, and the open fretwork of branches, limbs, and trunks, beyond which all winter we had seen sky, hills, and snow, has become an eye-stopping mass of green. The roaring of the streams diminishes, but the velocity of green increases until the interlocking leaves can't claim another inch of sunlight except by slow adjustment and the killing of rival growth. Now the animal presence is spread widely through the woods, and Shawno runs this way and that, nose to the ground, excited and distracted by overlapping trails.

It was in this season of early summer that we came here. The woods were new to me. I was prepared for wonders. And there occurred a small but strange encounter that did indeed prove haunting. We had been walking a woods road, Shawno and I, or the ghost of a road, and came to a little dell, dense with ferns and the huge leaves of young striped maples. Shawno drew close to me and seemed disturbed. He stood still for a moment, sniffing the air instead of the ground, and then the fur rose on his neck and he began to growl. At that moment there emerged from the semi-dark of a dense leaf bank, perhaps thirty steps away, two dogs, who stopped silently and came no further. The smaller dog was a beagle, the larger a German shepherd, black and gigantic. His jowls on both sides and his snout in front bristled with white-shafted porcupine quills. He didn't seem to be in pain, but seemed helpless and pathetic, a creature without fingers or tools, and therefore doomed. The uncanny thing about the dogs was their stillness. Shawno continued to growl and to stamp his feet uncertainly. Just as silently as they had appeared, the beagle and the shepherd turned into the undergrowth and vanished.

I was to see these two dogs again. In the meantime, I learned that it was not uncommon for dogs to run wild, or to lead double lives;

and that such pairings of scent and sight were frequent. The beagle could follow a trail. The shepherd had sharp eyes, was strong, and could kill.

In the city there had been but one threat to Shawno's life. Here there were several. He was large and tawny, and though he was lighter in color, he resembled a deer far more closely than had the cows, sheep, and horses that in the memory of my neighbors had been shot for deer—certainly more closely than had the goat that had been gutted in the field and brought to the village on the hood of the hunter's car. With such anecdotes in mind, I discovered one day, toward the end of hunting season, that Shawno had escaped from the house. At least eight hunters had gone up our road into the woods. I know now that his life was not at quite the risk that I imagined, but at that time I was disturbed. I ran into the woods calling to him and whistling, and wondering how I could find him if he'd already been shot. Several hours later, he emerged into our field loping and panting, and came into the house, and with a clatter of elbows and a thump of his torso dropped into his nook by the woodstove. He held his head erect and looked at me. The corners of his lips were lifted. His mouth was open to the full, and his extended tongue, red with exertion, vibrated with his panting in a long, highly arched curve that turned up again at its tip. He blinked as the warmth took hold of him, and with a grunt that was partly a sigh stretched his neck forward and dropped his chin on his paws.

In February of that winter I saw the beagle and German shepherd again. We were sharing a load of hay with a distant neighbor, an elderly man whose bachelor brother had died and who was living alone among the bleached and crumbling remains of what had been once a considerable farm. He still raised a few horses and trained them for harness, though there wasn't a living in it. I had backed the truck into the barn and was tossing up bales to him where he stood in the hayloft when a car drew up and a uniformed man got out. I recognized the game warden, though I had never met him. He was strikingly different from the police of the county seat ten miles away, who walked with waddling gaits and could be found at all hours consuming ice cream at the restaurant on the highway south. The warden was large but trim, was actually an imposing figure, as he needed to be—he had made enemies, and they had tried to kill him, once by shooting through the window, another time by throwing a gasoline bomb that had brought down the house in flames, at night, in winter. He and his wife and adolescent son had escaped. He was spoken of as a fanatic, but hunters praised his skill as a hunter. A man who had paid a fine for poaching said to me, "If he's after you in the woods he'll git you. No man can run through the woods like him." His large round eyes were a pale blue. Their gaze was unblinking, open, disturbingly strange.

He addressed the elderly man by his last name. The warden, too, was a scion of an old, old family here.

"We'd all be better off," he said, "if you'd kept him chained."

His voice was emphatic but not angry. He spoke with the unconscious energy and loudness that one hears in many of the rural voices. "He's been runnin' deer, and you know it. I caught him at the carcass. It was still kickin'." The warden handed him the piece of paper he had been carrying, which was obviously a summons. "I've done away with him," he said.

We had come out of the barn. The warden went to his car, opened the trunk, and came around to us with the small stiff body of the beagle. Its eyes and mouth were open, its tongue protruded between its teeth on one side, and its chest was matted with blood. The warden laid the body on the snowbank by the barn and said, "Come back to the car a minute."

The black German shepherd lay on a burlap sack, taking up the whole of the trunk.

"You know who owns that?"

The elderly man shook his head. No emotion had appeared on his face since the warden had arrived. The warden turned his blue, strangely unaggressive eyes on me and repeated the question. I too shook my head. The shepherd had been home since I had seen him in the woods: someone had pulled out the quills.

Shawno was barking from the cab of the truck. I had left the window open to give him air. It was his questioning, information-wanting bark. The smell of the dead dogs had reached him.

After the warden left, my neighbor went into the house and came back with money for the hay.

"Obliged to you for haulin' it," he said.

That night, on the phone, I told a friend, a hunter, about the dogs.

"The warden was right," he said. "Dogs like that can kill a deer a day, even more. Jake Wesley's dogs cornered a doe in my back field last year. She was pregnant with twins. They didn't bother killing her, they don't know how; they were eating her while she stood there. She was ripped to shreds. I shot them both."

There was a crust on the snow just then. Dogs could run on it, but the sharp hooves of the deer would break through and the ice cut their legs. They spent such winters herded in evergreen groves, or "yards," and if the bark and buds gave out many would starve. Occasionally the wardens took them hay, but this introduced another problem, for if the dogs found the snowmobile trails and followed them to the yards, the slaughter could be severe.

And what of Shawno? I realized that I regarded him habitually with the egocentricity of a doting master, as if he were a creature chiefly of his human relations, though certainly I knew better. I thought of the many cats his ferocious mother had killed. And I remembered how, the previous fall, while our children were playing with a neighbor's children in front of our house, Shawno had come into their midst with a freshly killed woodchuck. He held his head high and trotted proudly among us, displaying his kill. It was a beautiful chestnut color and it dangled flexibly full-length from his teeth, jouncing limply as he trotted. He placed it on the ground under the large maple, where he often lay, and stretched out above it, lionlike, the corpse between his paws. I was tying a shoelace for one of the children. I heard a rushing growl of savagery and out of the corner of my eye saw Shawno spring forward. I shouted and jumped in front of him. One of the visiting boys had come too close.

I doubt that Shawno would have bitten him. Nevertheless, in that frightening moment I had seen and heard the animal nervous system that is not like ours, but is capable of an explosive violence we never approximate, even in our most excessive rages.

He was with me in the pickup one day when I went for milk to a neighbor's dairy. There were usually dogs in front of the barn and Shawno was on friendly terms with them. This time, however, before I had shut off the motor, he leaped across me in the cab, growling and glaring, his snout wrinkled and his front teeth bared to the full. His body was tense, and instantaneously had been charged with an extraordinary energy. Down below, also growling, was a large black hound with yellow eyes. The window was open. Before I could close it or speak to him, Shawno put his head and shoulders through the opening, and with a push of his hind feet that gouged the seat cover, dove down on the hound.

There were no preliminaries. They crashed together with gnashing teeth and a savage, high-pitched screaming.

The fight was over in a moment. Shawno seized him by the neck, his upper teeth near the ear, his lower on the throat, and driving forward with his powerful hind legs twisted him violently to the ground.

The hound tried to right himself. Shawno responded with siren-like growls of rage and a munching and tightening of teeth that must have been excruciating. The hound's yellow eyes flashed. He ceased struggling. Shawno growled again, and this time shook his head from side to side in the worrying motion with which small animals are killed. The hound lay still. Shawno let him up. The hound turned its head away. Shawno pressed against him, at right angles, extending his chin and entire neck over the hound's shoulder. The hound turned its head as far as it could in the other direction.

The fight was over. There was no battle for survival, as in the Jack London stories that had thrilled me in my youth. Survival lay precisely not in tooth and claw, but in the social signaling that tempered the dogs' savagery, as it tempers that of wolves. It was this that accounted for the fact that one never came upon the carcasses of belligerent dogs who had misconceived their powers, as had the hound.

The victory was exhilarating. What right had I, who had done nothing but watch, to feel exultation and pride? Yet I did feel these things. Shawno felt them too, I'm sure. He sat erect beside me going home, and there was still a charge of energy, an aura about his body. He held his head proudly, or so I thought. His mouth was open, his tongue lolled forward, and he was panting lightly. From time to time he glanced aside at me out of narrowed eyes. I kept looking at him, kept smiling, and couldn't stop. I reached across and stroked his head and spoke to him, and again he would glance at me. He was like the roughneck athlete heroes of my youth, who after great feats in the sandlot or high school football games, begrimed, bruised, and wet-haired, would walk to the locker rooms or the cars, heads high, helmets dangling from their fingertips or held in the crooks of their arms, riding sweet tides of exhaustion and praise. I remembered the glorious occasions, too, after I had come of an age to compete, when my brief inspirations on the field had been rewarded by teammates' arms around my shoulders.

But there was more to it than this. It was as if I had been made larger and stronger by his power; it was as if my very existence had been multiplied because he was my ally and loved me. These, so I take it, were the feelings of the boy who still lived in me and who looked with happy gratitude at this guardian with thick fur and fearsome teeth, who could leap nonchalantly over the truck we now rode in, and who had devoted his powers utterly to the boy's well-being.

Very little of this came into my voice when I said at home, "Shawno got into a fight!"

Ida and Patricia came close to me, asking, "What happened? What happened?"

Ida had never witnessed the animal temper I have just described. What she wanted to know was, had he been bitten?

If anyone had said to Shawno what the little boy says in Ida's *Mother Goose,* "Bow wow wow, whose dog art thou?" he could not have answered except by linking Ida's name with my own. He often sat by her chair when she ate. Three of the five things he knew to search for and fetch belonged to Ida: her shoes, her boots, her doll. When I read to her in the evening she leaned against me on the sofa and Shawno lay on the other side with his head in her lap. Often she fell asleep while I read, and we would leave her there until we ourselves were ready for bed. When we came for her Shawno would be asleep beside her. On the nights when I carried her, still awake, to her bed, she would insist that both Shawno and Patricia come kiss her goodnight, and both would. Usually he would leap into the bed, curl up beside her, and spend part of the night. When she was five or six we bought two shaggy ponies from a neighbor and having fenced the garden let them roam as they would. The larger pony had been gelded, but was still mischievous and inclined to nip. Late one afternoon I glanced from an upstairs window and saw Ida leading Liza and Jacob across the yard, all three holding hands. Jacob had just learned to walk and they were going slowly. The ponies came behind them silently. Starbright, the gelding, drew close to Jacob and seemed about to nudge him, which he had done several times in recent weeks, toppling him over. Shawno was watching from across the yard. He sprang forward and came running in a crouch, close to the ground. I called Patricia to the window. His style was wonderful to see, so calm and masterful. There had been a time when he had harried the ponies gleefully, chasing them up and down the road without mercy, snapping at their feet, leaping at their shoulders, and dodging their kicks with what, to them, must have been exasperating ease. I had had to reprimand him several times before he would give it up. Now silently, and crouching menacingly, he moved in behind the children and turned to face the ponies. Starbright knew that he would leap but didn't know when, and began to lift his feet apprehensively. Shawno waited . . . and waited . . . and the pony apparently breathed a sigh of relief, and abruptly Shawno leapt, darting like a snake at Starbright's feet. The pony pulled back in alarm, and wheeled, obliging the smaller pony to wheel too. Shawno let them come along then, but followed the children himself, glancing back to see that the ponies kept their distance. The children hadn't seen a bit of this. "What a darling!" said Patricia. "What a good dog!"

[down to searles.]

The owners of bitches, when their dogs were in heat, were often obliged to call the owners of males and request that they be taken home and chained. Four days went by once before we could locate Shawno. At last the call came. He had traveled several miles. When I went for him he wouldn't obey me, was glassy-eyed and frantic. The only way to get him home was to put the bitch in the car and lure him. It was pathetic. He hadn't slept for four days, was thin, had been fighting with other males, and had had no enjoyment at all: the bitch was a feisty little dachshund. For two days he lay chained on the porch, lost utterly in gloom. He didn't respond to anyone, not even to Ida, but kept his chin flat between his paws and averted his eyes. He had gone to bitches before, but I had been able to fetch him. He had suffered frustration before, but had recovered quickly. What was different this time? I never knew.

Apart from these vigils of instinct, his absences were on account of human loves, the first and most protracted of which was not a single person but a place and situation irresistible to his nature. This was the general store.

The one-story white clapboard building was near the same broad stream that ran through the whole of the valley. The banks were steep here and the stream curved sharply, passing under a bridge and frothing noisily over a double ledge of rounded rocks. There had used to be horseshoe pits by the road and games before supper and at night under the single light at the corner of the store. Three roads converged here. One was steep and on winter Sundays and occasional evenings had been used for sledding. That was when the roads had been packed, not plowed, and the only traffic had been teams and sleds. Searles's father—the second of the three generations of C. W. Searles—though he was known to be a hard and somewhat grasping man, would open the store and perhaps bring up cider for the sledders. There would be a bonfire in the road, and as many as a hundred people in motion around it.

Searles was sixty years old when we arrived. The store was wonderfully well organized and good to look at, crowded but neat and logical, filled with implements of the local trades and pleasures. Searles had worked indoors for his father as a boy. Later, as a youth, he had gone with a cart and horse to the outlying farms, taking meat, hardware, clothing, and tools and bringing back not cash but eggs, butter, apples, pears, chickens, shingles. Now when he ordered the pâté called *creton,* he knew it would be consumed by the Dulacs, Dubords, and Pelletiers. The five sets of rubber children's boots were for the Barkers and were in the proper sizes. He displayed them temptingly, brought down the price, and finally said, "Why don't you take the lot, Charlie, and make me an offer?" He knew who hunted and who fished, and what state their boots, pants, and coats were in. A death in the town affected his business. He saw the price of bullets going sky-high, put in several shell- and bullet-making kits, and said, "Verne, what do you figure you spend a year on shells and bullets?" "Oh, it's horrible. I don't practice no more, that's what's come to . . ."

In the summer there were rakes, hoes, spades, cultivators, coils of garden hose, sections of low white fencing to put around flower beds, and perhaps a wheelbarrow arrayed on the loading apron in front of the store. In the fall, on the same apron, one found crated woodstoves, sections of black stovepipe, rolls of asphalt sheeting, rolls of plastic sheeting for window insulation, while inside, on racks, were checkered red-and-black hunting coats of thick wool, orange vests, orange caps, boxes of shells. When the getting-ready time was past and winter was really here, one saw stacks of broad shovels out front, and two or three of the large, flat-bottomed snow scoops that had to be pushed with both hands. Set up in rows on the window shelves were insulated rubber boots with felt liners, and two styles of snowshoes, glistening with varnish. Late in winter the sugaring supplies appeared: felt filters, wooden and metal spigots, zinc buckets with creased lids; and these were followed shortly by the racks of seeds to be started indoors, and the new fishing rods, new reels, the same old lures and hooks. At all times there were axes and axe handles, bucksaws, wooden wedges and iron wedges, birch hooks, a peavey or two, many chainsaw files and cans of oil. For years he kept a huge skillet that finally replaced, as he knew it would, the warped implement at the boys' camp. He carried kitchenware and electrical and plumbing supplies, and tools for carpentry, as well as drugstore items, including a great deal of Maalox. All this was in addition to the food, the candy rack, the newspapers, the greeting cards, and the school supplies.

People stopped to talk. Those he liked—some of whom he had sat beside in the little red schoolhouse up the road, long unused now—would stand near the counter for half an hour exchanging news or pleasantries. One day I heard Franklin Mason, who was five years older than Searles, say testily, "I seen 'em, I seen 'em." He was referring to the shingling brackets that had been propped up prominently at the end of the counter. Searles had known for two years that Mason wanted to replace his roofing; he had just learned that Mason had decided on asphalt shingles. "I might borrow Mark's brackets," said Mason, but he added, in a different tone, scratching his face, "these are nice, though. . . ."

People didn't say "Searles's place," but "down to Searles." "Oh, they'll have it down to Searles." "I stopped in down to Searles." "Let me just call down to Searles." He was C. W. the third, but had been called Bob all his life.

Of the men in the village he was certainly the least rural. He had grown up on a farm, loved to hunt and fish, play poker, drink whiskey, and swap yarns. But he had gone away to college, and then to business school, and had worked in Boston for three years. He was not just clever or smart but was extremely intelligent, with a meticulous, lively, retentive mind. He had come home not because he couldn't make a go of things in the city, but because he loved the village and the countryside and sorely missed the people. He subscribed to the *Wall Street Journal* and the *New York Times,* read many periodicals, was interested in politics and controversy and changing customs. When I met him his three children were away at college. We disagreed irreconcilably on politics. I was aware of his forbearance and was grateful for it. And I was impressed by his wit, and by his kindliness, as when, without reproach or impatience he would allow certain impoverished children to cluster for long, long minutes before the candy rack, blocking his narrow aisle; and as when he built a ramp for the wheelchair of a neighbor who could no longer walk but was still alert and lively. He was not a happy man. He drank too much to be healthy, and his powers of mind by and large went unused. Yet one could sense in him a bedrock of contentment, and a correct choice of place and work. He was tall and bony, carried far too large a stomach, and was lame in one leg. In damp weather he used a cane and moved with some difficulty about the store. I came to see that most of his friends were old friends and were devoted to him. I learned too that he had forgiven many debts and had signed over choice lots of land to the town, one for a ball field, another for picnics. His gregarious cocker spaniel, who possessed no territorial sense at all, lounged in the aisles and corners, and on sunny days could be found on the loading apron under the awning. And it was here, in front of the store, beside the caramel-colored spaniel, that one sunny day I encountered my own dog, who had vanished from the house.

He leaped up gaily, showing no guilt at all, and came beside me when I went into the store.

Searles, on the high stool, was leaning over the *Wall Street Journal* that was spread across the counter. The moment he raised his head, Shawno looked at him alertly.

Searles smiled at me. "I've got a new friend," he said; and to the dog, "Haven't I, Shawno? What'll you have, Shawno? Do you want a biscuit? Do you?" Shawno reared, put his front paws on the counter and barked.

"Oh, you do?" said Searles. "Well, I happen to have one."

He put his hand under the counter, where he kept the dog biscuits that had fattened the spaniel.

"Will you pay for it now?" he said. "Will you? Will you, Shawno?"

Shawno, whose paws were still on the counter, barked in a deep, almost indignant way. Searles was holding the biscuit, not offering it.

"Oh, you want it on credit?" he said. He held up the biscuit, and at the sight of it the dog barked in lighter, more eager tones. "What?" said Searles. "You want it free?" Again Shawno barked, the eagerness mixed now with impatience and demand. "All right," said Searles. "Here 'tis. On the house." He held it out and Shawno took it with a deft thrust of his head.

I had watched all this with a long-lasting uncomfortable smile.

I said that I hoped the dog wasn't a nuisance.

"Oh no," said Searles. "He's a good dog. He's a fine dog."

And I looked at Shawno, who was looking at Searles, and I thought, "You wretch, you unfaithful wretch! How easy it is to buy you!"

Yet I let him go back there again and again. He'd trot away in the morning as if he were going off to work, and then at suppertime would appear on the brow of the hill, muddied and wet, having jumped into the stream to drink.

I didn't have the heart to chain him. And I couldn't blame him. What better place for a gregarious dog than this one surviving social fragment of the bygone town? There were other dogs to run with, there was the store itself with its pleasant odors, there was Searles, my rival, with his biscuits, there were children to make much of him, and grownups by the score. Moreover, there were cars, trucks, and delivery vans, and all had been marked by the dogs of distant places. We

would arrive for groceries or mail and find him stretched on the apron
in front of the store, or playing in the road with other dogs, or standing in a cluster of kids with bikes, or stationed by the counter inside,
looking up inquiringly at customers who were chatting with Searles.

My jealousy grew. I was disgruntled and seriously ill-at-ease.
Somewhere within me I was saying, "Don't you love me anymore?
Have you forgotten how I raised you and trained you? Have you forgotten those mornings in the park when I threw sticks for you and
taught you to leap? Have you forgotten our walks here in the woods,
and the thousand discoveries we've made together?"

Most serious of all was his absence while I worked. I had built a little cabin half a mile from the house. He had been a presence, almost a
tutelary spirit, in the very building of it, and then he had walked
beside me every day to and from it, and had lain near my feet while I
wrote or read. Often when I turned to him he would already have
seen the movement and I would find his eyes waiting for mine.

Those inactive hours were a poor substitute for the attractions of
the store, and I knew it, in spite of our companionable lunches and
afternoon walks. But what of me?

One day, several weeks after his first visit to the store, I jumped
into the car and went down there rather speedily, ordered him rather
firmly into the back seat, and took him home. I did the same thing
the following day. The day after that I chained him, and the day after
that chained him again.

Life returned to normal. I took away the chain. He was grateful
and stopped moping. I saw that he had renounced his friends at the
store, and I was glad, forgetting that I had forced him to do it.
Anyway, those diversions had never canceled his love for me—so I
reminded myself, and began to see fidelity where I had established
dependence. But that didn't matter. The undiminished, familiar love
wiped out everything—at least for me.

[eddie dubord. sawyer's labrador.]
quills.

Just below us in the woods the stream was speeded by a short channel of granite blocks, though the mill wheel was gone that once had turned continuously during thaw, reducing small hills of cedar drums to stacks of shingles. There had been trout for a while in the millrace, but chubs, which eat the eggs of trout, had driven them away.

Upstream of this ghost of a mill, just beyond the second of two handsome waterfalls, one stringer of a rotted bridge still joined the banks. Snowmobilers had dropped a tree beside it and had nailed enough crossboards to make a narrow path. I had crossed it often on snowshoes, and then on skis, and the dog had trotted behind, but there came a day in spring, after the mud had dried, when Shawno drew back and stood there on the bank stamping his feet, moving from side to side indecisively, and barking. He had seen the turbulent water between the boards of the bridge. I picked him up and carried him across, and couldn't help laughing, he was so big, such a compli-cated bundle in my arms, and I remembered how he had nestled there snugly as a pup, lighter and softer than Ida.

Beyond the bridge a grassy road curved away into the trees. In somewhat more than a mile it would join the tarred road, but halfway there, on the inside of its curve, a wagon trail branched off, now partly closed by saplings. It was here at the corner of this spur that my neigh-bor Eddie Dubord built a small cabin similar to my own.

It was summer. The dog had gone with the children to the swim-ming hole and I was walking alone carrying a small rod and a tin of worms. I saw two wedges of smoke ahead of me, expanding and thin-ning in the slight breeze, and then I saw a parked car and a man working at something. The smoke was blowing toward him and came from two small fires spaced twelve feet apart. The man was blocky and short. He wore a visored cap of bright orange and a chore jacket of dark blue denim. His movements were stiff and slow, yet there was something impressive and attractive about the way he worked. Every motion achieved something and led to the next without waste or repetition. He went to one of the fires carrying an axe, which he used only to lift some pine boughs from a pile. He threw several on each of the fires. I walked closer, but stopped again and watched him. We had never met, but I knew that it was Dubord. He was seventy-four years old. He had driven the corner stakes to mark the floor of a cabin, had tied a cord on one of them and had carried it around the others. Evidently he had already leveled the cord. I watched him as he picked up a five-foot iron bar and went away dragging a stoneboat that was simply the hood of an ancient car turned upside down and fitted with a rope that could be used as a yoke. He stopped at a pile of stones, and with his bar levered a large flat stone onto the car hood. With the same bar he lifted the yoke to where he could reach it. He stepped into the yoke, placed it across his chest and under his armpits, and angling his substantial weight sharply forward, using the heavy bar now as a staff, set the skid in motion and dragged it easily to one of the corner stakes. When I walked by he was on his hands and knees firming the stone and didn't see me.

Several days later I went that way again, and again stopped to watch him. He had finished the floor and had built a low platform the length of it, and had equipped the platform with steps. He would be able to work on the rafters and roof without resorting to a ladder.

He had assembled several units of studs, rafters, and cross braces, and now as I watched he pushed one erect with a stick, and caught it in the fork of a long pole that held it while he adjusted it for plumb. He nailed bracing boards at the sides, and drove in permanent nails at the base. His concentration was remarkable. It was as total and self-forgetful as a child's. Later, after I had come to know him well, I marveled more, not less, at this quality. I had seen him at work on all kinds of things: radios and TVs, pop-up toasters, lawn mowers, snow-blowers, Rototillers, outboard motors, locks, shotguns, clocks. On several occasions I had come close to him and had stood beside him wondering how to announce my presence . . . but it had never mattered how—he had looked up always with a start of panic, and then had blushed. It was not merely as if his concentration had been disturbed, but as if some deep, continuous melody had been shattered. Then he would smile shyly and greet me in his unassuming, yet gracious, almost courtly way.

He had already roofed the cabin and was boarding the sides—on the diagonal, as the old farmhouses were boarded—when we finally met. And, as has often happened, it was the dog who introduced us, ignoring utterly the foolish shyness on both sides.

The smudge fires were going again to drive away the bugs. A small stack of rough-cut boards lay on a pallet of logs. Dubord had just hung the saw on a prong of the sawhorse and was carrying a board to the wall when Shawno trotted up to him and barked. He was startled and backed away defensively, ready to use the board as a weapon. But Shawno was wagging his tail in the extreme sweeps of great enthusiasm, and he did something he had almost abandoned since our coming to the country: he reared up, put his paws on Dubord's broad chest, and tried to lick his weathered, leathery face with its smokehaze of white stubble beard. By the time I reached them Shawno had conquered him utterly. Dubord was patting the dog, bending over him, and talking to him in that slurred, attractive baritone voice that seemed to have knurls in it, a grain and dark hue as of polished walnut, and that he seemed to savor in his throat and on his tongue, just as he savored tobacco, black coffee, and whiskey. And of course he knew the dog's name, as he knew my name, and as I knew his. It was the simplest thing in the world to shake hands and be friends.

To hold Dubord's hand was like holding a leather sack filled with chunks of wood. His fingers seemed three times the size of ordinary fingers. He scarcely gripped my hand, but politely allowed me to hold his. Gravely he said, "Pleased to meet you," and then his small blue eyes grew lively behind the round, steel-framed spectacles. "I'd ask you in," he said, "but there ain't much difference yet between out and in. You got time for a drink?" I said I did, and he opened the toolbox and handed me a pint of Four Roses.

His skull was shaped like a cannonball. His jaw was broad and gristly. Everything about him suggested strength and endurance, yet his dominant trait, I soon came to see, was thoughtfulness. He listened, noticed, reflected, though it was apparent, even now, that these deliberations must often have been overwhelmed in his youth by passions of one kind or another. He had come from Quebec at the age of twenty, and for almost two decades had worked in lumber camps as a woodcutter and cook. He had farmed here in this valley, both as a hired hand and on his own—had dug wells, built houses, barns, and sheds, had installed his own electric lines and his own plumbing, had raised animals and crops of all kinds. In middle age he had married a diminutive, high-tempered, rotund, childishly silly, childishly gracious woman. They had never had children. They had never even established a lasting peace. Her crippled mother lived with them in the small house he had built, knitting in an armchair near the TV while her daughter dusted the china knickknacks and photographs of relatives, straightened the paper flowers in their vases, and flattened the paper doilies they had placed under everything. Dubord liked all this, or rather approved it, but felt ill at ease with his heavy boots and oil-stained pants, and spent his days in a shed beside the house. There, surrounded by his hundreds of small tools, he tinkered at the workbench or table saw, repairing things or building them, listening to cassettes of French Canadian fiddle music, and occasionally putting aside the tools to play his own fiddle. The camp in the woods served the same purposes as the shed, but promised longer interludes of peace.

I got to know him that summer and fall, but it was not until winter—our family's third in the little town—that Dubord and I realized that we were friends.

The deep snow of our first winter had made me giddy with excitement. The silence in the woods, the hilly terrain with its many streams, most of them frozen and white, but a few audible with a muted, far-off gurgling under their covering of ice and snow, occasional sightings of the large white snowshoe hares, animal tracks—all this had been a kind of enchantment and had recalled boyhood enjoyments that once had been dear to me. I went through the woods on snowshoes, and Shawno came behind. The following year I discovered the lightweight, highly arched, cross-country skis, my speed was doubled, and our outings became strenuous affairs for the dog. Often he sank to his shoulders and had to bound like a porpoise. Except in the driest, coldest snow, he stopped frequently, and pulling back his lips in a silent snarl, bit away the snow impacted between his toes. His tawny, snow-cleaned, winter-thickened fur looked handsome against the whiteness. When we came to downhill stretches I would speed ahead, and he would rally and follow at a run.

We had taken a turn like this through the woods in our third year, on a sunny, blue-skyed day in March, when I decided to visit Dubord.

I could smell the smoke of his tin chimney before I could see it. Then the cabin came in view. His intricately webbed, gracefully curved snowshoes leaned against the depleted stack of firewood that early in the winter had filled the overhang of the entranceway.

I could hear music. It was the almost martial, furiously rhythmic music of the old country dances—but there seemed to be two fiddles.

Shawno barked and raced ahead . . . and Dubord's pet red squirrel bounded up the woodpile. When I reached the camp, Shawno was dancing on his hind legs barking angrily and complainingly, and the healthy, bright-eyed squirrel was crouching in a phoebe's nest under the roof, looking down with maddening calm. The music stopped, the door opened, and Dubord greeted us cheerfully—actually with a *merry* look on his face.

"You won't get that old squirrel, Shawno," he said. "He's too fast for you. You'll never get 'im. Might's well bark . . .

"Come in," he said. "I just made coffee. Haven't seen those for a while. Where'd you get 'em?"

He meant the skis. He had never seen a manufactured pair, though he had seen many of the eight- and nine-foot handmade skis the Finns had used. He didn't know why (he said later) only the Finns had used them. Everyone else had stayed with snowshoes, which were an Indian invention.

"Nilo Ansden used to take his eggs down to Searles on skis," he said. The Searles he meant was Bob Searles's father. "He took a short-cut one day down that hill 'cross from your place. We had a two-foot storm all night and the day before. He got halfway down and remembered Esther Barden's chicken coop was in the way, but he thought, *There's enough snow to get up on the roof* . . . and there was. Once he was up there there was nothin' to do but jump, so he jumped. Had a pack-basket of eggs on's back. Didn't break a one."

In the whole of any winter there are never more than a few such sunny days, gloriously sunny and blue. One becomes starved for the sun.

He left the door open and we turned our chairs to face the snow and blue sky and the vast expanse of evergreen and hardwood forest. He stirred the coals in the woodstove, opened the draft, and threw in some split chunks of rock maple. There was a delicious swirling all around us of hot, dry currents from the stove and cool, moist currents from the snow and woods. Occasionally a tang of wood smoke came in with the cold air.

As for the fiddle music—"Oh, I was scratchin' away," he said. "I have a lot of fiddle music on the cassettes. I put it on and play along."

His cassette recorder stood on the broad worktable by the window. The violin lay beside it amidst a clutter of tools and TV parts.

"If I hear somebody's got somethin' special or new, I go over an' put it on the recorder. Take a good while to play the ones I got now. You like that fiddle music, Shawno?"—and to me: "That was a schottische you heard comin' in."

He was fond of the dog. He looked at him again and again, and there began a friendship between them that pleased me and that I never cared to interrupt.

Shawno lay on the floor twisting his head this way and that and snapping at a large glossy fly that buzzed around him. He caught it, cracked it with his teeth, and ejected it with a wrinkling of the nose. Eddie laughed and said, "That's right, Shawno, you catch that old bastard fly." The dog got up and went to him and Eddie gave him a piece of the "rat cheese" we had been eating with our coffee. For a long time Shawno sat beside him, resting his head on Eddie's knee.

We laced our coffee with Four Roses whiskey and had second cups. The squirrel looked in at the window, crouching eagerly, its forepaws lifted and tucked in at the wrists, and its feathery long tail arched forward like a canopy over its head.

"I built that platform to feed the birds, but he took over, so I let him have it. That's where the birds eat now."

He pointed to a wooden contraption hanging by a wire from a tree out front. Several chickadees fluttered around it angrily. It was rocking from the weight of the blue jay perched on its edge, a brilliant, unbelievable blue in the sunlight.

Eddie had hinged a tiny window in one of the panels of the side window. He opened it now and laid his hand on the feeding platform, a few peanuts and sunflower seeds on the palm. The squirrel shied away, but came back immediately and proceeded to eat from Eddie's hand, picking up one seed at a time. Shawno went over and barked, and the squirrel snatched up one last morsel and leaped into the eaves. Dubord closed the window, chuckling, and again the dog sat with him, this time stretched at his feet with his chin extended over one wide rubber boot.

I saw his packbasket in the corner. He used it daily to bring in water and whiskey and a few tools. The handle of his axe protruded from the basket.

The basket was of ash strips, such as the Indians make. I had bought several two towns away. Dubord had made this one himself.

"The Indians can take brown ash wherever they find it," he said. "Did you know that? They used to camp every summer on the

Folsom place. Diamond National owns it now. There's brown ash down there, downhill goin' toward the pond. I used to trap beaver with one o' the men, and he showed me."

The basket was thirty years old.

He sipped his coffee.

"Have you met Mister Mouse?" he said.

"Who?"

"Don't know if he'll come while Shawno's here."

Smiling like a little boy, he said, "Keep your eyes open, but don't move. Don't even blink. He can see it."

He put a peanut on the two-by-four at the upper edge of the far wall, stepped back from it and stood there making a strange little whimpering sound. Shawno perked up his ears and became excited, but I whispered to him, *no, no . . . stay.*

Again Dubord made the squeaking sound, sucking air through his lips. Presently, quite soundlessly, a round-eared gray mouse appeared on the ledge, sniffing. It crept forward a few inches and froze, sniffing alertly and angling the delicate long antennae of its whiskers this way and that. It nibbled the peanut rapidly, listening while it ate, its bulging black eyes glinting with light from the windows and the door.

Shawno got to his feet . . . and that huge movement and the sound of his claws on the floor put an end to the performance.

Dubord came back chuckling, and stroked the dog's head.

We stayed for two hours. He talked of his early days in the States, and his years in the woods. I could hear the French Canadian and the Yankee accents alternating in his speech, the one stressing the final syllables, the other drawling them. Shawno sat close to him, sometimes upright with his chin on his knee, sometimes lying flat with his nose near the broad booted foot. Until now all his friendships had been friendships of play. This was a friendship of peace. It was one of those rare occasions on which, perhaps only momentarily, a little family of the spirit is formed.

It was good sapping weather. The days were sunny, the snow melting, the nights cold. When we saw Dubord several days later he was gathering sap from the huge maples near his camp.

A rapidly moving cloud of light-gray smoke rolled over and over in the lower branches of the trees. I skied closer and saw that it was not coming from the cabin, as I had feared, nor was it smoke, but steam from a large tray of bubbling maple sap.

He had shoveled away some snow and had built a fireplace of fieldstones he had gathered in the fall. The sides were lined with scraps of metal. The back had been cut from a sheetmetal stove and was equipped with a metal chimney five feet high. A shallow tray, two feet by four, rested on top of the fieldstone walls. It was from this tray that the clouds of steam were rising.

While I was examining all this Dubord came in sight, plodding blockily on snowshoes, pulling a toboggan that I recognized, since I had helped at all stages in the making of it, first splitting out boards from a squared-off log of ash, then boiling the tips, and finally nailing them around a log to cool and set. On the toboggan were two five-gallon white plastic jugs, each half-filled with sap. A tin funnel bounced against one of them, secured by a wire to its handle.

He glanced at me in a furious and bitter way. I didn't inquire what the trouble was, but took it for granted that he had been quarreling with Nellie. His teeth were clamped and his mouth was pulled down. How long he would have maintained this furious silence I don't know, but it was more than he could do to hold out against the dog. A deep blush suffused his weathered round face. He dropped the toboggan rope, and smiling helplessly bowed his head to the uprearing dog, petting him with both hands and allowing his face to be licked.

He took off the snowshoes and put more wood on the fire. The four-foot strips of white birch—edgings from the turning mill—had been stacked in the fall and covered with boards and scraps of asphalt roofing. Papery white bark still clung to them. The wood was well dried and burned hot—the "biscuit wood" of the old farmhouse kitchens.

The tray was slanted toward one of its forward corners, and there, with his brazing torch, Dubord had attached a little spigot. He drained some syrup into a large spoon, blew on it, and tested it with his finger.

I poured one of the jugs of new sap into the noisily bubbling syrup. The steam was sweet and had a pleasant odor.

Several galvanized buckets stood by the fire and Eddie divided the rest of the sap between two of them. I noticed that just as he had not filled the plastic jugs he did not fill the buckets—an old man's foresight, avoiding loads that might injure him.

I went with him back to the maple trees, and at last he broke his silence.

"'Twas a damn good farm fifty years ago," he said. "I wanted to buy it but I couldn't meet the price."

The huge, slowly dying maples lined the road. There were smaller trees around them, some in the road itself, but the maples, in season, were leafy, and were well exposed to the sun, and their sap was far richer than that of forest maples. The boiling ratio would be forty to one, or even better.

Buckets, four to a tree, clung to the stout, coarse-barked trunks waist high, as if suspended from a single belt. They hung from short spouts of galvanized metal that had been driven into the tree, and were covered with metal lids that were creased in the middle and looked like roofs.

Since I was helping, we filled the jugs, and soon had sledded sixty gallons to the fire.

Nellie's canary had been killed that morning. The quarrel had followed its death.

She had been cleaning its cage and had let it out to stretch its wings.

"She could've put it in the other cage," he said.

He was stirring the boiling sap with a stick of wood, and in his anger he splashed it again and again.

"'Twas right there under the bed," he said. "Damn thing shittin' all over the place! If I come in with one speck o' mud on my boots she raises hell! I wanted to go out. 'Don't open the door!' 'Well, put 'im in the cage!'"

He thumped the tray as if he meant to drive holes through it.

"Freddie Latham was outside fillin' the oil tank," he said. "Nellie's mother'd knitted some mittens for the new baby, so Nellie says to me over her shoulder, 'Git Buddy,' and she comes right past me and opens the door. 'Yoo hoo, Freddie.'"

He ground his teeth awhile.

"Git the bird!" he muttered explosively. "What'd she expect me t'do, fly up an' catch it? Damn thing flew out the door right behind her and she didn't even notice. She opened the porch door and it flew out that one too. Damn! If I had a stick o' wood in my hand I'd heaved it at 'er! You could o' heard her down t'village. 'Save Buddy! Here, Buddy! Git Buddy!'"

Dubord glared at me. "Damn thing perched on the roof o' the shed," he said, "I got some birdseed in my hand and got the ladder and started up. Freddie hauled out my smeltin' net and tried t'hand it to me. Fat lot o' good that did! Soon as Buddy saw me gittin' close he flew over an' perched on the ridgepole o' the house. Then he flew up to the antenna, and Nellie's whistlin' to him an' suckin' her lips. 'Eddie, git that canary record, maybe if we play it Buddy'll come down.' Now ain't that a goddamn smart idea! If he could hear it up there what'd he want t'come down for?

"By the time I come off the ladder the bird'd flew up to the electric wire. He was just gittin' settled . . . wham! Some damn ol' red-tail hawk been watchin' the whole thing. I never seen 'im. Where he come from I don't know. Couple o' yella feathers come down like snowflakes. I thought, here's your canary, Nellie. An' I thought, enjoy your dinner, mister hawk. You just saved me two hund'd dolluhs."

Eddie faced me and stood absolutely still. "Yessuh!" he said. "That's what I said! Two hund'd dolluhs! That's what I spent for birdseed! I'm tellin' the truth, I ain't makin' it up! And I ain't sayin' Buddy et that much, I'm saying we BOUGHT that much! You seen him do that Christly trick! You and the Missus seen that trick the first time you come down. Sure you did! You had the girl with you. . . ."

The trick he was referring to was something Nellie had taught the bird, or had discovered, namely, that when she put his cage up to the feeding platform at the window, he would pick up a seed from the floor and hold it between the bars, and the chickadees outside would jostle one another until one had plucked the seed from his beak, and then Buddy would get another. Nellie had loved to show this off.

Eddie was glaring at me. "WHERE DID YOU THINK THEM BIRDS COME FROM?" he shouted. "We had t'have them birds ON HAND! We was feedin' a whole damn flock right through the year so Buddy could do his Christly trick two or three times a month!"

He paced back and forth by the evaporating tray grinding his teeth and glaring. "I guess I warn't upset 'nough t'suit 'er," he said. "God damn! Hasn't she got a tongue!"

One last wave of anger struck him and he howled louder than before, but there was a plaintive note in his voice and he almost addressed it to the sky.

"IT WAS NELLIE HER OWN GODDAMN RATTLE-BRAIN SELF OPENED THE DOOR!" he cried.

And then he calmed down. That is to say, he walked around the steaming tray panting and lurching and thumping the sides and bottom with the little stick.

He had brought some blankets in his packbasket and was planning to spend the night.

He drained off some thick syrup into a small creamery pail and set it aside to cool. He drained a little more into an old enamel frying pan and with a grunt bent down and thrust it under the evaporator tray right among the flames and coals. After it had bubbled and frothed awhile, he knelt again and patted the snow, and scattered the hot syrup over it. When Shawno and I went home I had a jar of syrup for Patricia and a bag of maple taffy for the kids.

At around two o'clock the next afternoon I answered the phone and heard the voice of Nellie Dubord, whose salutation, calling or receiving, is always *Yeh-isss,* as if she were emphatically agreeing with some previous remark.

Eddie had not come home. She knew that he had taken blankets to the camp, but she was worried.

"I just don't feel right," she said. "I can't see any smoke up there. I should be able to see the chimney smoke, though maybe not. Ain't he boilin' sap? I should see that smoke too. Can you see it up there? Take a look. I guess I'm bein' foolish, but I don't know . . . I just don't feel right."

I went upstairs and looked from the west windows. There wasn't any smoke. I skied across.

There was no activity at the cabin, no smoke or shimmering waves of heat, no fire out front. Shawno sniffed at the threshold. He chuffed and snorted, sniffed again, then drew back and barked. He went forward again and lowered his head and sniffed.

The door was locked. I went around and looked in the window. Dubord lay on the floor on his back beside the little platform bed. He was dressed except for his boots. The blankets had come away from the bed, as if he had clutched them at the moment of falling. I battered the door with a piece of stovewood and went to him. He was breathing faintly, but his weathered face was as bloodless as putty.

He was astonishingly heavy. I got him onto the bed, covered him with the blankets and our two coats, and skied to the road. I saw his car there and cursed myself for not having searched him for the key: the nearest house was three-quarters of a mile away. I telephoned there for an ambulance, and made two other calls besides, then went back and put him on the toboggan and set out pulling him over the packed but melting trail, dreadfully slowly.

I hadn't gone twenty paces before the men I had called appeared. The two elder were carpenters, the young man was their helper. They were running toward us vigorously, and I felt a surge of hope.

But it was more than hope that I felt at that moment. Something priceless was visible in their faces, and I have been moved by the recollection of it again and again. It was the purified, electric look of whole-hearted response. The men came running toward us vigorously, lifting their knees in the snow and swinging their arms, and that unforgettable look was on their faces.

Ten days later Patricia, the children, and I went with Nellie to the hospital. The children weren't allowed to go up, and Nellie sat with them in the lobby.

Dubord was propped up by pillows and was wearing a hospital smock that left his arms bare. I was used to the leathery skin of his hands and face; the skin of his upper arms, which were still brawny, was soft and white, one would say *shockingly* white.

"Sicker cats than this have got well and et another meal," he said. And then, gravely, "Nellie told me you went in for me. I'm much obliged to you."

"Did the girls like their candy?" he asked Patricia. She answered him promptly, but it took me a moment to realize that he was referring to the maple taffy, the last thing he had made before the heart attack. A few moments later he said to me, "How's my dog?" and I told him how the dog had known at once that something was wrong. A rapt, shy look came over his face.

A neighbor leaned in at the doorway, Earl Sawyer. He joined us, and after chatting briefly, said to Eddie, "Well, you won't be seein' Blackie no more."

Dubord asked him what had happened.

"I did away with him," said Sawyer. "I had to. He went after porcupines three times in the last two weeks. Three times I took him to the vet, eighteen dollars each time. I can't be doin' that. Then he went and did it again, so I took him out and shot 'im, quills and all."

Sawyer was upset.

"If he can't learn," he said. ". . . I can't be doin' that. Damn near sixty dollars in two weeks, and there's a leak in the goddamn cellar. He was a nice dog, though. He was a good dog otherwise."

Sawyer was thirty-three or -four, but his face was worn and tense. He worked ten hours a day as a mechanic, belonged to the fire department, and was serving his second term as road commissioner. He had built his own house and was raising two children.

"I don't blame you," said Dubord. "You'd be after 'im every day."

"He went out an' did it again," said Sawyer.

There was silence for a while.

"I can't see chainin' a dog," Sawyer said. "I'd rather not have one."

"A chained dog ain't worth much," Eddie said.

Months went by before Eddie recovered his spirits. But in truth he never did entirely recover them. I could see a sadness in him that hadn't been there before, and a tendency to sigh where once he had raged.

The change in his life was severe. He sold the new cabin he had liked so much, and spent more time in the little shed beside the house. I drove down to see him frequently, but it wasn't the same as stopping by on skis or walking through the woods. Nor was he allowed to drink whiskey anymore. Nor did I always remember to bring the dog.

[a walk with ida.
wandering dogs.]

Most of the snow was gone by the end of that April. One night Shawno failed to appear for supper, and there was no response when I called from the porch. I called again an hour later, and this time I saw movement in the shadows just beyond the cars. Why wasn't he running toward me? I went out, calling to him. He crept forward a few paces on his belly, silently, and then lay still. When I stood over him, he turned his head away. His jowls and nose were packed with quills. He couldn't close his mouth. There were quills in his tongue and hanging down from his palate. The porcupine had been a small one, the worst kind for a dog.

He seemed to be suffering more from shame than from the pain of the quills. He wouldn't meet my eyes, and the once or twice that he did he lowered his head and looked up woefully, the whites showing beneath the irises.

I was afraid that he might run off, and so I picked him up and carried him into the house. This too was mortifying. His eyes skittered from side to side. What an abject entrance for this golden creature, who was used to bounding in proudly!

The black tips of the quills are barbed with multiple, hair-fine points. The quills are shaped like torpedoes and are hollow-shafted, so that the pressure of the flesh around them draws them deeper into the victim's body. They are capable of migrating then to heart, eyes, liver . . .

He wanted to obey me. He lay flat under the floor lamp. But every time I touched a quill with the pliers, a helpless *tic* of survival jerked away his head.

Ida was shocked. He was the very image of The Wounded, The Victimized. It was as if some malevolent tiny troll had shot him full of arrows. She knelt beside him and threw her arms around his neck, and in her high, passionate voice of childgoodness repeated the words both Patricia and I had already said: "Don't worry, Shawno, we'll get them out for you!"—but with this difference: that he drew back the corners of his open mouth, panted slightly, glanced at her, and thumped his tail.

I took him to the vet the next day, and brought him back unconscious in the car.

I thought of Sawyer and his black Labrador, and saw from still another point of view the luxury of our lives. I didn't go to bed exhausted every night, I wasn't worried about a job, a mortgage, a repair bill, a doctor's bill, unpaid loans at the bank. And here was another of the homely luxuries our modest security brought us: he lay on the back seat with his eyes closed, his mouth open, his tongue out, panting unconsciously. Great quantities of saliva came from his mouth, and the seat was wet when we moved him.

Spring comes slowly and in many stages. The fields go through their piebald phase again and again, in which the browns and blacks of grass and wet earth are mingled with streaks of white—and then everything is covered again with the moist, characteristically dimpled snow of spring. But soon the sun comes back, a warm wind blows, and in half a day the paths in the woods and the ruts in our long dirt road are streaming with water.

Black wasps made their appearance on a warm day in March, then vanished. This was the day that a neighbor left his shovel upright in the snow in the morning and in the evening found it on bare ground. It was the day that a man in his seventies, with whom I had stopped to talk while he picked up twigs and shreds of bark from his south-facing yard, turned away abruptly and pointed with his finger, saying, "Look! Is that a bee? Yes, by gurry! It's a bee! The first one!"

But there was more rain and more snow, and then came the flooding we had hoped to be spared, as the stream jumped its banks and poured down our lower road, to a depth, this time, of two feet. For several days we came home through the woods with our groceries in packbaskets, but again the snow shriveled and sank into the ground, and high winds dried the mud. I saw a crowd of black starlings foraging in a brown field, and heard the first cawing of crows. The leaves of the gray birches uncurled. There were snow flurries, sun again, and the ponies followed the sun all day, lolling on the dormant grass or in the mud. Shawno, too, basked in the sun, like a tourist on a cruise ship. He lay blinking on a snowbank with his tongue extended, baking above and cooling below. I pulled last year's leaves out of culverts, and opened channels in the dooryard mud so that the standing water could reach the ditch. Early one morning six Canada geese flew over my head, due north, silently, flying low; and then just before dusk I heard a partridge drumming in the woods.

Several days after Easter, when the garden was clear of snow and the chives were three inches high, Ida came striding into my room, striking her feet noisily on the floor and grinning.

"Wake up, dad!" she called. "It's forty-forty!"

She was seven. I had told her the night before how when she was four years old and could not count or tell time she had invented that urgent hour, forty-forty, and had awakened me one morning proclaiming it.

When she saw that I was awake, she said eagerly, "Look out the window, daddy! Look!"

I did, and saw a world of astonishing whiteness. Clinging, heavy snow had come down copiously in the night and had stopped before dawn. There was no wind at all. Our white garden was bounded by a white rail fence, every post of which was capped by a mound of white. The pines and firs at the wood's edge were almost entirely white, and the heavy snow had weighted down their upward-sweeping branches, giving the trees a sharp triangular outline and a wonderfully festive look.

The whiteness was everywhere. Even the sky was white, and the just-risen sun was not visible as a disk at all but as a lovely haze of orange between whitenesses I knew to be hills.

An hour later Ida, Shawno, and I were walking through the silent, utterly motionless woods. We took the old county road, which for decades now had been a mere trail, rocky and overgrown. It went directly up the wooded high ridge of Folsom Hill and then emerged into broad, shaggy fields that every year became smaller as the trees moved in. We gathered blueberries there in the summer, and in the fall apples and grapes, but for almost two years now we had been going to the old farm for more sociable reasons.

After breakfast Ida had wanted to hear stories of her earlier childhood, and now as we walked through the woods she asked for them again, taking my bare hand with her small gloved one, and saying, "Daddy, tell me about when I was a kid."

"You mean like the time you disappeared in the snow?"

This was a story I had told her before, and that she delighted in hearing.

"Yes!" she said.

"Well . . . that was it—you disappeared. You were two years old. You were sitting on my lap on the toboggan and we went down the hill beside the house. We were going really fast, and the toboggan turned over and you flew into a snowbank and disappeared."

She laughed and said, "You couldn't even see me?"

"Nope. The snow was light and fluffy and very deep."

"Not even my head?"

"Not even the tassel on your hat."

"How did you find me?"

"I just reached down and there you were, and I pulled you out."

She laughed triumphantly and said, "Tell me some more."

While we talked in this fashion the dog trotted to and fro among the snow-heavy close-set trees, knocking white cascades from bushes and small pines. Often he would range out of sight, leaping over dead-falls and crouching under gray birches that had been pressed almost flat by the snows of previous years, and then he would come back to us, sniffing at the six-inch layer of wet snow, and chuffing and snorting to clear his nose. Occasionally, snorting still more vigorously, he would thrust his snout deep into the snow, and then step back and busily pull away snow and matted leaves with his paws.

Watching all this, I understood once again that the world of his experience was unimaginably different from the world of mine. What were the actual sensations of his sense of smell? How could I possibly know them? And how were those olfactory shapes and meanings structured in his memory? Snout, eyes, tongue, ears, belly—all were close to the ground; his entire life was close to it, and mine was not. I knew that in recent weeks complex odors had sprung up in the woods, stirring him and drawing him excitedly this way and that. And I could see that last night's snowfall had suppressed the odors and was thwarting him, and that was all, really, that I could know.

After three-quarters of a mile the trail grew steep. We couldn't walk side by side; I let Ida go in front, and our conversation now consisted of the smiles we exchanged when she looked back at me over her shoulder. I watched her graceful, well-proportioned little body in its blue one-piece snowsuit, and felt a wonderful happiness and peace.

Milky sky appeared between the snowy tops of the trees. A few moments later there was nothing behind the trees but the unmarked white of a broad field—at which moment there occurred one of those surprises of country life that are dazzling in much the way that works of art are dazzling, but that occur on a scale no artwork can imitate. I called to Ida, and she too cried aloud. The dog turned to us and came closer, lifting his head eagerly.

The sight that so astonished us was this: several hundred starlings, perhaps as many as five hundred, plump and black, were scattered throughout the branches of one of the maples at the wood's edge. The branches themselves were spectacular enough, thickened by snow and traced elegantly underneath by thin black lines of wet bark, but the surprising numbers of the birds and their glossy blackness against the white of the field were breathtaking.

I threw a stick at them. I couldn't resist. The entire tree seemed to shimmer and crumble, then it burst, and black sparks fluttered upward almost in the shape of a plume of smoke. The plume thinned and tilted, then massed together again with a wheeling motion, from which a fluttering ribbon emerged, and the entire flock streamed away in good order down the field to another tree.

Shawno, who had remained baffled and excluded, resumed his foraging. He stopped and raised his head alertly, then leaped forward in a bounding, enthusiastic gallop, and in a moment was out of sight. When Ida and I came to that very place, she too brightened, and with no more ceremony than had been shown me by the dog, let go of my hand and ran.

And if I had been a child, I would have followed, since it was here, at this very point, that due to the lay of the land, that is, the acoustics of the field, the playful gaiety of two voices could be heard quite clearly, a girl's voice shouting, "I *did*, Leo! I *did!*" and the voice of her brother, who was eight, replying, "Ha, ha, ha!" and then both shouting, "Shawno! Shawno!" I stood there and watched Ida's diminutive figure as she ran by herself across the snowy field toward the house that had not yet come in sight.

I looked back for a moment down the long slope of the field, toward the woods, the way we had come. I had intended to look for the birds, but our three sets of footprints caught my eye, and I couldn't help but smile at the tale they told. They were like diagrams of our three different ways of being in the world. Mine seemed logical, or responsible, or preoccupied: they kept on going straight ahead. Ida's footprints, in contrast to mine, went out to the sides here and there; they performed a few curlicues and turns, and were even supplanted at one place by a star-shaped bodyprint where she had thrown herself laughing onto the snow.

But the footprints of the dog! . . . this was a trail that was wonderful to see! One might take it as erratic wandering, or as continual inspiration, or as continual attraction, which may come to the same thing. It consisted of meandering huge loops, doublings, zigzags, festoons. . . . The whole was traveling as a system in the direction I had chosen, yet it remained a system and was entirely his own.

The voices of the children grew louder. I saw the dark gray flank of the made-over barn that was now their home, and then saw the children themselves, running with the dog among the whitened trees of the orchard.

These two, Gretl and Leo Carpenter, together with Ida and me and Eddie Dubord, complete the quintet of Shawno's five great loves.

Gretl is Ida's age, Leo a year older. They are the children of Waldo and Aldona Carpenter, whom Patricia and I have known for years. But I have known Waldo since the end of World War II, when we both arrived in New York City from small towns to the west.

Aldona was evidently waiting for me. She was standing in the doorway, and when she saw me she beckoned. I hadn't planned to stop, except to leave Ida and the dog, since in all likelihood Waldo would be working, but Aldona had no sooner waved to me than the broad window right above her swung open and Waldo, too, beckoned to me, cupping his hands and shouting. Aldona stepped out and looked up at him, and they smiled at one another, though his expression wasn't happy.

Aldona was fifteen years younger than Waldo. By the time I came into the kitchen she was standing at the stove turning thick strips of bacon with a fork.

"Waldo was up all night," she said to me. "I hope you're hungry enough to eat." The large round table was set for three.

She looked rested and fresh—it was one of the days, in fact, that her entirely handsome and appealing person seemed actually to be beautiful. She wore a dark blue skirt, a light sweater-blouse of gray wool, and loose-fitting boots from L. L. Bean. Her long brown hair, which was remarkably thick and glossy, was covered with a kerchief of deep blue.

She said to me, in a lower voice, "We *are* going back."

She meant back to New York.

I had known that they wanted to. Waldo's excitement, coming here, had had nothing to do with country life. He had been fleeing New York and an art world that had become meaningless to him. His own painting, moreover, after two periods of great success, was in a crisis of spirit, and he had begun to mistrust his virtuosity. Country life had relieved him, but something was lacking, and he had said to me several times in the last two months, "We won't be staying forever."

I wasn't surprised, then, by Aldona's remark. Nevertheless, it was saddening, and I knew that the loss for Ida would be severe.

I said as much to Aldona.

"We'll certainly miss you," she said. "All of you. All of us. But we'll be back every summer."

"When are you going?"

"Soon. I don't know."

"How do the children feel about it?"

"We haven't told them yet," she said. "They've been happy here . . . but there's so much to do in New York . . ."

I could hear Waldo walking on the floor above our heads, and moving something. I asked him, shouting, if he needed a hand. "I'll be right down," he called back.

Aldona looked into the oven. She closed it quickly, but warm air and the delicious fragrance of yeast rolls reached me.

The kitchen had been the stalls of the old barn. The ceiling was low and was heavily beamed. Narrow horizontal windows ran the length of two sides and gave fine views of our mountains, though today nothing could be seen but snowy woods and a misty white sky. Intricate leaves of plants, overlapping this way and that from suspended pots, were silhouetted against the whiteness. By the kitchen door stood a battered upright piano, on which Waldo, with his large hands, played Scott Joplin. At the far end of the room, beyond the open stairs that led to Waldo's studio, a large window was fitted with a window seat, on which were a cushion and many pillows. There were plants hanging in front of the window. A stool was drawn up to a small, neatly arranged table, on which there were some books and some sheets of paper, jars of ink, tubes of paint, and an earthenware crock holding a cluster of small brushes. For two years, in this pleasant nook, Aldona, who was fluent in Lithuanian, had been translating a cycle of folktales for a children's book. She had done a great many gouache illustrations, and I knew that the project was nearly finished.

I heard Waldo on the stairs. He stopped part way down, and leaning forward called across to me, "Do you want to see something?"

After the whites and blacks and evergreen greens of the woods the colors of his work were dazzling.

Small abstract paintings on paper were pinned to the white work wall, as were clippings from magazines and some color wheels he had made recently. Larger paintings on canvas, still in progress, leaned here and there, and two were positioned on the wall for work. A stack of finished paintings, all of which I had seen, leaned against the wall in the corner.

Waldo had placed the new painting on the seat of a chair, and we stood side by side studying it. The paint was still wet and gave off a pleasant odor of oil and turpentine.

Waldo's manner was that of an engineer. Physically he was imposing. He was large but trim, with a stern, black-browed, bristly-mustached face that was actually a forbidding face, or would have been except that an underlying good humor was never entirely out of sight. When he was alight with that humor, which after all was fairly often, one saw an astonishing sweetness and charm. Aldona, at such times, would rest her hand on his shoulder, or stroke the back of his head; and the children, if they were near, would come closer, and perhaps climb into his lap.

The studio windows were sheeted with a plastic that gave the effect of frosted glass, shutting off the outside and filling the space with a shadowless white light. Beyond one of those milky oblongs we heard a sudden shouting and loud barking. Ida and Gretl were shouting together, "Help, Shawno! Help!" in tones that were almost but not quite urgent, and the dog was barking notes of indignation, disapproval, and complaint, a medley that occurred nowhere else but in this game, for I knew without seeing it that Leo was pretending to beat the girls with his fist, and was looking back at the dog, who in a moment would spring forward and carefully yet quite excitedly seize Leo's wrist with his teeth.

"It's a total dud," Waldo said dispassionately, "but it's interesting, isn't it? Kerosene light does such weird things to the colors. It's like working under a filter. Look how sour and acidic it is. It's overcontrolled, too, and at the same time there are accidents everywhere. That's what gives it that moronic look. I should have known better—I've done it before. *When you rob the eye you rob the mind.*"

Abruptly he turned to me and lowered his voice.

"We're going back to the city," he said. "I'm going down in a couple of days and see what has to be done. . . ."

I knew that he had not sublet his studio, which he didn't rent but owned—a floor-through in a large loft building.

"We haven't told the kids yet," he said, "but I think they'll take it pretty well. There's so much to do there. . . ."

Aldona's voice came up from below. We cut short our conversation and went down into the warm kitchen, the very air of which was delicious now with the smells of bacon, rolls, just-brewed coffee, and fried eggs.

The rosy, bright-faced children stormed in just as we sat down. Leo and Gretl clamored for juice, while Ida looked at them joyfully. Shawno came with them. He trotted to Aldona, and to Waldo, and to me, greeting us eagerly but without arresting his motion or taking his eyes from the children. "Hi. Hi," they said to me. "Hi, daddy," said Ida. All three tilted their heads, took on fuel, and with the dog bounding among them rushed out again as noisily as they had entered.

The sky was beginning to clear when I left half an hour later, and it was blue now, but a pale, wintry blue. A light, raw breeze was blowing.

I crossed the dooryard without calling to the children. They were throwing snowballs at Shawno, except for Ida, who was tagging along. Gretl hit him and shouted, "Bull's eye!" and witty Leo, throwing quickly but missing widely, shouted, "Dog's eye!" They dodged among the budded but leafless apple trees, while the dog, who didn't understand that he was their target, kept leaping and twisting, biting the snowballs with swift snaps that reduced them to fragments.

I went alone down the snowy road to the right, toward the river. Little clumps of snow were falling wetly from the roadside trees.

I had been cheerful coming through the woods with Ida and the dog, and cheerful talking with Waldo and Aldona though their imminent departure was troubling, but now as I walked away alone, I passed into a mood of sadness-without-a-present-cause, a twilight mood I knew to be somewhat obsessional, and that I had learned not to take so very seriously, yet often I had to pass through it to reach the solitude of my work.

My footprints were the only markings between Waldo's house and the larger road, but as soon as I made the turn I found myself walking between the muddy tracks of a car. In ten minutes I stood on the high ledge that overlooked the river.

The river was broad in this stretch, and was flowing heavily. The water was dark. Huge pieces of ice were strewn in a continuous line on the steep bank across from me. The ice had been dirty and interspersed with debris a week ago, but now the entire bank was white.

Two miles downriver lay the town, on which all such villages as ours were dependent. There were its hundreds of houses, its red roofs and black roofs, snow-covered now, its white clapboard sidings, its large, bare-limbed shade trees, all following the slopes of the hills. I could see the gleaming bell towers and white spires of the four churches, the plump wooden cupola of the town hall, also white, and several redbrick business buildings. It was a lovely sight from this height above the river, but it no longer stirred me. The town was spiritless and dull, without a public life of any kind, or much character of its own, but the usual brand names in the stores and the usual cars on the streets.

Just this side of the town, the timbered latticework of a railroad trestle crossed the river high in the air, emerging from evergreens on one bank and plunging into evergreens on the other.

I had grown up in a town of hills like these. At the top of one, in the branches of a large maple, my friends and I had built a platform. I was then just twelve. I used to lie there alone at times, looking out through the leaves, dreaming of the future, except that there weren't any dreams, or rather the dreams consisted entirely of the marvelous town that I could see in the distance: white houses in a sea of trees, rising up in terraces on both sides of a valley. The town was larger than ours, more various, and more attractive. A white, winding highway led to it through a vista of wooded hills, large pastures, and cultivated fields. To see all this was tantamount, really, to dreaming awake. If there were events in those reveries I have forgotten them, but I remember the almost painful yet joyful yearning stirred by that sight.

Halfway to the trestle before me now the hills gave way to lowland for a short distance. There must have been oxbow bends here at one time, but the river had jumped them and simplified its course, and now a sweeping arc of water bounded a large flat field. Black-and-white cows, a good-sized herd, moved almost motionlessly across their white pasture toward the river.

There came a loud metallic scraping and banging from the gravel pit below me. A bucket loader was scooping up gravel. It swiveled and showered the stones heavily into a waiting truck, which crouched and shuddered under the impact. Another truck, as I watched, drove down the long incline to the riverbank.

I went home by the same route, thinking now chiefly of the work that I had in hand.

Shawno and the children were still playing, but they were no longer running. Ida and Gretl were holding the two sides of a flattened cardboard box, quite large, and Leo, wielding a hammer, was nailing it to the rails of the broken hay wain by the house, apparently to be the roof of a hut. The dog sat near them, more or less watching. I didn't call or wave, but Shawno saw me. He responded with a start . . . and then he did something I had seen him do before and had found so touching I couldn't resent it. He pretended that he hadn't seen me. He turned his head and yawned, stood up and stretched, dropped abruptly to the ground with his chin on his paws, and then just as abruptly stood up again and moved out of sight around the house. What a display of doggy craftiness! It makes me smile to remember it—even though I must now say that this was the last that I saw him in the fullness of his life. I did see him again, but by our bedtime that night he was dead.

I went back alone through the woods, walking on the footprints we had made that morning. In a scant three hours the snow had shriveled and become wetter. It was no deeper than three inches now, and was falling noisily from the trees, leaving the branches wet and glistening.

At the bottom of the first hill, where I had to jump a little stream, and where that morning I had lifted Ida, I noticed a complicated track: the footprints of a deer and of two dogs. The deer had gone somewhere along the stream and then had come back, running, evidently pursued by the dogs.

Instead of going home, I turned in to the little field at the far end of which my cabin studio was situated. Everything was quiet, the fresh snow untouched. I was halfway across the field when I caught a movement in the sky. High up, drawing a broad white line behind it, a military jet drifted soundlessly. A moment later the thunderclap of the sonic boom startled me . . . and as if it had brought them into being, two dogs stepped out of the woods behind my cabin. Or rather, one stepped out, a brown-and white collie, and came toward me. The other, a solemn-looking rabbit hound, stood motionless among the trees.

I thought I recognized the collie and called to it. It came a few steps, and then a few steps more. It stood still when it heard my voice, then it turned and went back to the other dog, and both vanished into the woods.

I built a fire in the cabin, in the cast-iron stove, and spent the rest of the day at my work.

$$\Big[\text{before the house.}\Big]$$

As was my custom, whether I had done the cooking or not, I mixed some scraps and pan rinsings with dry food and went to the door to call Shawno, who ate when we did and in the same room. Ida had come home that afternoon with Patricia, but Shawno had not.

Half an hour later, after we had finished eating, and while the water was heating for coffee, I went outside again and called him, but this time I went across the road and stood before the barn. The lay of the land was such that in this position, and with the help of that huge sounding board, my voice would carry to Waldo's fields, at least to the sharp ears of the dog. I shouted repeatedly. As I went back to the house I thought I saw movement on the woods road we had traveled that morning. I was expecting to see him come leaping toward me, but nothing happened and I went into the house.

We finished our coffee and dessert. Liza was staying overnight with the twins who had become her friends. Patricia sat on the sofa with Jacob and Ida and read first a picture book and then a story of Ernest Thompson Seton's, which enchanted Ida and put Jacob to sleep.

I telephoned Aldona. She said that the dog had left them shortly after Patricia had come in the car for Ida. He had stayed like that often with Leo and Gretl and had come home through the woods at suppertime.

I put the porch light on and went across to the barn again. I was preparing to shout when I saw him in the shadows of the road. A turbulence of alarm, a controlled panic raced through me, and I ran to him calling.

He lay on his belly. His head was erect, but just barely, and was not far above the ground. He pulled himself forward with his front paws, or tried to, but no motion resulted. His hind legs were spread limply behind him. His backbone seemed inert.

I knelt beside him and took his head on my knees. He was breathing so faintly that I doubted if any air was reaching his lungs. I heard my own voice saying in high-pitched, grievously astonished tones, "Oh dog, dog . . ."

I ran my hand down his body. Near his lower ribcage, even in the shadows, I could see a dark mass that here and there glistened dully. It was smooth and soft, and there jutted out of it numerous fine points sharper than a saw. I was touching the exit wound of a large-caliber bullet.

I put my face close to his and stroked his cheek. He was looking straight ahead with a serious, soft, dim gaze. He gave a breath that sounded like a sigh because it wasn't followed by another breath, and instantaneously he was heavy to the touch.

I stayed there a long while with his head on my knees, from time to time crying like a child.

I heard the front door open and heard Patricia calling me. A moment later she was kneeling in the mud beside me saying, "Oh, oh, oh . . ." in a voice of compassion and surprise.

We conferred briefly, and I went into the house.

Ida sat on the sofa, in the light of the floor lamp, looking at the pictures in the Seton book. Jacob lay asleep at the other end of the sofa.

I said to her, "Ida, something has happened . . ." and knelt in front of her. She saw that I had been crying, and her face became grave.

I said, "Shawno has been hurt very badly." I did not want to say to her that he was dead. "He's out front," I said. "Come."

She said, "Okay" quickly, never taking her eyes from mine. She gave me her hand and we went outside, into the road, where Patricia still knelt beside him just beyond the light from the porch. She was bowed above him and was stroking him. She looked up as we approached, and held out one hand for Ida, but with the other kept stroking his head, neck, and shoulders.

In the morning, though she had cried herself to sleep the night before, Ida asked Patricia, "Is Shawno dead?" and hearing her say, "Yes, honey, he's dead," threw herself on the sofa, sobbing. We explained to her that Shawno had been killed because he was chasing deer. She understood very little of that, but didn't question us until weeks later. She thought about it probably for years.

I went out after we had eaten and tested the ground with a spade. I could dig down only six or seven inches; after that the ground was frozen.

All three children came outside. Ida had hugged him the night before, and had cried at breakfast, but now she only stared. I too looked without much feeling at the wet and muddy corpse, though when I glanced uphill toward the barn my expectation of seeing Shawno come running into sight was so complete that the fact of his death was more real in my thoughts than in the motionless body on the ground, which in some way seemed to be an impostor.

I had dug a temporary grave under an apple tree near the sauna. We wrapped him in some old blankets and plastic sheets and laid him in the damp depression. I had thought of performing some sort of ceremony, but I decided against it. We said goodbye to him, covered his wrapped body with soil and rocks, and went back to the house.

Two months later we got a golden retriever, and I made a point of saying to Ida, "He's not Shawno, honey, he can't be—but he's a real nice pup."

Her acceptance of the new dog was similar to mine: she simply didn't invest it with so much love, didn't draw it so ardently into relation as in her great love she had drawn Shawno.